Y0-CBZ-428

BAYOU BAD BOYS

BAYOU BAD BOYS

JoAnn Ross

Nancy Warren

E.C. Sheedy

KENSINGTON PUBLISHING CORP.

BRAVA BOOKS are published by

Kensington Publishing Corp.
850 Third Avenue
New York, NY 10022

ISBN 0-7394-6014-5

Printed in the United States of America

CONTENTS

CAJUN HEAT

by JoAnn Ross
1

YOU GIVE ME FEVER

by Nancy Warren
125

IN GOOD HANDS

by E. C. Sheedy
207

Cajun Heat

JoAnn Ross

One

If anyone had told him, back in his hormone-driven teenage days, that a guy could get paid sinfully big bucks for making love to the world's sexiest women, Gabriel Broussard would've hightailed it out of South Louisiana's bayou country a helluva lot sooner.

The morning after what would permanently be etched in stone as the worst night of his life, he'd loaded up his truck, just like the Clampetts had done in that old sixties sitcom, (though in his case it'd been a black Trans Am), and moved to Beverly.

Hills, that is.

Swimming pools.

Movie stars.

Okay, so technically this house wasn't actually in the Hills, but on the beach at Malibu, which in Gabe's mind was a lot cooler and still included its share of swimming pools and movie stars. Of which, though it still blew his own mind to think so, he just happened to be one.

Which explained the panties. Sort of.

"Six pairs," Angela Moreno announced as she dropped the lacy undies in front of him.

Gabe morosely eyed the pile of silk and satin lace. They

were all just like all the others this week—either red or black. Whatever happened to girly pastels? A soft, feminine pink? Or even a sweet virginal white? Though it'd been years since he'd had any interest in virgins, with the right woman, it could make a nice fantasy.

These were flat out forward.

Big fucking surprise. Like throwing underwear with pinned-on telephone numbers over his gate wasn't?

He plucked a black triangle with two strings the width of dental floss from the pile and held it up to the scant bit of sunlight that was managing to slip through the storm shutters he'd closed to keep out of the range of the vultures—tabloid photographers—who'd been circling ever since Tamara Templeton had tearfully announced on *Inside Edition* that she was breaking their engagement because she could no longer deal with Gabe's "addiction to kinky sex."

That's when the panty attacks had begun. This particular pair was as transparent as Tamara's ploy. When the sight of his hand showing through the sheer black fabric didn't strum a single sexual chord, Gabe wondered if he might getting old.

Christ, wasn't that a fun thought?

"Six pair are less than yesterday," he said.

"The day's still young." His assistant had to raise her voice to be heard over the *whump whump whump* of the rotors from the helicopter circling overhead. It was as if he was under siege. She dropped a blizzard of pink messages atop the underwear.

"Diane Sawyer's already called three times this morning, Katie Couric twice, and Barbara Walters didn't exactly come right out and say so, but I got the distinct impression that if you'd throw your interview her way, you'd be a shoo-in for one of her celebrity shows. If I were you, I'd hold out for the Oscar special."

"If you were me, you wouldn't be in this mess," Gabe muttered.

"Good point. And one I was too polite to mention." She ignored his snort. "Oh, and Leno's producer called and suggested that coming clean on *The Tonight Show* could really help your damage control campaign."

"I don't have a damage control campaign," Gabe ground out. Not being nearly as wild as his bad boy reputation made him out to be, he'd never needed one.

"Maybe you ought to get one. I vote for calling Barbara. Hardly anyone makes it through her interviews without crying."

"And how would me crying like a girl on national television help my image?"

"It'd make you look sensitive. Women love that. Besides, you might pick up some sympathy."

"I fail to see how accusing America's sweetheart of lying would gain the sympathy vote."

Tamara Templeton had literally grown up in viewers' living rooms. She'd made her first appearance as a plucky orphan sent from New York to live with her aunt and uncle and numerous cousins on the family farm somewhere in the nameless Midwest when she was nine years old.

Amazingly, in a competitive business where the average television show had a shelf life between milk and yogurt, bolstered by its saccharine "family value" stories set in "simpler" times, *Heartland*—which, in Hollywood high concept terms, had initially been dismissed by critics as *Little House on the Prairie* meets *The Waltons*—was still running strong twelve years after its debut.

And Tamara was a multimillionaire several times over.

She had her own clothing line, a perfume label, a series of best-selling books about her fictional character's adventures, and a doll whose period prairie dresses probably cost more than the average parents spent on their own kids' clothes.

Her movies, which to Gabe's mind were even more likely to give their young audience cavities than the damn TV show, were guaranteed blockbusters, and Gabe had heard tales of studios refusing to set a release date for their summer movies until *her* opening weekend was set in stone.

She was young, beautiful, rich, and appeared, to her legion of fans worldwide, to have everything any young woman could wish for. But there was one thing she was lacking. The respect of her acting peers.

Which is where Gabe had come in.

"Your mistake was letting her announce your engagement in the first place," Angela pointed out what Gabe had been telling himself over and over again since this mess had started.

"Like I knew she was going to pull a stunt like that." Gabe clenched his jaw. "Hell, we'd only been out twice." Both "duty dates" set up by the agent they shared.

Angela shrugged. "Sometimes it happens that way. People meet, heartstrings zing, and the next thing you know, you're in some Vegas chapel, pledging to love and honor until death do you part, while an Elvis impersonator belts out 'Burning Love.'"

Knowing that Angela had actually done the Elvis impersonator wedding bit, Gabe refrained from pointing out that he'd rather go skinny dipping with gators.

"Read my lips. Nothing went zing. Nothing fucking happened. Period."

Not that Tamara hadn't tried. And she was a fine one to talk about kinky, leaning over and telling him, just as they'd left the limo to do the red carpet walk into the Golden Globes, that she wasn't wearing any underwear.

There'd been a time when an announcement like that would've given him a boner the size of Alaska, but ever since his first movie, where he'd been cast in the starring role of the rogue pirate Jean Lafitte, a virtual Aladdin's cave of gorgeous, available women had opened up to him. In the beginning, he'd done what any healthy male would do when gifted with such a scrumptious smorgasbord of female dessert—he'd feasted.

Unfortunately, it hadn't taken him long to discover that even the sweetest desserts could become boring. And it was hard to value anything that came too easily.

"Hell." He dragged his hand through the shaggy hair he'd

been growing for an upcoming role as a borderline crooked, New Orleans cop. "I've got to get out of town."

"Like there's any place on the planet the paparazzi won't find you."

He'd spent a sleepless night thinking about that.

"There's one place."

Gabe had never planned to return to his hometown of Blue Bayou. Then again, he sure as hell hadn't planned to end up in a mess like this, either.

Besides, it wasn't as if he had anywhere else to go.

Two

It was funny how life turned out. Who'd have thought that a girl who'd been forced to buy her clothes in the Chubbettes department of the Tots to Teens Emporium, the very same girl who'd been a wallflower at her senior prom, would grow up to have men pay to get naked with her?

It just went to show, Emma Quinlan considered, as she ran her hands down her third bare male back of the day, that the American dream was alive and well and living in Blue Bayou, Louisiana.

Not that she'd dreamed that much of naked men back when she'd been growing up.

She'd been too sheltered, too shy, and far too inhibited. Then there'd been the weight issue. Photographs showed that she'd been a cherubic infant, the very same type celebrated on greeting cards and baby food commercials.

Then she'd gone through a "baby fat" stage. Which, when she was in the fourth grade, resulted in her being sent off to a fat camp where calorie cops monitored every bite that went into her mouth and did surprise inspections of the cabins, searching out contraband. One poor calorie criminal had been caught with packages of Gummi Bears hidden beneath a loose floorboard beneath his bunk. Years later, the memory of his frightened eyes as he struggled to plod his way through a punishment lap of the track was vividly etched in her mind.

The camps became a yearly ritual, as predictable as the return of swallows to the Louisiana Gulf coast every August on their fall migration.

For six weeks during July and August, every bite Emma put in her mouth was monitored. Her days were spent doing calisthenics and running around the oval track and soccer field; her nights were spent dreaming of crawfish jambalaya, chicken gumbo, and bread pudding.

There were rumors of girls who'd trade sex for food, but Emma had never met a camper who'd actually admitted to sinking that low, and since she wasn't the kind of girl any of the counselors would've hit on, she'd never had to face such a moral dilemma.

By the time she was fourteen, Emma realized that she was destined to go through life as a "large girl." That was also the year that her mother—a petite blonde, whose crowning achievement in life seemed to be that she could still fit into her size zero wedding dress fifteen years after the ceremony—informed Emma that she was now old enough to shop for back-to-school clothes by herself.

"You are so lucky!" Emma's best friend, Roxi Dupree, had declared that memorable Saturday afternoon. "My mother is soo old-fashioned. If she had her way, I'd be wearing calico like Half-Pint in *Little House on the Prairie*!"

Roxi might have envied what she viewed as Emma's shopping freedom, but she hadn't seen the disappointment in Angela Quinlan's judicious gaze when Emma had gotten off the bus from the fat gulag, a mere two pounds thinner than when she'd been sent away.

It hadn't taken a mind reader to grasp the truth—that Emma's former beauty queen mother was ashamed to go clothes shopping with her fat teenage daughter.

"Uh, sugar?"

The deep male voice shattered the unhappy memory. *Bygones*, Emma told herself firmly.

"Yes?"

"I don't want to be tellin' you how to do your business, but maybe you're rubbing just a touch hard?"

Damn. She glanced down at the deeply tanned skin. She had such a death grip on his shoulders. "I'm so sorry, Nate."

"No harm done," he said, the south Louisiana drawl blending appealingly with his Cajun French accent. "Though maybe you could use a bit of your own medicine. You seem a tad tense."

"It's just been a busy week, what with the Jean Lafitte weekend coming up."

Liar. The reason she was tense was not due to her days, but her recent sleepless nights.

She danced her fingers down his bare spine. And felt the muscles of his back clench.

"I'm sorry," she repeated, spreading her palms outward.

"No need to apologize. That felt real good. I was going to ask you a favor, but since you're already having a tough few days—"

"Don't be silly. We're friends, Nate. Ask away."

She could feel his chuckle beneath her hands. "That's what I love about you, *chère*. You agree without even hearing what the favor is."

He turned his head and looked up at her, affection warming his Paul Newman blue eyes. "I was supposed to pick someone up at the airport this afternoon, but I got a call that these old windows I've been trying to find for a remodel job are goin' on auction in Houma this afternoon, and—"

"I'll be glad to go to the airport. Besides, I owe you for getting your brother to help me out."

If it hadn't been for Finn Callahan's detective skills, Emma's louse of an ex-husband would've gotten away with absconding with all their joint funds. Including the money she'd socked away in order to open her Every Body's Beautiful day spa. Not only had Finn—a former FBI agent—not charged her his going rate, Nate insisted on paying for the weekly massage the doctor had prescribed after he'd broken his shoulder falling off a scaffolding.

"You don't owe me a thing. Your ex is pond scum. I was glad to help put him away."

Having never been one to hold grudges, Emma had tried not to feel gleeful when the news bulletin about her former husband's arrest for embezzlement and tax fraud had come over her car radio.

"So, what time is the flight, and who's coming in?"

"It gets in at five thirty-five at Concourse D. It's a Delta flight from L.A."

"Oh?" Her heart hitched. Oh, please. She cast a quick, desperate look into the adjoining room at the voodoo altar, draped in Barbie-pink tulle, that Roxi had set up as packaging for her "Hex Appeal" love spell business. Don't let it be—

"It's Gabe."

Damn. Where the hell was voodoo power when you needed it?

"Well." She blew out a breath. "That's certainly a surprise."

That was an understatement. Gabriel Broussard had been so eager to escape Blue Bayou, he'd hightailed it out of town without so much as a good-bye.

Not that he'd owed Emma one.

The hell he didn't. Okay. Maybe she did hold a grudge. But only against men who'd kissed her silly, felt her up until she'd melted into a puddle of hot, desperate need, then disappeared from her life.

Unfortunately, Gabriel hadn't disappeared from the planet. In fact, it was impossible to go into a grocery store without seeing his midnight blue eyes smoldering from the cover of some sleazy tabloid. There was usually some barely clad female plastered to him.

Just last month, an enterprising photographer with a telescopic lens had captured him supposedly making love to his co-star on the deck of some Greek shipping tycoon's yacht. The day after that photo hit the newsstands, splashed all over the front of the *Enquirer*, the actress's producer husband had filed for divorce.

Then there'd been this latest scandal with Tamara the prairie princess . . .

"Guess you've heard what happened," Nate said.

Emma shrugged. "I may have caught something about it on *Entertainment Tonight*." And had lost sleep for the past three nights imagining what, exactly, constituted kinky sex.

"Gabe says it'll blow over."

"Most things do, I suppose." It's what people said about Hurricane Ivan. Which had left a trail of destruction in its wake.

"Meanwhile, he figured Blue Bayou would be a good place to lie low."

"How lucky for all of us," she said through gritted teeth.

"You sure nothing's wrong, *chère*?"

"Positive." She forced a smile. It wasn't his fault that his best friend had the sexual morals of an alley cat. "All done."

"And feeling like a new man." He rolled his head onto his shoulders. Then he retrieved his wallet from his back pocket and handed her his Amex card. "You definitely have magic hands, Emma, darlin'."

"Thank you." Those hands were not as steady as they should have been as she ran the card. "I guess Gabe's staying at your house, then?"

"I offered. But he said he'd rather stay out at the camp."

Terrific. Not only would she be stuck in a car with the man during rush hour traffic, she was also going to have to return to the scene of the crime.

"You sure it's no problem? He can always rent a car, but bein' a star and all, as soon as he shows up at the Hertz counter, his cover'll probably be blown."

She forced a smile she was a very long way from feeling. "Of course it's no problem."

"Then why are you frowning?"

"I've got a headache coming on." A two-hundred-and-ten pound Cajun one. "I'll take a couple aspirin and I'll be fine."

"You're always a damn sight better than fine, *chère*." His grin was quick and sexy, without the seductive overtones that had always made his friend's smile so dangerous.

She could handle this, Emma assured herself as she locked up the spa for the day. An uncharacteristic forty-five minutes early, which had Cal Marchand, proprietor of Cal's Cajun Café across the street checking his watch in surprise.

The thing to do was to just pull on her big girl underpants, drive into New Orleans and get it over with. Gabriel Broussard might be *People* magazine's sexiest man alive. He might have seduced scores of women all over the world, but the man *Cosmo* readers had voted the pirate they'd most like to be held prisoner on a desert island with was, after all, just a man. Not that different from any other.

Besides, she wasn't the same shy, tongue-tied, small-town bayou girl she'd been ten years ago. She'd lived in the city; she'd gotten married, only to end up publicly humiliated by a man who turned out to be slimier than swamp scum.

It hadn't been easy, but she'd picked herself up, dusted herself off, divorced the dickhead, as Roxi loyally referred to him, started her own business and was a dues paying member of Blue Bayou's Chamber of Commerce.

She'd even been elected deputy mayor, which was, admittedly, an unpaid position, but it did come with the perk of riding in a snazzy convertible in the Jean Lafitte Day parade. Roxi, a former Miss Blue Bayou, had even taught her a beauty queen wave.

She'd been fired in the crucible of life. She was intelligent, tough, and had tossed off her nice girl Catholic upbringing after the dickhead dumped her for another woman. A bimbo who'd applied for a loan to buy a pair of D cup boobs so she could win a job as a cocktail waitress at New Orleans' Coyote Ugly Saloon.

Emma might not be a tomb raider like Lara Croft, or an international spy with a to-kill-for wardrobe and a trunkful of glamorous wigs like *Alias*'s Sydney Bristow, but this new, improved Emma Quinlan could take names and kick butt right along with the rest of those fictional take-charge females.

And if shc were the type of woman to hold a grudge, which she wasn't, she assured herself yet again, the butt she'd most like to kick belonged to Blue Bayou bad boy Gabriel Broussard.

Three

There was no way she could have missed him. Emma supposed that he'd chosen the plain white T-shirt, faded jeans, scuffed cowboy boots, red Ragin' Cajun baseball cap and RayBans in order to blend into the locals crowding the terminal, but there was no way Gabriel would ever blend in anywhere.

He was six feet one before tacking on the added height from those wedged heels of the boots and his body beneath that tight shirt appeared as lean and hard as it'd been when he was eighteen. The shaggy black hair curling at the nape of his neck was as black as a moonless night over the bayou and the thin white scar running across his cheekbone added a dashing, dangerous look reminiscent of the pirates who'd once used the bayou as a home base while raiding merchant ships out in the Gulf.

A sexy stubble of beard darkened his jaw, and his mouth was set in a firm, no-trespassing line designed to discourage anyone who might recognize him from speaking to him. He made his way past the newsstands, take-out Cajun food counters, and souvenir stands selling Tabasco sauce and plastic alligators on the loose-hipped predatory stride of a swamp panther.

Emma was wondering if Nate had informed Gabriel about the change of plans, that she'd be the one picking him up, when he honed in on her like a heat-seeking missile.

"Hey, *chère.*"

His drawl was as rich as the pralines being sold next to those grinning plastic gators. Emma had read that when he'd first gone to Hollywood, he'd been told to sound more "American," to which he'd responded that the last time he'd looked at a map, Louisiana *was* in America, and besides, having an accent sure as hell hadn't hurt Antonio Banderas, Pierce Brosnan, or Sean Connery.

After *The Last Pirate* was released, and all those earlier detractors realized how sexy moviegoers found that bayou drawl, Gabriel Broussard's name rocketed to the top of every A list in town.

Case closed. As they say in the movie business, *A Star Was Born.*

His sensually chiseled lips tilted into a weary, all-too memorable half smile that hinted at dark secrets. The smile that made women want to take him into their arms, coddle him, and make the pain go away. The smile that had coaxed more than one willing female into the backseat of the Batmobile black Trans Am he'd roared around the bayou in back in high school.

Then, even as she braced against it, he folded her in his strong arms.

Because the feel of that hard, male, built-for-sin body against hers made her want to hold on, Emma stiffened.

If he noticed her resistance, Gabe didn't show it as he put her a little away from him, keeping his long dark fingers curved around her shoulders as he subjected her to an openly masculine appraisal, from the top of her dark head, down to her Sunset Poppy lacquered toenails. The little toe was smeared a bit from putting her brand-new sandals back on before it dried, but from the way his gaze lingered on her breasts, Emma didn't figure he'd notice the flaw.

"Damned if you haven't turned into one hot female, you."

The intimate growl was more suited for a bedroom than the crowded concourse in Louis Armstrong International Airport. As for the words . . . well, they shouldn't have given her such a secret thrill.

They shouldn't.

But, heaven help her, they did.

They also gave her a rash, reckless idea.

While Emma wasn't one of those people who actually believed those tacky supermarket tabloid stories about bat boys and alien babies, and who in Hollywood was sleeping with whom, it was more than a little obvious that while he might no longer be the town's bad boy from the wrong side of the tracks, one thing about Gabriel Broussard hadn't changed. Seduction still came as naturally to him as breathing.

So, what if she turned the tables? What if *she* seduced *him*?

After all, he owed her. Big time.

Emma was proud of how she'd moved on after her divorce from Richard, the adulterous, tax-dodging, embezzling dickhead. But some old habits died hard, and in many ways, although there were times when she aspired to be promiscuous, she was still a good girl. Sometimes too much so, if her best friend could be believed.

Roxi, who could have written a modern girl's guide to hooking up, had taped all six seasons of *Sex and the City* and every Wednesday evening, while Richard had supposedly been at his Rotary Club meetings, she and Emma had gotten together to watch them. Unfortunately, while Roxi memorized Samantha's pick-up lines, Emma identified with the hopelessly romantic Charlotte.

It wasn't as if Roxi hadn't tried to liven up Emma's life, encouraging her to push the sexual envelope, to act on impulse.

Ha! Easy for *her* to say. Emma didn't do impulsive. She made lists. Lots and lots of lists. All of which were color coded by day of the week, month of the year, and whether they were business or personal.

Not only was she diligent about crossing items off as she accomplished them, if she did something that wasn't on one of those pieces of yellow lined legal paper, she'd add it to the bottom of the list, just for the satisfaction of drawing a line through it.

After going back to school to become a professional masseuse, she'd worked on her business plan for Every Body's Beautiful for eighteen months before buying so much as a towel. Much to Roxi's frustration, most of Emma's evenings were spent alone, poring over the day spa's books and spreadsheets, looking for ways she could improve her cash flow.

Reminding her on an almost daily basis that you didn't have to be in love with a man to sleep with him, Roxi was all the time also repeating her favorite bumper sticker slogan: Well-Behaved Women Seldom Made History. But being mostly content with the life she'd made for herself after the divorce debacle, Emma didn't feel a need to make history.

Still, what woman didn't have a few things in her past she might have done differently? Like marrying the dickhead.

Or believing, back when she'd been a naïve eighteen-year-old wallflower, that Gabriel Broussard would eventually grow tired of all those nymphets who were only attracted to his bad boy aura and tragically beautiful good looks.

Having harbored a secret crush on him for years, Emma had spent long lonely hours fantasizing scenarios where he'd suddenly recognize that there was a gleaming pearl amidst all the flashy cubic zirconium he'd been wasting his time with.

That pearl being her. A nice, caring, good girl who truly loved him for the sensitive, emotionally wounded heart that dwelt inside that devastatingly sexy body. For the man she'd known he could become.

A helluva lot of good that did you.

Maybe it was time, just for the few days he'd be in town, she ditched Emma, the good girl. And tried being Emma, the *good-time* girl.

Besides, part of Gabriel's appeal was that he'd always been a forbidden pleasure. Like all things forbidden, the fantasy undoubtedly surpassed the reality. Maybe it was time to find out if the bad boy of Blue Bayou could actually live up to his reputation.

And then, once she'd gotten a long overdue satisfaction, she'd just leave. The same way he had.

Later, when she was thinking clearly again, Emma would remind herself that her own reputation wasn't exactly that of a wild-woman seductress. And her body certainly wasn't Hollywood tucked, buffed, and toned.

But it was hard to even think at all when her mind was being bombarded by pheromones from a damn testosterone bomb.

Feeling uncharacteristically reckless—not to mention lightheaded—she backed two steps away to give him a good look. Trying not to teeter on the ridiculously high fuck-me stilettos that had seemed like a good idea when she'd seen them in the window of The Magic Slipper, and resisting the urge to lick her suddenly dry lips, Emma smoothed her palms over the hips of the brand-new flowered silk skirt she'd bought after closing up today.

She hadn't bought the outfit for Gabe. The timing was only coincidence. No way would she risk maxing out her AMEX for any man.

Apparently the money, which could have paid Every Body's Beautiful's electric bill for six months, had not been wasted. Emma experienced a sudden surge of feminine power as his gaze followed the provocative gesture.

Channeling her inner Samantha, Emma checked him out in turn, drinking in the mouthwatering sight of broad male shoulders, bulging biceps and the strong V-shaped torso that arrowed down into lean male hips. Allowing her gaze to linger suggestively on the button placket of his jeans, she watched his penis flex beneath the worn denim.

Oh. My. God.

An illicit thrill zinged through Emma. Hot damn if Roxi wasn't right.

Men were easy.

Wishing she'd known this feminine secret back in high school, Emma lifted her eyes back to his, which were still shaded by those damn sunglasses, and treated him to a bold, sultry look hot enough to melt steel.

"You're not looking so bad yourself, sugar," she said on a throaty let's-get-naked drawl Emma figured Samantha would use in this situation, if New York City's most famous bad girl had been born in bayou country.

When Gabe's lips twitched in a faint smile, Emma's rebellious mind conjured up an X-rated fantasy of them tugging at her suddenly sensitive nipples.

"Nate called me just as I was leaving for the airport this morning," he said.

In Emma's fantasy, his mouth was moving south, trailing wet hot kisses over her naked flesh. And she'd begun to tingle in places she'd forgotten *could* tingle.

"I wasn't real thrilled when he started in explainin' about havin' to go out of town, since that meant I was gonna have to rent a car, me," Gabe continued.

In her fantasy, he was nudging her dampening panties down with his beautiful white teeth. His words were beginning to be drowned out by the thundering hoofbeat of stampeding hormones.

"Which wasn't real high up on my Top Ten things to do right now since I'm trying to stay under the radar. Then he told me he'd found a stand-in."

"That stand-in being me."

Standing in. Standing up. Lying down. Against the wall, on the floor, the ceiling. Emma didn't care how. Or where. She just wanted him. Any which way.

"*Mais,* yeah." His slow, lazy gaze traveled slowly, erotically, down the length of her again. "If I'd known certain things about Blue Bayou had gotten so appealing, I'd have come back a helluva lot sooner."

What on earth would Samanatha say to that? Emma's mind stalled; her breath caught.

Think!

Since her brain seemed to have crashed, more vital regions leaped into the breach. "Some days a guy gets lucky," she heard herself cooing in a very unEmma-like way.

Emma realized she'd hit the bull's-eye when an ebony brow lifted above the frames of those wraparound shades. "You sayin' this is going to be one of those days, *chère*?"

Emma had spent most of her teenage years—and later, even after a marriage that should have been declared dead at the altar—dreaming about Gabriel looking at her this way, as if she were the most desirable woman he'd ever seen. As if she were a whiskey-drenched bread pudding smothered in whipped cream he wanted to eat up.

Amazingly, this reality was proving even more exciting. She took her time, pretending to think it over, while, relying on age-old feminine instincts she hadn't even realized she possessed, she slowly trailed her fingers along the V-neck of her silk blouse.

"That's for me to know."

His shielded gaze followed the deliberately languid gesture, honing in on her cleavage.

Easy.

"And you to find out."

He moved closer, the pointy tips of his boots touching her bare toes. "Sounds like a treasure hunt."

His deep, rumbling voice caressed every nerve.

"It just might be." She cocked her head. Electricity was sparking all around them. "Do you enjoy treasure hunts?"

He rubbed his square jaw, drawing her gaze to that cleft just beneath his lower lip. "That depends on the treasure."

He moved even closer, so that there wasn't a breath of air between them, and toyed with a strand of auburn hair, wrapping it around his hand in a way that had her imagining him dragging her by the hair below deck to his pirate captain's quarters, where he'd force her to do all sorts of wicked, wild, wonderful things.

His hand—his large, dark hand—skimmed down her neck, sliding over her shoulder like warm silk. "If I have enough motivation, I can be very, very good at them."

Emma gave him the fluttery Scarlett O'Hara smile Roxi used to practice in the mirror back when they were thirteen. "I'll just bet you can."

Emma was hot, hot, hot.

So blisteringly hot she was on the verge of melting into a pitiful puddle of need right here in front of a display tower of Mean Devil Woman Cajun Hot Sauce.

"What do you say we blow this place and get started?" Gabriel suggested, lowering his head until his mouth was hovering just above hers. So close she could feel his hot breath against her lips.

Some faint vestige of reason in Emma's mind managed to break through the hormones that were jumping up and down, screaming yes, yes, yes! to remind her that this was no longer her own private erotic fantasy.

The game she was playing with Gabriel Broussard was all too real. What on earth made her think she was up to playing in this man's league?

Still, the part of her mind that was still functional asked, what was the worst that could happen? That he might reject her? So? Wasn't it better to have loved and lost than to never have loved at all?

Not that they were talking about love.

It was lust. Pure and simple.

What would Samantha say?

It'd be his loss.

Good answer.

"So," she asked brightly, with renewed confidence, "do you have luggage?"

"Just this." He held up a scuffed leather duffle bag that looked as if it'd been around the world at least a dozen times. Emma wondered if it was the same one he'd packed before leaving her sleeping in his bed.

You're a survivor. You can do this.

"I'm parked outside," she said.

Duh! Where the hell else would she be parked? A blonde with a cotton candy mass of frosted and over-teased hair and a dangerous spark in her overly made-up blue eyes was headed toward them. If they hung around here any longer, any opportunity to escape unnoticed would be lost.

"We'd better get going before we draw a crowd and you end up on the front of some tabloid." She turned and started walking toward the exit.

"Wouldn't be the first time." He smiled like an unrepentant sinner and fell into step beside her, shortening his stride to match hers.

His response brought to mind Tamara Templeton's alleged reason for breaking her engagement to Gabe. Which, in turn, had Emma wondering what kind of kinky situation she was getting herself into, driving this man out to that isolated camp in the bayou.

This was insane.

Amazing.

Insanely amazing.

Heat, thick with moisture, hit like a fist as they left the terminal. Emma could feel her hair, which she'd spent twenty minutes this morning blow-drying to a smooth, auburn sheen, spring into a mass of wild, unruly curls.

It figured. Even her hair couldn't control itself around Gabriel Broussard.

Four

What the hell had he been thinking? Coming on to Emma Quinlan that way? Christ, Emma, of all people.

As he'd followed that magnificent J.Lo butt out of the terminal, to the sporty, cherry red Miata convertible that fit the bold, adventurous female Emma Quinlan seemed to have metamorphosed into, Gabe was having trouble reconciling this lushly curvaceous, sexy, incredibly hot female with the shy, plump girl who'd so openly adored him back in high school.

That Emma had followed him around like a puppy, and although it probably had been selfish of him, he'd let her. Emma had been the only person he could talk to. The only person he could share his impossible dreams with. The only person, besides Nate Callahan—who'd been struggling to start up his construction business and take care of his dying mother in those days—whom Gabe trusted.

And, although there'd occasionally been times when he'd felt a little sexual tug, and known that she would have been more than willing to let him do anything he wanted, getting naked in the backseat of his Trans Am with a friend would've been just too weird.

Like their one night together hadn't been?

Shit.

"What are you going to do for a car out at the camp?"

"Can't see that I'll need one. Nate stocked the place with groceries and the pirogue's there. It's not like Blue Bayou's got a lot of nightlife I'm going to be missing out on."

"You might be surprised. We're celebrating Jean Lafitte Days this weekend."

"Yeah, Nate mentioned something about that. But as much as I hate to miss all the fun, I think I'll pass."

"You don't have to be sarcastic. A parade and a dance probably don't seem that big a deal to a jet-setting movie star," she said. "But people enjoy it. And the money from the tickets goes to an after-school recreation program for the kids of the parish, so it's all for a good cause."

"I'm not sayin' it isn't. In fact, I'll write you a check. I'm just not feelin' real sociable right now."

"Speaking as deputy mayor, I'll be happy to accept any contribution you'd like to make," she said stiffly, sounding, Gabe thought, uncomfortably, like her mother.

"I've gotta admit to bein' surprised you're not still pissed off at me."

"About what?" Her tone was casual enough, but the slight tightening of her fingers on the steering wheel gave her away.

"My last night in town. The one we spent together."

"It may come as a huge surprise to your movie star ego, but it's been years since I even thought about that." She kept her gaze directed out the windshield. "Besides, it wasn't as if anything happened."

"That's not the way I remember it."

Her skirt, colored in a bright tropical print, was calf-length. Which was the bad news since it had him salivating like one of Pavlov's pups for a look at her long legs.

The good news was that it was cut like a sarong. As she stepped on the gas to pass a minivan, the silk parted, giving him a view of thigh that caused his insides to tingle and heat up.

Speaking of heating up . . .

"I recall you bein' hot as a Mardi Gras firecracker, you."

"You were so drunk I'm surprised you remember anything about that night."

"I might have been tanked, sure enough. But it's hard to forget giving a girl her first orgasm."

Her deep, rich laugh sent the heat in his belly traveling south. "You are so full of yourself, Gabriel Broussard. What makes you think that was my first?"

He'd tried to forget most of the things that had happened that night, but one thing had remained vividly etched on his mind: the memory of Emma writhing beneath his plundering mouth, her bare back bowed off the soft, Spanish-moss stuffed mattress, the breathless cries—almost like keening—that were ripped from her ravished lips as he drove her higher and higher until she'd come, screaming his name.

Even now, ten years later, the mental picture of her, flushed and uncharacteristically wanton, was so vivid, it was all he could do to keep from licking the pale flesh exposed by that sexy slit in her skirt.

"Solo flying doesn't count," he said.

A corner of her mouth turned down in a frown, but she didn't deny his point that he'd been her first. First man. First orgasm.

"Speaking of flying, along with all that booze, you also had enough Demerol in your system to fly to the moon." She tossed him a look. "Solo."

She'd warned him against mixing drugs and alcohol. But had he listened? Hell, no. He'd been on a crazy, self-destructive binge that night and by the time they'd reached the camp after the emergency room visit, he'd had to lean on her to stagger into the cabin.

He'd fallen onto the bed, taking her with him in a tangle of arms and legs. Her dress—an unflattering, black taffeta—had crackled when he'd delved beneath it. That sound had, for some inexplicable reason, generated such a hot spurt of lust that years later, while filming the scene in *The Last Pirate*, where Jean

Lafitte attends a ball in the French Quarter, the sound of all those rustling petticoats the costume designer had put the actresses in caused him to walk around with a boner for two days.

His reaction had not gone unnoticed; several conservative religious groups had had a field day posting close-ups of his groin on the Internet as yet another example of the erosion of the national morality.

"I sure as hell wasn't feeling any pain, me." Not when he'd left the ER anyway. And certainly not later, when he'd been rolling around on that fragrant mattress with Emma. "Like I said, I don't remember much about that night. But I've got the feelin' I never thanked you for all you did."

"We were friends," she said simply. "You would have done the same thing for me."

The bitch was, Gabe wasn't real sure he would've. He'd been a pretty self-centered bastard in those days. A '90s James Dean retread. Rebel without a clue.

Gabe sighed.

"So," he said, deciding to change the topic, "I guess you heard about the little mess I'm in."

"Which mess is that?"

"Excuse me. I hadn't realized you'd been away on Mars the past week." Of all the topics he could have chosen, why the hell had he brought that one up? What was wrong with the weather? That was always a safe topic. Or sports.

"So, do you think the Saints are going to be able to capture the NFC South this season?"

"I've no idea." Her tone suggested she didn't give a rat's ass, either. "Football isn't real big up on Mars—it's hard to mark the yardage lines in all that red dust—so I'm a little out of the loop." They were crossing the old iron bridge over the Mississippi. "So, what mess are we talking about?"

"The one about my so-called engagement."

"Ah." She nodded in a way that told him she'd known exactly what he'd been referring to. "The one your little television star fiancée called off."

Gabe ground his teeth and felt his penis, which had gotten semi-hard at the memory of Emma lying beneath him, deflated like a three-day-old balloon. Timing, he thought, was effin' everything. "Tamara Templeton was never my fiancée."

"I see." She nodded again, obviously not buying his denial. "And you bought her that ten carat Tiffany diamond why?"

"I didn't buy it."

That captured her attention. She glanced over at him. "Mary Hart said you did."

"Mary Hart may be one helluva television personality. She's also fairer than most of her breed." Because for some reason it was important that Emma understand he wasn't a total son-of-a-bitch, he yanked off the shades and looked her straight in the eye. "She's been known to get her facts wrong."

He watched the wheels turn around in her bright head as she processed that little bit of information. Then she turned her attention back to the narrow road. "If Mary Hart's so fair, why didn't you tell her what you've just told me? That you weren't really engaged?"

Good question. "Dammit, because it's fuckin' complicated."

"You don't have to shout at me, Gabriel. After all, you're the one who brought it up," she reminded him.

"You've not only gotten damn sexy, *chère*. You're a helluva lot tougher than you used to be." Sassier. And damned if it didn't look good on her.

"From necessity." She shot him another look. "Do you have a problem with tough women?"

"Actually, I like them." He especially liked picturing Emma wearing only a pair of black leather thigh-high boots and a wicked smile. "Under the right circumstances." Like in his bedroom with flames crackling in the fireplace, and some slow, sultry tenor jazz flowing from the Surround sound speakers. "When they play fair."

"And your fiancée didn't?"

"She wasn't my goddamn—"

"Right. Tamara Templeton wasn't your real fiancée. Just your fake one. Which is funny—"

"There's nothing funny about this."

"Funny odd. Not funny ha-ha," she corrected calmly. "Although I'm admittedly no expert on precious gems, that Texas-size rock weighing down her left hand sure didn't look like a fake diamond."

Gabe could tell from her tone that she wasn't ready to suspend all disbelief. Hell, he didn't blame her.

"You're right. It was real. But I didn't buy it." He yanked off his Ragin' Cajun cap and dragged his hand through his hair. "Hell, we'd only gone out twice. Both times set up by our agent to maximize press coverage."

"I wouldn't think you'd need that."

"It wasn't really my choice. But Tamara was hot to change her image—"

"So she figured the best way to do that would be to go out with Hollywood's bad boy?"

Okay, now they were back to dealing with major disbelief.

"That reputation is overrated," he ground out through clenched teeth. "It's typecasting. Because I tend to choose roles that look at the dark side of human nature, people figure I'm a son of a bitch in real life."

"If you say so."

He still wasn't convincing her. Gabe mentally added a whip to the image of her wearing those dominatrix boots. "My agent, asked me to accompany Tamara to a couple public events. Since Caroline was the first person in the business to take me seriously, and stuck with me when I refused to play the teen idol card after the pirate flick, I figured I owed her one."

"I can see why you wouldn't want to be typecast as a teen hunk. But *The Last Pirate* was a very good movie."

"You saw it?" Gabe found himself liking that idea.

"Of course. It played to a packed house at the Bijou for five weeks. I doubt there was anyone in the parish who didn't see it at least once."

"Which is surprising, since I'm sure as hell not Blue Bayou's favorite son."

"Jean Lafitte was from around here. That gave it a local connection. Plus, I think a lot of people were curious to see how Blue Bayou's favorite juvenile delinquent turned out." Her plump, made-for-sin mouth curved in a smile that sent a lightning bolt of heat straight to his groin. "You were very good. Not that I ever had any doubts."

"That made three people in town who thought I might have a future other than landing my ass behind bars."

He wondered what she'd thought while watching the erotic scene where the pirate ravished the Spanish ship captain's wife. Had she gotten turned on by the forced seduction? Had she watched the pirate take a jeweled dagger and cut open the woman's bodice to gain access to her breasts and remembered when he'd torn open her dress and taken her soft and yielding flesh in his mouth?

And when his dark and dangerous character had surged between the woman's fleshy white thighs that had opened willingly for him, had Emma remembered how he'd pinned her to the mattress and, using his mouth, his teeth, his tongue, made her come?

The view outside the window became hazed with the red lust shimmering before his eyes as he imagined lashing Emma's wrists and ankles to his bed and fucking her hard and fast and deep. But only after he'd driven her crazy enough to beg for it.

Jesus. If he kept on this runaway sex train of thought, he was going to come in his jeans before they even got to the camp.

"Three people," he repeated, his voice raspy with pent-up lust. He would have cleared his damn throat, but didn't want her to realize that somehow, when he hadn't been paying close enough attention, she'd captured control over not just the situation, but his damn mutinous dick, as well. "You, Nate, and Mrs. Herlihy."

The high school drama teacher had rescued Gabe from detention when Raul Dupree had come down with flu. She talked him into auditioning for the role of Sweeny Todd in the spring musical, and literally changed his life.

"She's retiring this year," Emma said conversationally.

"No shit? Isn't she a little young to quit teaching?"

"She's sixty-eight. And she's not retiring, exactly. She's going to volunteer at the Boys and Girls Club after-school program."

"That sounds like something she'd do."

Rescuing more at-risk kids. They might not grow up to be Hollywood stars—which to Gabe's mind was a mixed blessing—but they also might avoid going to prison, which is where he probably would've ended up if it hadn't been for the teacher's intervention.

"We're giving her an award after the Jean Lafitte parade on Saturday," Emma said.

Gabe tensed, sensing what was coming.

"A plaque isn't all that much to pay her back for all she's done for the town." She paused another beat. "It'd probably make the ceremony a lot bigger deal if you were the one presenting it."

This time it was he who paused. "I don't think that'd be a real good idea, *chère*. Seems I'd be taking the spotlight off the person who really deserved it."

It was a not so artful a dodge. "And we both know how you hate the spotlight," Emma murmured. "Which is undoubtedly why you chose a low-profile career like acting."

"Got me there," he said.

"You just want to hide out from the press. Which brings us back to those dates—"

"They weren't dates, in the traditional sense of the word." The woman was like a damn pit bull. Why couldn't she just let the thing go? "And I was a perfect gentleman."

She laughed at that idea.

"Hey." He held up three fingers in the sign of a pledge. "Scout's honor."

"Funny. I don't remember you being a Boy Scout."

True enough. Even if he had been able to afford the uniform, which he hadn't, there's no way the other parents would have allowed the kid of the town drunk to have anything to do with their churchgoing sons. Thinking back on the wild, angry kid he'd been back then, Gabe couldn't really blame them.

"I don't remember you bein' so sarcastic." Or offering him anything less than her unwavering support, including, that one night, when he'd opened a forbidden door he should've just kept locked.

Hell, maybe she was holding a grudge. He couldn't deny she had every right to.

"I'm sorry. The scout remark may have been hitting below the belt. So, don't leave me hanging."

"Like I did that night?" Gabe decided there was no more point in beating around the bush. "When I left you a virgin?"

A soft flush, like a late summer rose, filled her cheeks as she realized her inadvertent double entendre. "I meant I want to know the rest of the story that brought you back home."

The woman wasn't just hot. She was damn pretty. And, since he didn't believe people really changed all that much, Gabe suspected that beneath her sexy new attitude, Emma was still that sweet, caring girl who had, for one suspended night in time, made him feel things he'd never thought he'd feel. Wish for impossible things beyond his reach. Ache for the kind of love he hadn't thought a guy like him could ever have.

"Gabe?"

She was looking at him again, her expression quizzical.

"Sorry." He shook his head, like his old retriever, Beau, used to do when climbing out of the water with a duck. Emma wasn't the only one puzzled by the feelings bombarding him. She'd stirred something in him. Something he couldn't quite put a name to. "Looking at the color in your pretty face got me sidetracked. I can't remember the last time I've been with a woman who blushed."

He took hold of her hand, which smelled a bit like almonds, and nibbled on her knuckles. "Watching your cheeks go all pink makes me wonder what it'd take to make the rest of you blush all over."

She shivered. Not, Gabe suspected, because she was suddenly finding the air-conditioning blasting from the dashboard vents too cold.

"You were telling me about those dates that weren't really dates." She tugged her hand free. Her gaze fixed on a mirage shimmering like a phantom pool on the black asphalt ahead.

"Anyone ever tell you you've got a one-track mind, *chère*?"

"Why am I not surprised an actor would have something against linear thought?"

"Hey, I can do linear thought. In fact, my mind's been pretty much runnin' on a single track since I walked off that plane and saw you standing there lookin' like you'd stepped out of a Gauguin painting."

The blush he'd found so appealing in her cheeks bloomed across the magnificent cleavage revealed by her neckline. The blouse was silk. Remembering all too well that her perfumed flesh was softer, Gabe was suddenly burning with the need to touch. To taste. To cup those lush breasts in his hands, to stroke her nipples, which, he couldn't help noticing, were pressing against the flowered silk.

They weren't the only thing that had gone hard. No friggin' doubt about it, his cock had taken on a mind of its own. And if it had its randy way, they'd be pulling over to the side of the road, and he'd be lifting that skirt while her long legs straddled him, while she took him deep inside her wet, slick womanly warmth. He fantasized nipping at those pebbled nipples, sucking on them hard enough to make her body tighten around him, as she rode him hard and fast.

"That sounds suspiciously like a line from some movie," she accused.

"It's no line." He'd never been one to pretty sex up with sweet words and silken promises. Never had to. But damned if she didn't remind him of the painter's lushly feminine Tahitian subjects. And he should know, since two of the paintings were currently hanging on his bedroom wall. "You ever have anyone film you, *chère*? While you're making love?"

"Of course not." Her eyes widened; she sounded properly scandalized. But perhaps intrigued?

There was a half beat of silence. Then . . .

"Have you ever?" she asked. *Oh, yeah,* Gabe thought, definitely intrigued. "Filmed someone while you were making love?"

"Not yet. But there's always a first time." He nodded in the direction of the duffle bag he'd thrown into the backseat when he'd climbed into the car. "I brought along my video camera." Unable to resist the lure of her soft, fragrant skin, he slipped his hand into that enticing slit in her skirt and began trailing small, concentric circles just above her dimpled knee. "I've been thinkin' of getting into directing, me."

That was true enough. Although he enjoyed acting, he was beginning to tire of living in some other character's skin for weeks, sometimes months, at a time. And then there was the issue of control. It wasn't that he was a control freak or anything—hell, damn straight he was.

There wasn't much in the movie business under anyone's control. It was, he'd often considered, like playing one of those flying trapeze artists without a net. But directing offered more opportunity for calling the shots than acting ever would.

"How would you like to star in my first film?" Encouraged that she hadn't yanked the slit in her skirt closed, he trailed his fingers up petal-soft skin.

"You want me to star in a porno film?"

"An erotic film," he corrected huskily, getting turned on by the imagined sight of a nude Emma in his viewfinder. "One with limited distribution. Just the two of us."

"I don't think—"

"I'll take a page from Gauguin's book and film you outdoors," he said reflectively, overriding her refusal as creative wheels started turning. The more Gabe thought about it, the more it seemed like a perfect way to while away the days he was going to be stuck out in the bayou.

"Maybe on that old swing at the camp, lying on your back, your hair loose, flowing over your breasts, your rosy pink nipples thrusting through those long wild curls."

With his free hand, he plucked the clip from her hair, allowing the curls to tumble riotously free, shining like a bright copper penny in the stuttering rays of sun managing to break through the gathering clouds.

"Gabe." His name shuddered out from between glossy pink lips. "Don't."

"Don't what, *chère*? Don't touch you?" When his fingers continued their sensual quest, she trembled, but did not pull away. "Don't imagine how you'd look, with the sun setting at your back, your long sexy legs spread over the wooden arms of the swing, your lower lips all lush and wet, and—"

"Dammit, Gabriel," she complained. "Please."

"Please, *oui*?" He skimmed a feathery touch back down to her knee, this time on the inside of her thigh, and watched her unconsciously rub her thighs together.

Gabe wanted to be there.

Between those long, wraparound legs.

Inside her.

"Or please, *non*?"

"How am I supposed to think when you're doing that"—she arched her back against his touch as he lightly scraped the warming flesh with a fingernail—"let alone drive."

Realizing that if he wasn't careful, he could be responsible for them ending up in the water, Gabe reluctantly reclaimed his hand and turned back to the idea of filming Emma in the throes of passion.

"You'll need to be eating something. An apple fits Gauguin's *Eve in the Garden of Eden* theme, but it's too clichéd," he said thoughtfully, getting into the idea as creative juices stirred along with sexual ones. "A ripe peach." He nodded, pleased with the notion. "I'll feed it to you. Then lick the sweet, sticky juice off your sun-warmed naked flesh."

She actually moaned. The same way he imagined she would if he were trailing his tongue down her torso, over the soft feminine swell of her stomach. Then beyond.

He was about to tell her just to pull over to the side of the road, when the front tire suddenly started going *thump thump thump*.

"Damn." The mood was shattered. Emma hit the steering wheel with the palm of her hand as she pulled over to the side of the road. "That's all we need," she complained. "That storm's getting closer, and this time of day, it'll take the auto club at least an hour to get out here from the city."

"No problem." It took all his acting talent to keep his tone even when what he wanted to do was bang his head against the dashboard at the way she'd been yanked out of the sensual spell his seductive words had wrapped around them. "You've got yourself a spare, right?"

"Well, of course, but—"

"I haven't changed a tire since my old days working at Dix's Automotive. But I'll bet it's one of those things you don't forget. Like ridin' a bicycle." He winked at her. "Or sex."

Now that the moment had been lost, the thing to do was get the damn tire changed so they could get to the camp.

Where he and the luscious, soft-skinned, sweet-smelling Emma Quinlan could begin driving each other crazy.

Five

As Gabe took the jack from the Miata's trunk, Emma tried to remember her former husband ever doing anything more physical than swinging a golf club and came up blank.

Richard had been too busy stealing money from his employer—who just happened to be his father-in-law—and screwing the bimbo to help out with any chores.

Now, watching Gabe work, she decided that there was something to be said for having a male around the house to do those manly things. Like change a tire. Mow the lawn. Tie you up.

Tie you up? Where had that come from?

From that damn Jean Lafitte movie. Emma had known she was in trouble the minute it had come up in the conversation and was vastly relieved that there was no way Gabe would ever know she'd sat in the dark of the Bijou, popcorn going uneaten, as she'd watched his larger-than-life character throw that woman over his shoulder, then leap from her husband's Spanish galleon to his own ship that was flying the bloodred flag feared throughout southern waters.

His captive had fought like a wildcat, kicking, biting, scratching, her nails leaving a scarlet trail down the dark skin of his back. But she'd been no match for the rapacious rogue.

Nor her own rioting female desires. By the time the actress was bucking beneath him, opening herself up to his invasion, Emma's panties had been drenched and her legs so weak, she'd had to stay seated until long after the credits had rolled and the theater emptied.

That night she'd dreamed of being held hostage by a pirate, who, unsurprisingly, looked exactly like Gabriel Broussard. Dressed in a pirate's black shirt, tight trousers, and high black leather boots, he'd tied her to the mast of his ship, his strong hands claiming her body at will, while his low, rumbling voice told her all the things he intended to do to her.

Wicked, outrageous things. Things that shocked her. Shamed her. And, dammit, excited her.

Just remembering that movie, and the dream, along with the scandalous way she'd allowed him to touch her in the car, was enough to make her so hot she was surprised she wasn't liquidizing from the inside out.

Watching him work wasn't helping. Who'd have guessed that changing a flat tire could be such a turn-on? As he crouched down and loosened the lug nuts with a speedy efficiency that a NASCAR pit mechanic might have envied, the faded denim pulled tight against strong, muscular thighs in a way that had Emma imagining naughty things. Kinky things.

She was used to seeing men without clothes on. Her days, after all, were spent with nude men who wore nothing but a towel and a blissful expression as her hands brought them to ecstasy. Or, as close to it as a person could get without having sex.

But, Emma was discovering, there was a huge difference between nude and naked. Nude was when a man wasn't wearing clothes. Naked was when he wasn't wearing clothes and was up to no good.

And, heaven help her, naked was how she wanted Gabe.

When he bent over to jack up the wheel, any lingering desire to kick his butt evaporated. It was a gold medal, world-class butt and what Emma wanted to do, was aching to do, was bite it.

Do it, that devilish Samantha perched on her damp shoulder, advised.

I can't just maul him!

"*What world do you live in,* chica*?*" A new voice, sounding a lot like Gabrielle, from *Desperate Housewives,* chimed in.

Terrific. Now they were ganging up on her.

"It's not that easy, dammit." Emma was appalled when she heard the words come out of her mouth.

"Something wrong?" Gabe glanced back at her.

"No." She forced a smile. "I was just saying that didn't look very easy."

He shrugged. "Like I said, some things you never forget. Who'd have thought a past working as a grease monkey would ever come in handy?"

Thunder rumbled ominously on the horizon; black clouds raced in from the Gulf. The dense air was thick enough to drink. As he returned to work, sweat dampened his shirt, causing it to cling to his back, revealing every corded muscle. More muscles bunched in his arms as he pumped the jack.

Lightning crackled across the darkening sky. Emma could taste the electricity on her tongue, beneath her skin, scorching along her nerve endings. She'd lived in south Louisiana all of her life. She was accustomed to the heat and constant humidity. But never had she been so hot she felt on the verge of fainting.

Her head grew light. White spots, like paper-winged moths, fluttered in front of her eyes. She placed a hand against the back fender of the Miata to steady herself. Gabe, who'd replaced the flat with the spare and was tightening the lug nuts, glanced up at her.

"You sure you're okay?"

"Of course."

If you didn't count the fact that she was on the verge of

falling flat on her face. Her hair was clinging to her forehead; more unruly curls had escaped to stick to the back of her damp neck. Swaying a bit, she tried to brush it away with the hand that wasn't holding onto the car for dear life, but her fingers were shaking.

Deep blue eyes framed by long, sooty lashes that would have appeared feminine were it not for the lean, hungry lines of his face, studied Emma with an intensity that did nothing to help clear her head.

"You look as if you're about to pass out, *mon ange*."

He'd called her his angel that night. When he'd drawn her down onto that mattress and kissed her. A deep, searing kiss that had scorched away a lifetime of inhibitions. A kiss she'd been fantasizing about since she'd been twelve years old. But the reality had far surpassed those romantic, junior high school daydreams.

"I've never fainted in my life." The spots swirled like snowflakes as she tossed her head.

"There's always a first time for everything."

He tossed aside the jack, stood up and curled his hands around her upper arms to steady her.

The wind picked up, rattling the sugar cane in the fields on either side of the road. "You're tremblin' like a willow in a hurricane, you."

Emma was far from willowy, but at this moment, with this man, she felt strangely, uncharacteristically fragile.

"You scared of storms, *chère*?"

"No." She swallowed.

"You're not scared of me?" His hands were moving up and down her arms, the gesture, which was meant to soothe, made her ache with the need to feel them everywhere.

"No." She shook her head.

Emma was afraid of herself. Of this dizzying, hot way only this man had ever made her feel. Despite her little internal pep talk about rejection being no big deal, the truth was that while Richard's very public affair had wounded her pride, Gabe's taking off without so much as a good-bye kiss had been like an arrow shot into the center of her heart.

It had taken her a long time to get over that night; now, what she feared was risking her foolish heart again.

She lifted her hand, skimmed her fingers over his face. Even with that scar cutting across his cheekbone, it was beautiful, the face of a fallen angel which could have been washed off the ceiling of a cathedral.

"Should I be? Afraid of you?"

"*Mais, non.*" He touched her in turn, his fingertips feeling like sparklers as they traced the line of her mouth, brushed her cheek, her temple, into her hair. "I'd never hurt you, Emma."

But he would. Oh, he honestly wouldn't mean to. But she could see the heartache coming as clearly as the storm barreling toward them across the bayou.

As she felt herself drowning in the midnight blue of his eyes, Emma suspected that the pain could be well worth the risk.

Lightning forked across the sky, sparking inside her. The rumbling answer of thunder was echoed in Emma's own heart as she stood there, looking up at him, knowing that her wildly foolish heart was glowing, unguarded, in her eyes.

He framed her face with his hands. "I'm going to kiss you now, *chère.*" His deep voice was tender, yet roughened with arousal.

Emma had to remind herself to breathe as his mouth, slowly, inexorably, moved downward, toward hers.

Having never forgotten the last time they'd been together, she braced herself for the heat.

Six

Prepared for an invasion of teeth and tongue, Emma was surprised when he began kissing her gently—little licks and nips up her cheek, over her eyelids, which closed at the touch of his lips, her temple, the hollow beneath her lower lip—which no other man had ever taken the time to discover—was somehow directly connected to that hot, damp place between her legs.

"Gabe?"

"What, *chère*?"

The tip of his tongue touched hers, then retreated, while he trailed a hand down her throat, to where she knew he could feel the out-of-control beat of her blood.

Her arms felt heavy as she lifted them, linking her fingers together behind his neck. "I thought you were going to kiss me."

"That's what I'm doing."

"But I want . . ."

Her voice trailed off as his caressing touch dipped into the warmth between her breasts.

"What do you want, Emma?"

Taking hold of her hair, he pulled her head back, to give his mouth access to her throat.

"I want you to *really* kiss me."

She felt his smile against her tingling lips.

Then his tongue thrust between her lips, sweeping deep to mate with hers, and his mouth, which had been so gentle only a moment before, ground against hers hard enough to bruise, the plundering kiss one of raw, sexual possession.

"*Mon Dieu*, you taste good," he rasped as he pinned her between the hot metal of the car and the even greater heat of his body. "I could eat you up."

She wrapped a leg around his; her skirt fell open, baring her thigh all the way up to her panties and she managed to get a hand between them, curving her fingers around his length.

"You're killing me here, Emma," he groaned when she began stroking the erection that swelled even larger, hotter, against the denim.

He yanked his head back just long enough to look down at her. The masculine hunger darkened, like molten cobalt flowing over obsidian.

"Where the hell have you been hiding?" His voice was low and guttural, his hands thrillingly rough. Relentless.

"I wasn't hiding. I've been right here. In Blue Bayou." Waiting for him, Emma could have said, but didn't because it would be too hard to explain how that could be true when she didn't understand it herself.

Gabe might have been her first man, but he hadn't been her last. She had, after all, been married.

But she'd never forgotten their night together and now she was discovering that some secret, hidden part of her heart had been awaiting his return.

As for her body . . . it wanted him. Everywhere. In every way.

"I've been here," she repeated breathlessly beneath the plundering mouth that had branded her on a stormy night ten years ago.

A clap of thunder caused the ground beneath them to tremble. The black sky overhead opened up.

As a hot, stinging rain pelted down on them, Gabe dragged

her hand from his groin. Her body might be lush, but her bones were narrow, allowing him to wrap his fingers around both slender wrists. Lifting her hands, he held them against the roof of the car, forcing her body into a taut, trembling bow.

She didn't fight against his dominant male behavior. Didn't try to free herself. Yet there was nothing submissive about the way she was rotating her pelvis against his, or the way, somehow managing to stand on those spindly little fuck-me-big-boy high heels, she lifted her leg even higher, wrapping it around his waist.

He ran his free hand up her smooth bare leg. The crotch of her panties was soaked. And not from the rain.

He felt her suck in an expectant breath as he pushed the elastic band of the high cut leg aside.

He paused.

She whimpered.

"Dammit." She arched her hips even higher, straining, seeking. "Touch me."

Obliging Emma, pleasing himself, Gabe stroked the slick, hot flesh.

One of them trembled as he slipped a finger into the welcoming wet warmth. Gabe wasn't sure whether it was Emma. Or him.

He slipped another finger inside her, at the same time flicking her swelled clitoris with a searing stroke of his thumb.

"Oh, God." She rolled her head against the window as he swallowed her moan with a long deep soul kiss.

"Tell me." He bit her bottom lip, then soothed the sting with the tip of his tongue. "Tell me that you want this as much as I do."

"Of course I do." A sound, somewhere between a laugh and moan was ripped from her throat as he thrust deeper. Harder. "Can't you tell?"

She was flowing over his hand. Her avid lips ate into his, her breasts pressed against his chest.

"*Mais*, yeah." He ripped open the top button of his jeans, wondering why he'd never before noticed that the 501s he'd worn since high school were like a fucking chastity belt.

Maybe, he conceded, as his fingers, which were not nearly as steady as he was accustomed to, struggled with button number two, the reason he'd never noticed was that having always preferred to be the one in control, he'd never been so desperate, so damn needy to bury himself inside a woman. Up to the hilt in one hard, deep thrust.

But then again, he'd never known a woman as uninhibited as Emma. It wasn't that he wasn't accustomed to good sex. He always made sure the woman came, at least once, before he gave any thought to his own satisfaction; but there was always a part of him that remained an uninvolved observer, watching how the women beneath him moved, the expressions on their faces as he urged them higher and higher, the breathy little sounds they made when they came. The man in him was proud of his ability to satisfy; the actor in him recognized a performance when he saw one.

It wasn't that they were faking, exactly. Since practice made perfect, Gabe had been able to spot a phony orgasm before he was legally old enough to drink. But there was a certain artificiality about the way they arranged their bodies so as to always ensure they looked good, the way they never expended enough energy for their carefully coiffed hair to get sweaty, the way their faces, while portraying passion, never went lax with spent lust.

Emma was nothing like that.

Her eyes were closed, squeezed so tightly, lines fanned out from them, nearly into her hair. Her head was flung so far back, the tendons in her neck strained and her mouth was open, encouraging erotic thoughts of what those voluptuous ripe lips would look like surrounding his cock.

She was totally into the moment. Into him. Oblivious to the rain pelting down on her expressive, upturned face like stinging needles, oblivious to the fact that they were parked along the highway, risking discovery at any moment.

A sudden, ear-splitting blast of an airhorn blared through the rain.

Emma's eyes flew open as the eighteen-wheeler rumbled by. Her leg slid back down his to the ground.

"I can't believe I . . ." Her face, her lovely, flushed, wet face was bemused. "On a public road . . . Out in the open." She looked up at the sky. "In the pouring rain."

"Yeah." Timing, Gabe thought again with a frustration that did nothing to soothe his still rampant hard-on, was everything.

He released her hands. When she used one to cover her mouth, he braced himself for tears.

Emma surprised him yet again.

She laughed. "That was the most reckless thing I've ever done."

She put her freed hands against his chest. Then her eyes, which had begun to clear, started turning all sexy and soft focused again.

"Talk about reckless," Gabe groaned. "If you don't stop looking at me that way, I'm going to take you right here and now, and believe me, darlin', once I get inside you, not even an entire convention of long-haul truckers leaning on airhorns is going to be able to make me stop."

Her face lit up. "Even better."

It was Gabe's turn to laugh. Although his erection was still throbbing painfully, her unmasked excitement at the sexual threat was the first thing in a very long time he'd found to laugh about.

Her hair had tumbled down around her shoulders. The tangled curls looked like wet copper silk and smelled like peaches. Gabe ached with the need to feel them draped over his chest. His thighs. His penis.

"We're all wet," she murmured, seeming surprised at the discovery.

"Seem to be."

The flowered skirt clung damply to her womanly convex stomach, rounded thighs, and mound. Her blouse was rendered nearly transparent by rain. Beneath the silk she was wearing a white lace bra that matched the panties he'd nearly ripped off her. Her taut nipples were the same raspberry pink hue he hadn't even realized had remained imprinted on his memory all these years.

"But it sure as hell looks better on you," he said.

She tilted her head. Her lips tilted in a faint, somewhat indulgent smile. "What is it about men that whenever they see a woman they imagine her naked?"

"I don't."

She folded her arms beneath those amazing breasts. "Of course you don't." Her tone was a great deal drier than the weather.

"When men look at women they picture them in garter belts, silk stockings, and mile-high stiletto heels."

She rolled her eyes. "That is so chauvinistic."

"What can I say? Men are pigs," he agreed easily.

Gabe cupped her breasts, watching her eyes widen as he pinched those nipples. Hard.

She exhaled a short, surprised breath; the yielding flesh swelled in his hands.

"You are, without a doubt, the most responsive woman I've ever met."

Struggling against the urge to drag her into that little red car, rip their wet clothes away, throw his naked body on top of hers and devour her, Gabe lowered his forehead to hers and drew in a deep, painful breath that was meant to calm.

But damn well didn't even come close to tempering the male need to mate that was rampaging through every pore of his body.

"I'm going to put the jack in the trunk," he said. "Then we're going to the camp, where I'm going to take a long time to finish what we started ten years ago."

She shuddered against him; there was so much heat emanating from both their bodies, he was amazed they weren't surrounded by clouds of steam.

"After I have you, I'm going to feed you." He'd always liked to cook. The idea of cooking for Emma was nearly as appealing as making love to her. "Then we're going to spend the rest of the night seeing just how reckless we can be."

"I don't have any clothes with me."

"Don' worry 'bout it. You won't need any for what I have in mind."

"What if I have plans?"

"Do you?"

"Yes." She hooked an arm around his neck, went up on her toes, and gave him a quick, hard kiss. "I'm planning to spend the night with you."

Seven

Gabe offered to drive the rest of the way, but feeling the need to maintain some vestige of control over the situation, Emma declined.

"Just as well," he said agreeably. "This way I can play with your leg."

"Just my leg," she said.

"Spoilsport."

"Unless you want to end up in the bayou."

"Good point." He sighed. "And one I'd reluctantly already thought of myself right before we got that flat."

As she drove away from New Orleans, deep into bayou country, a comfortable silence surrounded them, the quiet of the night broken only by the metallic percussion of the rain on the roof of the Miata, the hiss of waters beneath the rolling tires, the music flowing softly from the car speakers.

They'd gone about two miles when Gabe unbuckled his seat belt, turned around and went up on his knees, giving Emma an up-close-and-personal view of threads beginning to unravel beneath his right cheek.

Down, girl.

Needing a distraction, she glanced up into the rearview mirror and watched him unzip the duffle bag, and figured he must be getting out a dry shirt. Which was a shame, because she really, really loved the way that white knit T-shirt clung to his chest, defining pecs and six-pack abs that had instilled lust in female moviegoers from Seattle to Shanghai.

It turned out he wasn't after a shirt, after all. But a CD.

"Thought we could use a change from the snooze stuff," he said, pressing the eject button on her dashboard player.

"That's Celtic Grace." The Irish group was hugely soothing as background music to her massages. "They're very popular."

"If you happen to like New Age." His dismissive tone put them right up there with polka bands and Barney tunes.

"A great many people do." Including her. "Life's become very hectic. New Age is relaxing."

"There's a difference between being relaxed and comatose."

He exchanged her CD with his, pushed play, leaned back in the leather bucket seat, stretched his long athletic legs out in front of him and laced his fingers behind his dark head.

Cutting him a surreptitious sideways glance, Emma found the sight of those dark biceps bulging anything but relaxing.

A smoky, female voice drifted out of the speakers.

"Now, that's music," he said approvingly. "Doesn't get any better than Lady Day."

Although they'd been about as intimate as two people could be only minutes before, being alone with him, in this dark car in the rain, with Billie Holiday's sultry, sex-tinged voice singing about how she couldn't help lovin' that man, caused Emma's stomach muscles to knot.

Did he remember playing that exact same CD on another drive to the camp ten years earlier? The night before he'd left for California?

Emma had never been so nervous. Not even the night before her wedding to Richard, when she'd tossed and turned, futilely chasing sleep, afraid that she was making a terrible mistake.

The next morning she'd told her mother that she wanted to postpone the ceremony, to give herself time to sort out her confused feelings, but Angela Quinlan had briskly pointed out that with five hundred of their "closest friends" arriving at the Church of the Holy Assumption within the next six hours, canceling was not an option.

So, behaving like the dutiful daughter she had always been, with the exception of those stolen hours with Gabe, Emma had walked down that long white satin runner on her father's arm, feeling like a condemned prisoner being led to her execution.

That was before she'd learned the hard way to stand up for herself. To make her own decisions.

Decisions like spending tonight with Gabriel Broussard.

Emma might feel like putty in his hands, but she didn't want Gabe to mistakenly believe that she was still that fat red-haired girl who would have done anything to get him to notice her.

To want her.

To love her.

No! This wasn't about love. Gabe was talking about sex, pure and simple.

Could she actually go through with it? Could she throw caution to the wind and share a night of mind-blowing passion, knowing that it wouldn't lead to anything but multiple orgasms?

And your point is? the Samanatha inside her head asked.

It was the right thing to do, Emma assured herself. The way to get the man out of her system once and for all. In fact, looking at it that way, having sex with Gabe wasn't so reckless, after all. It was eminently logical.

But, for the time being, if she didn't stop thinking about getting naked with him, she really was going to risk driving into the bayou.

"You know, I never doubted that you'd be a star," she said. He'd always had charisma, what Roxi had called his red-hot aura. "But it must have been difficult, breaking into a business as competitive as the Hollywood filmmaking industry."

"I doubt anyone has it that easy. And I know damn well I

wasn't the only wannabe actor to live in a car my first month in L.A.," he said.

"That sounds terrible."

"At the time it didn't seem like that big a deal. The weather was nice and I just kept driving around to different beach parking lots to stay ahead of the cops.

"My first place was a seedy apartment on Hollywood Boulevard, which is not, by the way, anywhere near as glamorous as it might sound. There were four of us crammed into a space not much bigger than the Trans Am."

"Were they actors, too?"

"Two of them were. The third was a wannabe screenwriter who moonlighted as a waiter at this trendy Rodeo Drive restaurant five nights a week. He also pulled in a few extra bucks making porno films under the name of Stone Mallet."

A laugh burst from her. "Stone Mallet? Really?"

"My hand to God." He grinned as he raised his right hand. "Porn names aren't exactly subtle. But, I suppose it looked better on credits than James Klozik, which was his real name. He offered to help me break into the business. Promised me that with all his connections, I could be a big star."

"Did you? Make any of those movies?"

"And have my dick turn green and fall off from some STD? Hell, no."

"I'll bet you could've," she said. "Not have your—uh—penis fall off. But be a porn star."

It was dark inside the car, but she could feel his smile. "Seen a lot of porn flicks, have you, *chère*?"

"No." She could feel the heat rise in her face. "But I have a very good imagination. . . . So, I remember reading that you got a job in construction?"

"As a day laborer." Gabe liked that she'd cared enough to read about him. "The work was hard and dirty, paid peasant wages, and most of the guys on the crews tended to take off running whenever *La Migra* showed up looking for aliens to deport; but the upside was that it gave me time to make the rounds of casting calls."

Where he'd discovered that the legendary casting couch did, indeed, exist, and women weren't the only ones having to dodge sexual harassment.

He'd managed to dodge the females with the bad boy grin that had charmed the panties off more than his share of females back here in Blue Bayou. Usually they'd shrug off his rejection, give him their home phone number, in case he ever changed his mind about tangling the sheets, show him the door, then call in the next guy

A big-shot agent famous for his A list parties, had not been so easily put off. Gabe hadn't been real comfortable with the way the interview was conducted in a circular conversation pit built into the office floor, but had already figured out that Californians weren't exactly like the folks he'd grown up with in Louisiana. And movie people were even more skewed than most.

His instincts had proved right on the money when, after glancing through the black and white glossies, Gabe had spent three weeks building a rock retaining wall. It was meant to keep a popular sitcom star's Pacific Palisades mansion from sliding down onto the Coast Highway and to pay for it, the guy lunged for Gabe's crotch.

Gabe left the agent rolling on the glacier white carpeting, hands cupping his balls, cursing like a drunken sailor and screaming that he might as well go back to the fuckin' swamp because the redneck trailer trash son of a bitch sure as hell wasn't going to ever work in this town.

Having been threatened by a lot tougher guys than the pervert wearing a pink and lavender paisley shirt, mauve leather pants and a toupee that looked like roadkill, Gabe hadn't been exactly trembling in his boots.

"So," he said, "how about you? Nate tells me that you run a massage parlor."

"Every Body's Beautiful is a day spa. Roxi Dupree's my

partner. We offer massages, manicures, pedicures, Tarot card and palm readings, love spells—"

"I'm not real familiar with spas, but are palm readings and love spells usually part of the business?"

"Not as a rule," Emma allowed. "But Roxi's grandmother, Evangeline, who owned Hoo Doo Voo Doo—"

"That place on Magnolia, over by the cemetery, with all the gator heads and teeth in the window?"

"That's the one. Evangeline died about six months after we opened up. Roxi got rid of all the heads and teeth and was going to dissolve the business, but all these people kept showing up at the spa wanting spells like the ones they'd bought from her grandmother.

"She didn't want to turn them down, so she started studying Evangeline's shadow books—they're sort of like a witches' cookbook—and decided to concentrate on mixing up the lotions and oils, since they fit in nicely with the spa concept."

"Where do the spells come in?"

"A lot of our business comes from people who book massages for relaxation. Since romance tends to be one of the things that seems to stress people out, it only made sense to include Hex Appeal into our menu of treatments."

"You actually believe in magic?"

From his disbelieving tone, Emma suspected Gabe didn't. "I suppose everyone has their own idea of what magic is. I believe there's some invisible force that connects everything in the universe. And that everything we do affects that force, like ripples in the water. And I believe in destiny . . ."

She paused.

"And I'll bet you don't," she said, reading his silence.

"Sure. I just believe we all make our own destiny."

She wasn't surprised, given his own personal history. Gabe had not only grown up on the wrong side of the tracks, his father had been the town drunk.

According to Charlotte Cassidy, the day checkout clerk down at the Cajun Market, who served as Blue Bayou's unofficial town crier, Claude Broussard had once been considered the person in Blue Bayou most likely to become famous.

Supposedly—and the photographs in the trophy case at the high school backed Charlotte up on this fact—he'd been a mouthwateringly handsome quarterback on the Blue Bayou Buccaneers state high school championship football team.

He'd been recruited by every major football program in the SEC, and from other colleges as far away as Notre Dame and UCLA. Athletic shoe companies were salivating for a chance to sign the charismatic Cajun kid to an endorsement contract.

Then, on Homecoming Day, 1956, a tackle from Houma had broken through the offensive line and slammed into Claude while he was searching the field for a receiver. The hit the Baton Rouge *Advocate*'s headline referred to as "The Sack Heard Around Louisiana," not only shattered the promising quarterback's knee, it brought his entire world crashing down around him.

Things went downhill from there.

He began to drink. His cheerleader girlfriend, Angeline Beloit, got pregnant; rumor had it that it had taken Angeline's daddy's Ithaca 12-gauge to convince the high school dropout to marry the girl. Gabe was born six months after the shotgun wedding; he was eight months old when Angeline ran off with an oil rig worker from Houston.

Everyone knew Claude beat his son, but since a lot of people in the rigidly Catholic, conservative bayou town believed in that old maxim about sparing the rod and spoiling the child, authorities were never called in. Besides, no one in their right mind wanted to get on the wrong side of Crazy Claude Broussard.

So, he continued to drink and brawl, until that New Year's Eve, two years ago, when he drove his truck off the bridge leading into town. There was no funeral since the only people who might have shown up would have been those wanting to see for themselves that the bully of Blue Bayou really was dead.

No one, least of all Emma, had been surprised when Gabe didn't return home for his father's interment in the far corner of the cemetery once known as Paupers' Field.

Eight

While so much had changed in both their lives since the last time they were together, the cabin was exactly as Emma remembered it.

Like most other bayou camps, it had been built on stilts to allow for rising water to pass underneath; the cypress had weathered to a soft silver hue and a dark green metal roof slanted low over a front porch.

The narrow oyster shell road ended by the front door, but since land and water were always warring in this part of the country, one good storm could turn the road back into a waterway. Which was the reason for the flat-bottomed boat tied to the floating dock.

"This rain's going to have the ground more boggy than usual," he predicted. "No way you're going to be able to walk to the camp in those spindly shoes."

He was right. They'd also be ruined by the mud. "No problem. I'll take them off."

"You'll get your feet muddy."

"You have running water, right?"

"Yeah. Nate checked on that when he brought out the groceries." He rubbed his jaw. "I've got a better idea. I'll carry you."

It had not been easy, growing up a chubbette with Bayou Barbie for a mother. Emma had struggled against self-esteem issues most of her life, which, she'd realized with the twenty-twenty vision of hindsight, was how she'd ended up agreeing to marry Richard against her better judgment.

It wasn't that her mother had loved her ex-husband's slick southern charm. (Though she had.) Nor was it because her father had been impressed by his Vanderbilt degree. (Which, the FBI discovered during the embezzlement investigation, had turned out to be a forged document.) It was because a man who looked a bit like Brad Pitt—if you closed one eye and squinted just right with the other—professed to love her. A fat, shy wallflower who'd only gone to the graduation night cotillion because she'd been assigned to take pictures for the year-end edition of the school paper.

No, it hadn't been easy, but the good thing that had come out of her divorce was that she'd vowed never to let anyone—especially a man—make her feel insignificant again.

Still, for the first time in ages, she found herself desperately wishing Roxi had some magic spell that could make her instantly lose ten—okay, make that twenty—pounds.

"You can't carry me."

"Why not?"

Emma looked him straight in the eye. "Because I'm fat." There. She'd said it. It was a test and they both knew it.

"You're lush." Emma hadn't realized she was holding her breath until she noticed his gaze had drifted down to her breasts, which were in danger of popping out of the neckline of her blouse. "Voluptuous. Hell, darlin', if you'd lived back in pagan times, you'd have been declared a major goddess."

Well. That was definitely not what she'd been expecting to hear.

"Here's how we'll do it," he said with the absolute self-confidence she suspected had allowed him to believe a bad boy from the wrong side of the tracks in Nowhereville, Louisiana, could become the hottest hunk in Hollywood. "I'll come around to the driver's side. You'll get out and wrap those long gorgeous legs around my waist."

He skimmed a hand up her leg in a slow, hot path. "Then, if I can resist takin' you against the car, in the rain, like we almost did back there along the road, we'll make it inside without messin' up those pretty girly shoes or gettin' hit by lightning."

Feeling as if the lightning scenario had already happened, leaving her tingling from the inside out, Emma agreed.

Scarlett O'Hara, eat your heart out. Emma had always thought Rhett sweeping his unruly wife into his arms and up that famous movie staircase, was one of the most erotic moments in movies. But if Rhett had carried Scarlett the way Gabe was holding her—pelvis to pelvis, his hands digging into her bottom, the rock hard bulge of his erection thrusting against her crotch, her legs twined around him as the rain came down so hard and hot she feared she might dissolve from lust—they'd have never made it to the bedroom because Rhett would've taken Scarlett right there on those stairs. And she would have helped him.

Emma felt a momentary stab of loss when he put her back on her feet once they got to the porch so he could retrieve the key from above the lintel.

After warning herself that it was her last chance to back out, she took the hand Gabe held out to her and walked through the open door.

Gabe flicked the light switch by the door. Nothing.

"The electricity's out." Which wasn't any big surprise. Power was iffy this far from civilization. Especially during a storm.

It had been out that night, he remembered. When Emma had brought him here after the doctor had stitched up the slice made to his cheek by his father's state football championship ring. Having been drunk as usual, Claude had tracked him down after the graduation ceremonies. Having never made it out of Blue Bayou himself, he was damned if he'd let his kid get away.

If Emma, who'd been taking pictures at the cotillion, hadn't come along when she had, Gabe probably would have killed the bastard. Which would've landed his father in Paupers' Field years earlier, and him in Angola.

"Fortunately, I came prepared." He dug a lighter from the pocket of his jeans and began lighting the candles kept on hand for just such contingencies. Then, once the living room and adjoining bedroom were bathed in a flickering yellow glow, Gabe turned toward Emma, drinking in the sight of her rich, ripe body, showcased by the clinging silk.

Because his mouth was hungry for the once forbidden taste of her luscious lips, his hands desperate to explore every inch of her plush breasts, and his throbbing erection aching to bury itself deep inside her, he forced himself to back away. To take his time. To this time, do things right.

Gabe realized she'd mistaken his hesitation for second thoughts when she dragged a hand through her tangled hair.

"I must look like a drowned cat."

Something in his heart turned over. "There you go, being too hard on yourself, *chère.*"

Gabe had never considered himself a particularly sensitive person, but he would have had to have been dense as a stone not to understand some of what Emma was feeling.

Knowing that the lingering bit of insecurity was a legacy from that stick-thin, ice-hearted bitch of a mother who'd threatened to have his "trailer trash Cajun ass" thrown in jail if he ever so much as laid a finger on Emma, Gabe vowed that before tonight was over, Emma would realize exactly how desirable she was.

He pushed some wild curls away from her face, then lifted her round chin. "You look wet, you. And fuckin' hot."

"This is too fast," she said on a quick, shuddering breath as he bent closer. "Too much."

"No, *ma belle.*" He touched his mouth to hers. Her lips were soft as thistledown, as potent as whiskey. "It's not nearly enough."

The blood was pounding in his head. His cock.

God help him, he'd tried. She was right about things having gone too fast. Emma wasn't some one-night stand he'd picked up in a Melrose Avenue bar. She deserved better than a quick, hard, anonymous roll in the sheets.

After nearly taking her against the car, Gabe had vowed to slow things down. To take his time; do things right.

But he hadn't counted on her twining her arms around his neck. Or smashing her breasts hard against his chest as her hungry mouth opened beneath his.

Half crazed, desperate to touch her, he peeled away the wet silk from her skin.

"Lift your arms."

She did as instructed, allowing him to yank the blouse over her head and onto the floor.

Lacy cups framed her voluptuous breasts. Forget the Grand Canyon or Victoria Falls. Emma's breasts were the true natural wonders of the world. And even more amazingly, unlike all the ones he'd come across the past few years in California, they were real.

"Damn, Emma." He cupped her breasts in his hands, embracing the warm weight of them. "You're wearing white lace."

"Colored would've looked tacky beneath the blouse."

"You couldn't look tacky if you tried." Well, there *was* that fantasy of her wearing those black boots. Which wasn't so much tacky, he decided, as hot. Hot and wicked. "Do the panties match?"

"Of course."

"Thank you." He rocked forward on the toes of his boots, kissed her. "I fantasized about this," he murmured as he skimmed a fingertip over the white lace flowers covering her taut nipples.

"You fantasized about me?" Her eyes, which had fluttered down to half-mast, opened.

"Kinda." His touch circled, teased. Her nipples were the color of ripe strawberries, which brought up a fantasy of spreading chocolate on those amazing breasts and licking it off.

"After my fictional fiancée broke our fake engagement by telling the world I had certain, uh, predilections of the kinky kind, women started bombarding my house with panties."

He slipped the straps over her shoulders. "They came FedEx, UPS, in the U.S. mail." While his hands stayed busy with her breasts, his lips nuzzled her neck. "Some ladies were more direct and just tossed them over my gate."

"Those weren't ladies."

He chuckled. "At least not proper Southern ones," he agreed. He kissed her collarbone. "Most of the panties were black." Her shoulder. "The rest were red." The crest of her breast and inhaled her scent. "I was thinkin' it'd be nice if just one of those women had decided to show off her softer side." His lips dipped into the cleavage framed by the white lace. "And talk about soft."

Emma trembled as his tongue stroked over her straining nipple.

"*Bon Dieu*, you are one tasty female."

"It's the lotion." Emma gasped when his teeth closed around a tightened nipple and tugged. "Roxi blended it especially for me. From essential oil of peaches, vanilla, and coconut."

"What I'm tastin' sure isn't peaches. You taste like temptation, you. And sex. I've a mind to lick you all over."

Her skirt had an elastic waist, and fastened with a hook-and-eye and zipper in the back. Proving himself to be a man who definitely knew his way around women's clothing, he dispatched the hook with a simple twist of the fingers.

Emma drew in a sharp breath when his knuckles brushed against the bare skin of her back.

The sexy sound of the zipper, slowly lowering, tooth by tooth, had her wet with wanting.

The silk skirt whispered over her skin as it slid down her thighs to pool on the floor at her feet, leaving her standing there, in the center of the cabin, barely clad in a bra that was clinging to the tips of her breasts, a pair of panties, and those shoes, which must make her look like a porno actress in one of those Voluptuous Vixens DVDs she'd seen for rent in the back room of the Video Express.

Some women—like Roxi—might be able to get away with wearing barely there underwear and high heels. Emma had never believed herself to be one of them.

"Don't," he murmured when one hand instinctively went to her breasts, the other to conceal her crotch. "Don't cover up anything. And don't move. I want to see you."

Well, that was sure as hell going to blow her midnight-stuck-in-a-cabin-with-Gabe-Broussard fantasy right out of the water.

He was standing there, taking her in, studying her slowly, silently, as if memorizing every curve.

"I don't think this is such a good—"

"Shh." He touched a finger to her lips, forestalling her complaint at being looked at like a . . . what?

A sex object.

Which was impossible. No one had ever looked at her in this scorchingly hungry way Gabriel was looking at her. If even the smallest percent of what the tabloids were always saying was true, Gabe had slept with some of the most beautiful women in Hollywood. In the entire world. Women with "buns of steel" asses, Bowflex-tight stomachs, and pert, perfect breasts.

Emma didn't even want to think about how she might compare to all those past lovers.

It had been hard enough to make the decision to throw caution to the wind and sleep with Gabriel. To stand still for such an intense study from a man whose beautifully formed physique could have been immortalized in marble and gleaming bronze, chipped away at Emma's hard-won confidence.

"You are," he said, "without a doubt, the most—"

Fat, her mind jumped ahead of his words. Though she doubted it'd help all that much, Emma sucked in her oh-so-not-flat stomach.

"*Female* woman I've ever seen." His eyes, which lust had darkened to nearly a midnight black, looked into hers as he fondled her heavy breasts. *"J'aimete faire l'amour avec toi."* His deep voice was as thick as gumbo. "I wanna make love to you the way a woman like you deserves to be made love to."

Emma trembled when he ran those treacherously clever hands hand down her sides, then back down her spine, over the curve of her bottom.

"You've got a great ass, you." He splayed the fingers of both hands over each cheek, began kneading her flesh. Her white, abundant flesh.

"A big ass, you mean."

Emma wished she could take the words back the instant she'd heard them escape her lips. Talk about ruining the mood!

His fingers tightened. "I don't ever want to hear anyone put you down." He pressed her against him, hard. The bulge straining against the faded denim had the metal buttons pressing into her stomach. "Not even you, *chère.*" He thrust his hand between them, breaching the white stretch lace of her panties to tangle in the moist curls. "I wanted to take things slow. But I'm afraid this first time's going to be a hard, fast fuck." His free hand tangled in her hair, pulling her head back. "So if that's not what you want . . ."

She was burning from the inside out. If he didn't take her soon, Emma feared she'd self-combust. "Oh, God, yes."

Nine

Gabe's mouth took hers in a hard, claiming kiss, his tongue sweeping deep, mating with hers as he lifted her off her feet and carried her into the adjoining bedroom. The sweet-smelling mattress, stuffed with Spanish moss and herbs, gave way as they tumbled onto it, mouths fused, arms and legs entwined.

His mouth left hers to blaze a path down her throat, her breasts, her torso, with hot, openmouthed kisses that scorched her skin and made her blood flame.

Outside the cabin, the rain beat a strong, steady percussion on the tin roof. Inside, a storm swirled.

The last of Emma's clothes, and all of Gabe's, were ripped away, as if by gale-force winds. He proved to be a ruthless lover, forceful, demanding. His teeth scraped against her inner thighs, drawing a ragged moan from deep in her throat. He brushed a thumb over her swollen clit, then parted the wet pink folds of her ultrasensitive labia, spreading the moisture, exciting her, preparing her.

There was thunder. Emma could hear it in her heart, which was pounding so hard and so loud she was certain he must be able to hear it. There was lightning, blindingly bright, but she couldn't tell whether it was outside the cabin or inside her mind.

Another tempest, more dangerous than the one conjured up

by Mother Nature, swirled in the dark eyes that were watching her face intently as he slid first one finger, then another, deep inside her.

And when his hands dug into her hips, and he lifted her to his mouth to feast, the already all-consuming storm intensified.

Around Emma.

Inside her.

She writhed beneath him, her wet hair whipping across the bed as her head thrashed back and forth.

"More." The ragged word was half plea, half demand as she ground her mound against his ravenous mouth. "Please. I need . . . I want . . ."

Before her passion-hazed mind could fully form the coherent plea, Gabe's fiendishly talented tongue took one last, long, lascivious swath. She screamed his name, a full-throated scream of release that echoed out over the bayou.

Her tremors had not yet subsided when Gabe yanked open the condom he'd taken earlier from his jeans pocket. On some distant level, as he rolled the latex over his straining penis to the crisp dark hair at the broad base, Emma was grateful that one of them had thought of protection.

Taking hold of her ankles, he spread her legs wider, exposing her more fully. He was poised over her like a sleek jungle cat, every muscle taut, his dark flesh gleaming with a sheen of sweat, his sheathed erection jutting out with primal intensity.

He lifted her legs, hooking them over his shoulders.

Emma had never felt more exposed. Nor more aroused.

"Do you have any idea what I want from you?"

"No." She could barely hear her whispered answer over the hammering of rain on the roof and the pounding of blood in her ears.

His smile was swift. Carnal.

"Everything."

Gabe plunged into her with one strong swift stroke, slamming up against her cervix with a strength that ripped a hoarse cry from her ravished lips.

"Damn." He sucked in a deep, shuddering breath she could feel inside her. The muscles in his arms stood out in rigid relief as he braced himself above her body. "Are you okay?"

"I'm fine." The brief sharp pain had become an even sharper need. Her hips bucked, urging him on. "Oh, God. Don't stop."

"As if I could," he muttered between clenched teeth.

He began to move, thrusting, withdrawing, thrusting, pacing his movements with a perfection of power and timing that had her coming again. And again.

Outside, thunder boomed; the night wind wailed. Inside, bedsprings squeaked; the iron headboard pounded against the cypress wall. Rhythms matched. Breathless, Emma clung to him as they raced into the storm.

Finally, giving into the demands of his body, Gabe allowed his own release on a long, shuddering groan that echoed deep into Emma's bones.

Afterwards, they lay amidst the cooling, tangled sheets, arms and legs entwined, his large body sprawled over hers. He felt heavy, but not uncomfortably so. As she twined her still-unsteady fingers through his damp hair, Emma wondered if Gabe could feel her body's continued pulsations.

He could. The way her inner muscles kept clenching around his still throbbing cock was the sexiest thing he'd ever felt.

"Wow." Her breasts were a pillowy cushion, soft and bountiful. He turned his head and kissed the fragrant flesh. "That was more incredible than in my fantasies of you."

"You fantasized about me?" *Why?*

"*Mais,* yeah." He shared a reminiscent smile. "There was this one summer, when I was filming up in northern Ontario, in the lake district. The temperature was in the '90s, with a humidity just as high."

"I never thought of Canada being as hot as the bayou," she managed as his lips caressed a nipple.

"Neither had I. We spent seven weeks there making this movie about a guy who escapes from prison when the transport bus goes off the highway. He carjacks an SUV, takes the driver hostage and falls in love with her."

"*Ransom*," she murmured. It had been an edgy, yet romantic movie about two unhappy people who'd found each other at the impossibly worst time. Unfortunately, the screenwriter hadn't gone for a happily-ever-after ending, instead having Gabe's character killed in a hail of bullets.

When the Bijou's lights had gone back on, all the moist eyes in the theater revealed Emma hadn't been the only moviegoer who'd cried at the tragic final scene.

"That's the one, all right." He nodded. "There was this one scene, where she was cleaning the bullet wound he'd gotten during the breakout and the strangest thing happened."

His gaze took on a faraway look as if he was picturing the moment in his mind. "I had this flashback to when we were here at the camp. When you were putting the ice pack on my stitches."

The emergency room doctor had given Emma the gel pack, instructing her that keeping the wound iced would help keep down the swelling.

She lifted her fingers, traced them along the white scar which, rather than detract from his devastating good looks, only added to his rakish appearance, keeping his features from being impossibly perfect.

"That never should've been necessary. Someone should have done something to stop your father years earlier."

Gabe shrugged his broad shoulders. "You know how it is down here. Everybody pretty much minds their own business."

"A child being abused should be everyone's business." She smoothed a hand over his temple, and down his neck. The tightened tendons told her that he wasn't as nonchalant as he was trying to sound. "If you knew a father was beating a child—"

"I'd want to kill him," he responded on a deadly primitive tone that had goose bumps prickling on Emma's skin.

It was as if a bucket of ice water had been thrown on the warm, afterglow mood. With a muttered curse, Gabe rolled off her, left the bed, and went into the adjoining bathroom.

Ten

Gabe leaned a hand against the wall as he flushed the toilet, watching the condom swirling down the drain. Just like his life would've done that night if Emma hadn't come across him and his father beating each other's brains out. From the time he'd grown taller and stronger than Claude Broussard, Gabe had thought about killing him. But, not wanting to end up in prison, he'd mostly stayed out of his way as much as he could.

Nate's dad, who'd been Blue Bayou's sheriff, had tried to get him moved out of the house, but then he'd been killed in the line of duty. Nate had helped out by giving him a key to this place, where Gabe had essentially lived on his own from his thirteenth birthday.

Although he hadn't gotten drunk again since that long ago night of the showdown he and his father had been building toward all his life, Gabe suddenly wanted a stiff drink now. Jack Black, straight up, hold the ice. And keep them comin'.

Shit. How old did a guy get before he finally escaped the ghosts of his past?

He'd never thought of himself as a coward. But as unpalatable as the idea was, while he'd spent his entire life struggling not to grow up like his drunk of an old man, he'd ended up a lot like his mother.

Like her, he'd run away from Blue Bayou. Now, having also run away from Hollywood, he was right back here where he'd begun. Which meant that he'd spent the past decade running in circles.

Dragging his hand down his face, he took a deep breath and left the bathroom.

"Sorry about that," he said as he sat down on the edge of the mattress and ran a hand down her tangle of hair. "Guess the topic just hit a little too close to home."

"That's okay," she said with that unwavering loyalty that he now realized he hadn't fully appreciated when he'd been younger. The corners of her lips tilted in a faint, reassuring smile, but her eyes were as grave as they'd been that night.

"I'm glad you didn't kill your father, Gabe"—she smoothed a caress over his knuckles which, that night, had been bruised and bloodied—"not for his sake, but for yours."

"The bastard wasn't worth doing hard time for, that's sure enough," Gabe agreed. "But if you hadn't come along when you did, I'd probably be in prison and he'd have been in the ground ten years ago."

And not a soul in the parish would've mourned Claude Broussard's passing. Gabe hadn't felt so much as a twinge of regret when Nate's wife, Regan, who was now the sheriff, had called to tell him about the accident.

"You hungry, *chère*?" He didn't want to talk about his father anymore. Didn't want to think about him. "Since the power was on when Nate stocked the fridge this morning, things shouldn't have spoiled, and we've got plenty of wood for the stove. How does some crawfish jambalaya and dirty rice sound?"

"Wonderful."

"*Bien*. So, we'll have ourselves a little supper. Share some conversation." He nipped at her bottom lip and ran his hand down the silk of her bare back. "Then we'll go back to bed."

Her answering smile could've lit up the bayou for a month of Sundays. "That's the best idea you've had yet."

Deciding that things were definitely looking up since he'd

come back to Blue Bayou, Gabe paused in the act of buttoning up his jeans. "I don't suppose you'd like to save me the trouble of ripping off your clothes later, by just stayin' naked?"

That soft, lovely color he was beginning to love bloomed in her cheeks. Who would have suspected that a sexy, multi-orgasmic woman who could turn him every which way but loose, was capable of blushing? When choosing roles, Gabe had always been drawn to contradictions in character; Emma was a gorgeous, walking, talking tangle of intriguing contrasts.

He vowed by the time he left the bayou, he'd have explored every one.

"I am *not* eating without clothes on," she insisted.

He shrugged, even as he decided that Emma was going to make one bang-up dessert. "I had a feeling that's what you'd say. Though it's a damn shame, because you sure do pretty up the scenery, *tite chatte*."

He retrieved his duffle bag out of the car. Since he was a great deal taller than her, the oversize black and gold New Orleans Saints T-shirt hit Emma about mid-thigh. He heaved a deep sigh of regret when she put her panties back on.

"Spoilsport." He knew he should've just ripped the damn things when he had the chance. He liked the idea of Emma bare-crotched and bare-assed, available to him whenever he felt the urge to touch her. Take her. Pleasure her.

And she would be pleasured, Gabe vowed. In more ways than she'd ever imagined. Again and again.

Just thinking about all the ways he was going to have her, all the things he planned to do to Emma, *with* her, had sweat breaking out on his forehead and a hard-on of Herculean proportions straining against his jeans.

He was considering giving into the rampant testicular urge to drag her back to bed when his stomach grumbled.

If he was going to spend the rest of the night ravishing the delectable Emma Quinlan, he'd need to keep his strength up.

Food first.

Then, one hunger satisfied, he was going to claim her. Physically. Emotionally. Completely.

Emma was surprised at how well she and Gabe worked together. He gathered up the ingredients, assigning her the job of peeling the boiled crawdads while he started the rice.

"There was another time, up in Canada," he said, as he heated the oil in a large, cast-iron skillet, "when this actress and I were rollin' 'round the bed, supposed to be makin' love."

"I seem to recall a lot of that," Emma said.

"The couple were hot for each other, sure enough. But the time I'm talkin' about was when it was like I got zapped by a time machine and instead of bein' with her, it was like I'd ended up back here, with you.

"Jus' thinkin' about how pretty you looked, and those soft little sounds you made when you came, I got such a boner, me, that Clint had to call a break in action so we wouldn' end up with a triple-X rating."

"Things like that happen," she said with a brief, knowing nod. "To men."

His lips quirked in a smile as he added some flour to the oil, whisking the roux with smooth, deft strokes she couldn't help but admire. Although Emma had grown up in a part of the country known for its Cajun and Creole cuisine, since her mother's cook had never let her in the kitchen, her own culinary skills were self-taught and marginal, at best.

"Been with a lot of horny men, have you, darlin'?"

Hearing the laughter in his voice, Emma refused to look up from peeling the red-shelled crustaceans. "One of the first things you learn in massage school is not to take a male client's erection personally." She cringed inwardly as she heard her mother's prim tone coming out of her mouth.

"Sounds reasonable," he said easily. "Though, fair warning, Emma—any erection I get around you, you oughta take real personal."

The decadent smile he flashed her way was rife with sexual promise and sent a shiver of primitive awareness shimmying up Emma's spine. Carnal fantasies, each more kinky than the previous one, tangled hotly in her mind.

He turned down the heat beneath the pan and began dicing a fat yellow onion. "Nate left beer and wine in the fridge. Why don't you get something for us to drink while I finish peeling those mud bugs?"

Having been caught up in a fantasy of being dragged by rough-handed brigands before Jean Lafitte, Emma was momentarily disoriented to find herself in the camp kitchen, rather than in the pirate's private quarters.

"What would you like?"

"Now there's a tempting question." He put such blatant sexuality into the growled response that for a fleeting moment, Emma was back on the pirate's private galleon, naked, on her knees, forced to satisfy his every erotic demand.

"We seem to have Voodoo Beer," she reported in an uncharacteristic stammer. "And Chardonnay."

"I'll take the beer. For now." The timer he'd set for the rice dinged. "Then perhaps I'll drink the wine off your lush body for dessert."

As she opened the wine with the corkscrew she found in a drawer and unscrewed the cap of Gabe's beer, Emma couldn't decide whether to take his words as a promise or a threat.

The wine sparkled in the candlelight like sunshine on water. The robustly spiced jambalaya and dirty rice could've easily been served at one of the finest New Orleans Cajun restaurants.

While the south Louisiana culture could admittedly be accused of being chauvinistic from time to time, cooking had always been a rite of male passage for Cajun men, dating back to when they'd had to feed themselves during those long, lonely months at their camps when they'd supported their families by hunting and trapping.

As if by mutual, unspoken agreement, they kept the conversation casual over dinner. Gabe entertained Emma with anecdotes about the movie business, while she caught him up on the local gossip.

"Remember Dorothy Pettijohn and Pearl Duvall?" she asked as he cleared the table. She'd offered to help, but he'd refused, insisting that he'd rather she just stay in one place so he could enjoy the scenery while he worked.

"Sure. God, they must be at least seventy, by now."

"Seventy-three," she confirmed. The two women had lived together in a little house on Bayou Pettijohn for as long as Emma could remember. "They went off to Canada last year for a vacation and came back married."

"Good for them," Gabe said as he poured the coffee he'd turned on before they'd sat down to supper.

"A few people were scandalized." Emma's mother being one of them. "But most just figured it was their business." She smiled her thanks as he placed the heavy mug in front of her. "Turns out the ceremony took place on their fortieth anniversary."

"That's a helluva long time for any couple to be together," he said.

"Isn't it?" Emma remembered how happy they'd looked when they'd returned home from Toronto. Their faces, lined and weathered from seven decades of living, had been glowing. "I hate to admit it, but I envied them. Just a little."

"No shame in that." He took a drink of coffee, eyeing her over the rim of the earthenware mug. "By the way, in case you were wondering? That picture of me with that actress on that tycoon's yacht was a cut and paste. I don't fool around with married women. And I don't screw around on women I'm with."

Unlike some people. The unstated words hovered in the air between them.

"Nate sorta filled me in on what's been happening with you."

"It's not exactly a secret." Her fingers tensed on the mug's handle. She forced them to relax. "Given that Richard's in prison."

"For embezzling from your daddy."

"Yes. The ironic thing was that he'd married me to get in good with my father in the first place."

"Now, that's hard to believe."

"It's true."

Strangely, it didn't hurt now because it hadn't hurt then. Not really. Oh, Emma's pride had been wounded. But her heart had remained unscathed because while she'd been promising to love, honor, and respect, her heart hadn't been hers to bestow on her husband. Because she'd given it to Gabe years ago.

"He told me, the day he left me for Chandra, that he'd never really loved me."

"I'd call the guy a prick, but he'd give a bad name to penises everywhere." Gabe leaned back on the hind legs of the chair. "So, did you love him?"

"I thought I did." She'd almost managed to convince herself that she had. "I certainly wanted to."

"So, why did you marry him if you weren't sure?"

Because I finally gave up on you. "It's hard to explain."

"Was it the sex?"

Emma nearly choked on her coffee. "What?"

"The sex. I guess it was pretty good, huh?"

She was amazed to discover that she could laugh about something that had been so painfully embarrassing. "It wasn't anything to write home about." She dragged a hand through her hair and pretended a sudden interest in the well of darkness outside the window. "I wasn't his type."

"*Chère,* a woman like you is definitely the type of every male who has even one workin' nut."

Emma felt the heat—the bane of redheads—flood into her face. "That's nice of you to say—"

"It's not nice. It's the truth."

"I wasn't very good. You know," she said at his arched brow, "with the how-to part."

What was it about Gabe that had her telling him things she'd never told anyone but Roxi. Couldn't she just keep her mouth shut? Apparently not. She kept pointing out her flaws. Her big butt, her lack of sexual expertise, next she'd be telling him about the D she'd gotten in high school geometry and the bad perm that had caused her hair to break off at the roots two days before her wedding.

A rich, deep, sexy laugh exploded from him. "Emma, darlin', if you were any better at the how-to part, I'd be laid out on a slab down at Dupree's funeral parlor after dying from havin' my head blown off by that last climax."

She thought about the way he'd shouted her name as he'd come with a force that had driven her deep into the mattress and decided that even Gabe wasn't that good an actor.

"It was good, wasn't it?" she murmured.

"Better than good. It was gold-medal, world-class sex, and if I were a more generous man, I'd drive myself up to that prison and thank your dickless ex-husband for not bein' man enough to handle a woman of your vast sexual needs."

She might have laughed. Or argued. But for some reason, the hot and hungry way he was looking at her made her almost believe him.

"It was a good thing, in a way," she said, taking another sip of the chicory flavored coffee. "I'd gotten complacent, working as a bookkeeper down at Nate's construction company. I'd thought about opening my own business for a long time, but Richard didn't believe two careers were good for a marriage."

"Sounds like the guy was intimidated by strong, confident, sexual women."

"That's the same thing Roxi said."

"You should listen to your friend, you."

"Well, once he left—taking our joint bank account with him—I decided to open Every Body's Beautiful. We began as pretty much a typical fluff and buff operation, then I started expanding services. One of our most popular packages is the Rose Body Booster. It's an aromatherapy treatment that includes a rose petal massage. We get a lot of requests for that at Valentine's Day and Mother's Day. And just last week we did an entire bachelorette party."

Gabe tilted his chair back on its rear legs. "Maybe I'll sign up for one while I'm here. Just the idea of getting naked and having you rub rose petals all over my body makes me hot . . . But you know what makes me even hotter?"

Emma was already turned on by the mental vision of herself straddling his hips, crushing the scent of rose petals against his oiled, muscular back. The naked hunger in those sultry dark eyes had her breath catching in her lungs, and heat dampening the crotch of those panties he hadn't wanted her to put back on.

She swallowed. "What?"

"The idea of me rubbing those rose petals all over your luscious body." His eyes drifted from hers, to her lips, then lower, lingering on her breasts. "Everywhere." The molten heat in his gaze had an answering warmth uncurling deep inside her.

"Do you have any idea what it does to me, when you look at me that way, *chère*?" he murmured, leaning closer, until his lips were just a breath away from hers.

Unable to respond, Emma shook her head.

"It makes me want things." He brushed his knuckles around her jaw. Up her cheek. "Hot things." His fingers slid into her hair "Pelvis-grinding, dirty, blow-your-mind things."

The fingers of his other hand circled her wrist and he pressed her palm against the front of his jeans, where his swollen sex backed up his claim. Then he stood up, pulling her with him, his strong hands cupping her bottom, his pelvis grinding, just as he'd promised, against hers.

"Unfasten me," he said against her mouth as his hands delved beneath the T-shirt and cupped her breasts.

The top button was already unfastened. He was gloriously naked beneath the jeans. Emma unfastened two more metal buttons, exposing the ebony hair that continued from his chest to his groin.

Anticipation curled hotly between her thighs as she finished with the last two buttons, then, feeling a great deal like the captured woman in *The Last Pirate*, Emma knelt on the hard, heart-of-pine floor and slowly drew the jeans down over Gabe's lean male hips.

Then she sat back on her heels, devouring him with her eyes. Until this moment, Emma had not realized how beautiful the male penis could be.

"Touch me." His voice was thick with need.

"*Mais,* yes," Emma borrowed a bit of his Cajun French which, to her ear, sounded sexier.

Gabe bucked his hips forward, into her touch as she explored the satiny length. Holding her rioting hair back with one hand, so he could better view the action, she stroked his erection from base to knobbed tip.

A tiny drop of moisture gleamed like a pearl in the plump cleft. Leaning forward, Emma gathered it in with a swirl of her tongue.

He swelled in her hand. A groan, somewhere between a curse and a prayer, was ripped from his chest when she took the sleek silk into her mouth. Loving him with her tongue, Emma reveled at the power thrusting between her parted lips.

"Not that way." He grabbed her hair, urging her back to her feet. "Not this time."

His hand delved beneath the black T-shirt, tearing away her panties as if they were made of tissue paper.

"I'll replace them," he growled against her mouth as he plunged his fingers deep inside her.

"They're not important." She gripped his shoulders and sagged against the hard wall of his chest and she was rocked by a sudden, molten wave of pleasure. "Oh, God, what are you doing to me?"

"I'm taking you." Balancing her on one knee, he swept the coffee mugs off the table, and laid her on her back and pressed his palms against her inner thighs, spreading her legs apart on the pine planks. "And you're going to love it."

Eleven

The kitchen was compact enough for him to keep one hand on her mound while grabbing the pair of wooden handled shears stuck in a wooden knife block. After using the shears to snip the hem of the shirt, he tossed them aside and ripped it open.

He was standing over her, looking down at her with the dark, hungry eyes of a conqueror.

"Christ, you've got some amazing body, *chère*."

He cupped her breasts, then bent his head to scrape his teeth against a straining nipple.

Emma couldn't hold back the moan his caressing touch dragged from her throat as he rolled the turgid peak between his thumb and forefinger; nor could she stop her body from arching upward, offering his wickedly clever hands and mouth better access.

"You are so beautiful." His words vibrated against her burning hot skin as his mouth moved down her torso.

His caresses continued their treacherous trail downward, over the swell of her stomach, down her inner thighs, his fingers kneading the flesh that made swimsuit shopping such an exercise in masochism.

"Your skin's so white." His voice was rough as an oyster shell road. "Like magnolia petals."

Even more amazing than the fact that he could make her want him with a single hot look or a lingering touch, was that where she saw stretch marks and cellulite, Gabe saw flowers.

"I've been wanting to do this all during supper."

Grabbing a condom from the box he'd brought into the kitchen earlier, he sheathed himself, then, planting his long bare feet far apart, rubbed the latex-covered tip against the swollen lips of her labia, stroking in long, wet glides, teasing the tender flesh, while refusing to enter her until she was gasping, thighs quivering, heart hammering, begging him. "Please, Gabe. Oh, God, please, take me, now."

"I thought you'd never ask," he said with a satisfied chuckle against her mouth.

Emma could taste herself on his lips as he gave her a long, slow soul kiss that had white-hot stars wheeling behind her closed eyes. Then—thank you, God, finally!—he slipped into her, as smoothly as if they'd been created to fit together in just this way.

"*Dieu,* I love the way your body feels against mine." He moved his hips, sinking deeper. "All soft and welcoming." Then deeper still. "Ah," he breathed as his entire length was surrounded and they were fully joined. "That's so good."

Her senses swam. Her mind shut down.

Gabe laced his fingers with hers, moving their joined hands up, on either side of her head. "I wish I could stay inside you forever."

He began to move, slowly at first. Tenderly. Then faster and faster, hot flesh slapping against hot flesh as Emma scissored her legs around him, lifting her hips with each down-stroke, meeting him thrust for thrust as they both raced over that dark edge together.

Colors—fading from the red of a bursting star to rose to a cooling pinkish blue—floated peacefully in her mind. Gabe's mouth was against her throat. Their breathing, still in unison, gradually slowed. He lifted his head, combed the wet hair from her face. "I don't think I'll ever get enough of you," he murmured, seeming, Emma thought, a bit surprised at the notion.

She smiled at that, even though she knew it was only the pleasure of the moment speaking. What she and Gabe had shared was wonderful. Better than wonderful, it was the most exquisite thing she'd ever known.

But the man who was sprawled lazily on top of her like a satiated lion, had broken her heart once before. And would again, if she didn't guard her heart more carefully this time.

"Wait here," he said. "I'll be right back."

As if she were capable of moving. Every bone in Emma's body seemed to have turned to water. "Where are you going?"

"I promised to replace those panties."

She leaned up on her elbows. "You're not driving back into town? The stores will all be closed by now."

"I'm not going to the store." He opened the refrigerator and took out a tall red can. "I'm gonna give you a pair of whipped cream underpants, *chère*." He winked. "Then I'm going to eat them off you."

Impossibly, sexual tension sparked again, tightening muscles that had gone lax. "Is there enough whipped cream in that can for both of us to have dessert?"

He grinned. "I gua-ran-tee it."

It was dark when Gabe felt Emma slipping out of the bed. If he were the kind of man who kissed and told, which he wasn't, he would have thanked Nate for having bought that whipped cream. *Mon Dieu*, how he'd enjoyed spraying it onto her lush, rounded body. Enjoyed even more licking it off her.

And if she were worried about calories, she definitely hadn't shown it, as she'd done the same thing to him.

Which had, of course, left them so messy, they'd been forced to take a shower. Amazingly, he'd taken her yet again, up against the tile wall. He hadn't felt so horny, or been able to recover so quickly between rounds, since his high school days.

If only he'd known how hot the soft, sweet-smelling Emma

Quinlan was back then. He'd gotten a hint of the passion she kept banked beneath that shy, wallflower exterior on graduation night.

Would things have changed if he'd just given into his rebellious body's demands and taken her virginity? Would his life have turned out differently? Would hers?

Gabe had never been one to lie. Not even to himself. Especially to himself. The truth was, he probably wouldn't have appreciated her then. He might have even ended up hurting her more than that son-of-a-bitch embezzler she'd made the mistake of marrying.

Although he'd never believed in destiny, the past hours with Emma had Gabe wondering if perhaps there was some unseen force working here, some fate, that had led them down separate, individual paths, only to bring them back together once they were older, wiser, and even more hot for one another.

Whatever the reason, Gabe was determined to make up for lost time. The problem was, he considered, as he heard her rustling around in the dark, gathering up her scattered clothing, Emma didn't seem to be on the same page.

The door's hinges squeaked as she opened it. Gabe could feel her tense, like a deer fearing a predator's approach.

He could stop her. He was, after all, larger. Stronger. Not that he'd have to use force. Because it would only take a slow kiss, a lingering touch, a hand to that slick hot place between her legs, to have her back in his bed.

Gabe was still weighing his options when he heard the engine turn over. Heaving a weary sigh, he climbed out of bed, flipped open the cell phone and called his best friend.

"Hey, Nate," he said, when the sleep-husky voice on the other end of the line answered. "I need another favor. Yeah, everything went jus' fine. But Emma's on her way back to town from the swamp and I hate the idea of her driving through the bayou alone in the dark. Could your pretty sheriff wife send a deputy out to meet her on the highway and follow her home? Then let me know she got there okay? Thanks, *cher.*"

That little matter taken care of, Gabe pulled on a pair of boxers, and went into the kitchen to await the call letting him know that his *'tite chatte* had made it home safe and sound.

"If she thinks we're finished," he said, as the coffee dripped into the pot, "the lady has another think coming."

Having come to a crossroads in his life, Gabe wasn't entirely sure where his future was headed. But he knew damn well that Emma was going to play a starring role.

"I gua-ran-tee it."

Twelve

Emma was not having a good day. She'd mixed up her oils, using Mr. Lamoreaux's sandlewood and juniper on Mrs. Breaux, who preferred the relaxing scent of lavender. Rather than appearing unhappy, the elderly lady assured Emma that it was occasionally a good idea to get out of a rut. While Etienne Lamoreaux, who wore a gold hoop in his ear and rode an old chopper Harley, seemed to take smelling like a little old lady's sachet in stride.

All day long she jumped every time the phone rang. By closing time, she'd been forced to wonder if she wasn't putting too much importance on what had probably been to him nothing more than a convenient, one-night stand. Especially since that polite, green as spring grass deputy had informed her that he had instructions to follow her back from the camp to her house, which meant Gabriel had been aware of her sneaking away.

How difficult would it have been to keep her there, if he'd wanted her to stay? He wouldn't even have to use force. All it would've taken was a few kisses, some touches . . .

"Are you sure you want to do this?" Roxi asked.

Emma crossed her arms. "Absolutely."

"Because I can sure as hell think of worse things than daydreaming of that hot Cajun Gabriel Broussard."

"That's just the point," Emma argued. "I don't *want* to dream of him."

Her blood began to swim at the thought of Gabe touching her. Tasting her. "He's like a fever in my blood, Roxi. I can't concentrate. He's all I think about. I want him gone."

A moonstone ring, larger than the diamond one Gabe professed not to have bought for Tamara Templeton, glowed as Roxi tossed her long black hair over her shoulder. "You do realize, of course, that most of the time people want me to bring love to them. Not send it away."

"We're not talking about love. This is lust. Pure and simple."

Although, in truth, there was nothing simple about her feelings for Gabe. He stirred her up. But at the same time, during supper, she'd felt strangely relaxed with him. Okay, maybe not relaxed. But comfortable. As if she could be herself.

"Oh, God," Roxi groaned. "You went and did it, didn't you?"

"I told you we did. Several times."

"You said you had mind-bending, multi-orgasmic sex. You didn't tell me you did a pair bonding with him."

"There wasn't any bonding going on." At least not on Gabe's part. If there had been, wouldn't he have called by now?

Hell. She really wasn't any good at casual sex.

"Haven't I told you that you have to keep your emotions and your orgasms separate?"

"Easy for you to say. You haven't had sex with Gabriel Broussard."

"More's the pity. Though unfortunately, he's not my type."

Emma snorted disbelievingly.

"Really," Roxi insisted. "I have, when it comes to men, one steadfast rule: I refuse to sleep with any guy who has the whole package. The best way to keep sex a no-strings affair is to stick to only going to bed with a man who's got a below-the-belt package."

"Gabe has that, too." Emma was feeling feverish just remembering him inside her. Filling her. Loving her. "Oh, God, Roxi." She leaned her elbows on the table and dropped her face into her hands. "I love him." So much, it hurt.

"It's too bad I'm not into black magic, or I'd put a curse on that Hollywood stud muffin for seducing you."

"He didn't seduce me." He hadn't forced her to go buy that sexy outfit, that barely there underwear, those damn fuck-me-big-boy shoes, which had definitely lived up to their name. *"I seduced him."*

It was Roxi's turn to snort. "From what I've read, the guy doesn't need a lot of convincing."

"He's not like that."

"Not kinky?"

Emma thought about the way he'd taken her on the table. And later, the whipped cream. And she hadn't even realized that some of the things he'd done to her in the shower were physically possible. "Define kinky."

Roxi shook her head. "Shit. It just gets worse." She stood up, went over to the kitchen and took out a small wooden chest. "Short of putting a stake through Gabriel Broussard's manly chest, this is the most powerful 'go away, lover' spell I know." She paused as she took a small glass vial of essential oil from the box. "So, I'm asking one last time—you sure this is what you want to do, *chère*?"

Emma had entered into their one-night stand with her eyes wide open. She'd known Gabe would hurt her. And he had.

So, the downside was that her heart was broken. Shattered, like the white shards of pottery that had covered the wood plank floor after he'd swept their coffee mugs off the table.

The upside was that she'd experienced a night of passion few women would ever know. With the sexiest man alive.

And that was worth remembering.

Now the thing to do was to get rid of Gabriel Broussard so she could move on with her life.

She nodded. "Absolutely."

* * *

Gabe missed Emma.

And not just for the sex, which had been blow-your-mind incredible, but even before *People* magazine had named him the sexiest man alive, sex had been easy to come by. And, too often, easily forgotten.

Which was not the case with Emma. It was as if the woman had burned herself into his mind. Having given her mixed messages ten years ago, he spent all day and evening out on the *gallerie*, trying to logically sort out his feelings. Which wasn't that easy to do since his mind kept returning to last night, rerunning every thing they'd done in Technicolor and Surround sound.

Every little detail about her was scorched onto his mind: her scent—tropical flowers blended with womanly arousal—as he'd dragged her down onto the bed; the flame silk of her hair draped over his thighs as she'd taken him deeper, with more enthusiasm, than any woman had taken him before; the rosebud shaped birthmark at the base of her spine; the satin of her legs wrapped around his hips, the soft little sounds she made when he kissed that sensitive spot behind her ear; the way she screamed his name when she came.

But there was more. Much, much more. He liked the way her smile lit up her eyes; he admired the way she'd taken those lemons her ex had dumped on her and turned them into day spa lemonade. He enjoyed her enthusiasm when she talked about her business; got a kick out of knowing that she'd seen all his movies, and liked the fact that her opinions of each role were honest, even if they weren't always flattering. Such as her belief that he'd made a mistake with that comic action hero flick, something he'd figured out on the first day of filming.

He'd also been damned relieved that she hadn't seemed to hold a grudge against him for having taken off to California.

Which reminded him—he still owed her an explanation.

No time like the present, he decided.

Conveniently overlooking the fact that it was eleven-thirty at night, he flipped open his cell phone.

While Regan Callahan didn't sound all that thrilled to be awakened for the second night in a row, Nate remained his typically unflappable self.

"No problem," he said.

That little matter taken care of, Gabe left the cabin, climbed into the pirogue tied to the dock, and headed across the wine-dark water toward Blue Bayou.

And Emma.

Thirteen

Gabe admittedly hadn't formulated much of a plan about what he'd do after he got to Emma's house. The one contingency he hadn't even considered was the notion that she'd be pulling out of the driveway just as he'd turned the corner onto her street.

It was nearly midnight. Where the hell was she going? To meet another man?

"The hell she is."

He wasn't stalking her, Gabe assured himself as he took off after the Miata. Not really. Even here in Blue Bayou, a woman driving alone in the middle of the night could be asking for trouble. He was merely looking out for her; the same way he'd want to protect anyone.

"Yeah, right." And if anyone believed that, he just happened to have a bridge to sell.

Less than ten minutes later, she came to a stop in front of a pair of tall wrought-iron gates surrounded on three sides by water. Having followed at a discreet distance, just like that detective he'd ridden around with researching his upcoming cop role had taught him to do, Gabe cut the headlights of the borrowed Callahan and Son Construction truck, pulled over to the side of the road and watched as Emma climbed out of her car.

The cemetery gate, badly in need of oil, squeaked as she opened it, then it slammed shut behind her. Wondering what the hell kind of assignation the woman might have in a graveyard in the middle of the night, Gabe followed, hiding in the shadows.

The scent of impending rain rode a night air scented with night-blooming jasmine and damp brick. A ring circled a full white moon, casting a ghostly gleam over crumbling stone angels draped in a veil of thick gray fog.

Bullfrogs croaked; cicadas buzzed; fireflies winked on and off amidst the limbs of oak trees draped in silvery Spanish moss.

Gabe watched Emma make her way across the uneven, shell-strewn ground to a tomb covered with Xs. He recognized the tomb, which had over the centuries faded to a dusky pink and begun to sink into the marshy ground, as belonging to Marie Dupree, a nineteenth-century voodoo priestess and ancestor of Roxi Dupree. The Xs on the brick signified requests for spiritual intervention; the coins, shells, and beads littering the ground around the moss-covered stone were offerings in appreciation of wishes granted, or in hopes of spells yet to be spun.

Emma took a small spade from a black backpack she'd taken from the car, and removed a bit of earth from in front of the tomb. Gabe couldn't make out her softly spoken words, but suspected they must be some sort of incantation. She retrieved something else from the pack, placed it in the shallow hole, then covered it up with the soil she'd removed.

There were more words. The glint of metal as she scattered some coins and purple, gold, and green Mardi Gras beads onto the ground.

An owl hooted; a blue heron glided low over the night black water.

Gabe was tempted to step out from behind the broken-winged stone angel and ask what was going on. At the very least, he wanted to dig up whatever it was Emma had buried.

Later.

First he'd make sure she got home safely. Then he'd return to the graveyard and learn what the hell the woman had been up to.

The idea that she'd probably had her friend cook up a love spell had him smiling all the way back to Emma's blue and white shotgun house.

Fourteen

It was even better than a love spell.

Three times, Gabe read the piece of paper Emma had buried. The first time her words—written in that tidy hand the nuns at Holy Assumption school had tried to drill into their students—made him hard.

The second time made him ache.

The third time had him debating whether or not to yank open his jeans and take care of the throbbing hard-on himself.

He could do that.

There'd been a time he probably would've. It was a logical, practical solution to the problem.

But after being inside Emma, after feeling those silky moist walls tighten around his dick and milk him so hard he was amazed he had any fillings left in his teeth, Gabe didn't want practical. Or logical.

What he wanted was Emma. Lying beneath him. Writhing. Screaming his name to high heaven.

Mais, yeah.

He'd already discovered, firsthand, how down and dirty the lady could be. To literally unearth proof of her vivid sexual fantasy life was like icing on a very sweet cake.

He rolled the paper back up. Retied the scarlet ribbon and put the list in his shirt pocket.

Emma didn't know it yet, but she was about to get lucky. They both were.

Although she'd tried to put Gabe out of her mind after burying that list of fantasies in the graveyard last night, he'd billowed in her thoughts, taunting, teasing, and oh, God, yes tasting.

"A man with as much sexual energy as Gabriel Broussard isn't going to be all that easy to get rid of," Roxi said knowingly, after Emma had complained for the third time that day about the spell not working.

"So, what do I do?"

"Keep him?"

"Sure, that's a great idea." Emma glared over at the pink draped altar. "I don't suppose you have a spell that'll make him want to give up the high life in Hollywood, come back and live in his father's old trailer while he changes tires and rebuilds engines at Dix's Automotive."

"I think the bayou reclaimed Claude's trailer after that tropical storm hit last fall."

"Don't be so literal." Emma took a vicious bite of the shrimp po'boy sandwich she'd ordered out from Cajun Cal's. My point, and I do have one, is that there's nothing here for Gabe."

"There's you."

"Right." Emma held up her left hand, palm up. "Let's see. Glamorous Hollywood actresses, supermodels, and wild, hedonistic parties at the Playboy mansion." She lifted her right hand. "A former chubbette living in a dead-end town where the highlight of the entertainment week is Arlan Dupree changing the movie posters down at the Bijou."

"Blue Bayou isn't exactly a dead-end town."

"Does or does not the highway end here?"

Roxi shook the bottle of hot sauce over a red and white

cardboard container of popcorn shrimp. If she weren't her best friend, Emma would've envied the way she could eat fried food every day without gaining an ounce. "Now, who's being too literal? Besides, it was always obvious to anyone who wanted to notice that there was something between you and Gabe."

"We were just friends."

"Which was why you wrote Mrs. Gabriel Broussard all over your seventh grade science notebook. And why you volunteered to paint scenery the year Mrs. Herlihy cast him in Sweeny Todd."

"All right. I stand corrected. He just thought of me as a friend. While I had a schoolgirl crush on him. But that was a long time ago. Lives change. People move on. Grow up."

Roxi rolled her dark eyes. "You may as well change your name to Cleopatra Quinlan, girlfriend. Because you are definitely living in denial."

"It's not that easy." Emma wadded up the waxed paper wrapper and tossed it into the wastebasket. It was twelve fifty-five. Dani Callahan, Nate's sister-in-law and Blue Bayou's librarian, had a one o'clock appointment and unlike most of the people in town, Dani was unrelentingly prompt.

"Maybe it shouldn't be easy," Roxi suggested. Sympathy born from years of friendship darkened her whiskey-hued eyes. "Don't knock first loves," she said as she slurped down the last of her R.C. Cola. "Sometimes they're the strongest mojo of all."

It turned out to be a long day. Maybe it was because of the full moon, or some strange alignment of the planets, or perhaps someone had put something in the water supply, because it seemed that everyone in town was suddenly in need of a massage.

It was nearly eight by the time Emma managed to leave Every Body's Beautiful and with her mind focused on taking off her shoes and pouring herself a glass of wine, as she unlocked her front door, she failed to see the truck parked across the street from the house.

She stepped out of the white clogs she wore to work and padded barefoot into the kitchen, where she took out a bottle of wine from the refrigerator.

"Late day," a deep, all-too-familiar voice offered from the shadows.

Emma spun around, one hand gripping the neck of the green bottle, the other splayed across her breast. "You scared me to death."

"Sorry." The man sprawled in the kitchen chair she'd sponge-painted a cheery sunshine yellow one cold gray day last December didn't look the least bit apologetic. He was inexplicably wearing a white silky shirt that laced up across the chest, black leather pants, and high boots polished to a glossy sheen. His long legs were spread open in a blatantly male way that drew Emma's attention to his groin, where the leather cupped his sex like a lover's caress.

"What are you doing here, Gabe?"

"What am I doing?" He rubbed his cleft jaw with those long dark fingers that had created such havoc to her body and her mind.

"I believe that was my question." Emma had spent enough years being the recipient of her mother's scornful tone that she was easily able to borrow it now.

Apparently unwounded by the sharp edge in her voice, he flashed her a wickedly rakish grin. "I'm here to fulfill all your fantasies, *chère.*"

A premonition had the fine hairs at the back of her neck standing on end. Surely he didn't mean . . . he couldn't be talking about . . . he wouldn't have . . . couldn't have . . .

Oh, God. Emma's knees nearly buckled when he tossed the rolled up piece of paper onto her kitchen table.

"Where did you get that?" Surely Roxi wouldn't have given it to him?

"Where you buried it." He clucked his tongue "You should be more careful with your secrets, *ma belle*. Think what might happen if it fell into the wrong hands. Now I don't much care what folks say about me. But you might be a tad bit embarrassed if everyone in town were to find out that you secretly want to be ravished by Jean Lafitte."

"It's only a fantasy." Still unnerved by the outrageous idea of him following her out to the graveyard, Emma refused to give him the satisfaction of knowing that her fantasy wasn't of the pirate himself, but of Gabe playing the part. "And you had no business stalking me."

"I wasn't stalking." He folded his arms and had the effrontery to look annoyed. "I was lookin' out for your welfare, me."

"Of course you were." Not.

"It's the truth. I was on my way here to talk to you, when I saw you leaving the house—"

"You had a sudden need for a midnight chat?"

"Well, actually, if you want the unvarnished truth, the more driving need was for a midnight fuck. But I figured we could talk afterwards."

"Has anyone ever suggested you may possess a few Neanderthal tendencies?"

He shrugged. "Don't know about that. I am what I am."

"No kidding, Popeye."

The thing was, Gabe's claim about being his own man was absolutely true. Emma had never met an individual, male or female, with a stronger sense of self. Or with more self-confidence. How many other men, growing up with Claude Broussard for a father, would've taken the easy way out and become the juvenile delinquent the entire town, including her parents, had probably expected him to be? Her parents had certainly forbidden her to date him, which had been a moot point since she'd have been just as likely to be asked out by Brad Pitt.

"At first I thought maybe you were off to some assignation with another man."

"And what business would that have been of yours?"

"You know, sugar, that was the exact same thing I asked myself. And you know the answer I came up with?"

"What?"

"I don't like to share." The suddenly hard gleam in his midnight blue eyes echoed that claim.

"Even if you had any claim on me, which you don't, that attitude is *so* chauvinistic."

"Guess it's that pesky Neanderthal in me," he said agreeably. "The same old-fashioned guy who thinks maybe he ought to watch out for any woman crazy enough to be driving around alone on dark country roads in the middle of the night. Which, like I said, was why I followed you to the cemetery."

He rubbed the side of his nose. Shook his dark head. "I gotta tell you, darlin', you sure as hell threw me a curve when you pulled up outside that old iron gate. At first I wondered if maybe you were one of those females who get off doin' it in graveyards."

"I believe you're the one of us who's into kink."

"Now, see, before you got off on lickin' that fluffy white cream off my dick, I might've believed that." He untied the red ribbon, and smoothed the scroll with his palm. "You already had me tied up in sexual knots, *chère.* But reading this just made things a helluva lot more interesting."

"I'm so pleased I can provide you some entertainment while you're stuck here."

"You know, that uppity princess-to-peasant tone might work real well when we get down to playing voodoo queen and her obedient love slave."

He tapped the second item on her fantasy list. The damn list Roxi had instructed Emma to write out, claiming that by burying it in the cemetery at midnight, she'd be rid of the hot scenes that had been plaguing her mind. Scenes starring, of course, Gabriel Broussard. "But it just doesn't fit with the number one fantasy on your personal sexual hit parade."

"You had no right reading a private document." She lunged for the list.

He raised it just out of reach. "'Less things have changed in the last ten years, the cemetery's a public place. Shouldn't have left your *private document* there if you weren't willin' to risk someone coming along and reading it."

"Excuse me for not anticipating stalkers with shovels."

"*Dieu*, you sure got a sassy mouth on you." He leaned closer. Skimmed a hand over her shoulder. "I must be getting perverted in my old age, because for some reason, you abusing me this way is startin' to turn me on."

"So, what else is new?" She batted away his hand. "From what I can tell, everything turns you on."

"Everything 'bout you," he agreed. "Could've been worse if Harlan Breaux got hold of it."

Harlan Breaux was what Gabe, having grown up with Claude Broussard, might have become. A stereotypical Southern bully, Harlan had a beer belly and a bad attitude right out of *Deliverance*. He'd spent time in Angola for rape, returned with his arms covered with prison tattoos, and there wasn't a woman in town who'd want to come across him in a dark alley. Or even, for that matter, in the middle of the town square at noon.

"You're right." Emma blew out a breath. "Going out alone at midnight probably wasn't the smartest thing I've ever done."

"Lucky thing I just happened to be there when you buried your love spell."

"Shows how much you know." Emma folded her arms across her breasts. Breasts that had begun to ache for his touch. "It wasn't a love spell." Her smile was sweetly false. "It was a go-away love spell."

He laughed at that. "Like that's gonna happen." He bent down and retrieved a shopping bag bearing the name of a popular New Orleans costume shop from behind the chair. "I brought you a little present. To help you get in the mood."

Expecting some sort of barely there froth of Victoria's Secret satin and lace, she was surprised to pull out a wide leather belt and heavy brown muslin skirt.

"Well, this is certainly sexy."

"You don't need frou-frou stuff to be sexy. Besides, you're a pirate's captive." He reminded her of not only her fantasy, but the scene from *The Last Pirate*. "It wasn't as if you had time to pack before I stole you away from that Spanish captain's ship."

"That was a movie."

He shrugged. "A movie's just another way of lookin' at fantasies. How about it, *chère*? Tonight you'll be my captive." He tunneled his hand beneath her hair, cupped the nape of her neck and kissed her, a hard, predatory kiss that caused needs to well up inside her. "I'll do things to you. Wild, wicked things."

His arm curved around her, anchoring her against him; he was hard, urgent, but in no way did Emma feel truly threatened. "Impossible things." His hand bunched up the flowing, calf-length broomstick skirt she'd worn to work, caressing the back of her leg, her thigh, the curve of her hip. "I'm going to spend this entire weekend taking you places, Emma. Wonderful places beyond your most daring fantasies."

His fingers slipped beneath the waistband of her panties, reminding her that, having given up on being with him again in this way, she was—oh, damn!—wearing plain white cotton.

She sucked in a sharp breath as his teeth nipped at the tender cord in her neck at the same time his fingers tightened on her bottom.

"And then, since, despite what you consider my Neanderthal tendencies, I'm all for equality; when we get around to playing Voodoo Queen, you can call the shots."

Common sense told her that all he wanted was to fuck her.

And your problem with that is?

Good point. The truth, as much as she might like to deny it, was that Gabe had reawakened something inside Emma. Something that had remained dormant all during her marriage. Something that she'd only experienced once before.

So what if what he was offering was only about sex?

In all her nearly twenty-eight years, until the other night at the camp, she'd only experienced true passion once in her life.

But for some reason she'd never truly understood, he'd pulled back, leaving her virginity intact.

Hoping to recreate that passion, she'd married Richard, who'd left her believing she'd only imagined that hot, burning-up-from-the-inside-out way she'd felt with Gabriel.

But then Gabe had come back to town. And all it had taken was one knowing look from those fathomless blue eyes, one touch of those wickedly clever hands, for Emma to realize that she hadn't imagined a thing.

And, amazingly, the fever was burning hotter than it had ten years ago.

Some things hadn't changed.

Gabriel still wasn't offering forever after.

But he was offering a sexual experience women all over the planet could only dream about.

"I can't spend the entire weekend with you. It's Jean Lafitte Days," she elaborated at his arched brow. "I'm Deputy Mayor. I have responsibilities."

She watched him process that, even as she tried to decide what she'd do about the ultimatum she feared was coming.

"These responsibilities," he said slowly. Thoughtfully. "How much time they gonna take?"

Emma blinked. "Well, Nate can open the festival by himself. And the food and carnival booth committees have those things pretty well covered." Roxi had been bubbling up potions for the past month to sell at her pink and gold Hex Appeal tent. "I'm supposed to be co-grand marshal of the parade." She had been looking forward to riding in that powder blue Caddy convertible rumored to have belonged to Elvis. But compared to having sex with Gabe, it was no contest. "But Roxi can do that." After all, she already had the wave down pat.

"But, I'm not going to miss giving Mrs. Herlihy that plaque." Emma lifted her chin, prepared for an argument.

"Which is when?"

"Sunday night."

"Well, then." He nodded, surprising her by accepting the compromise. "Sounds like we should stop wasting time and get on with workin' our way down this list."

"I have a hard time picturing you doing whatever I say." It was hard—make that impossible—to imagine Gabriel in a submissive role.

"I'll do whatever gives you pleasure, *chère,*" he said in a rough, deep voice. "They're your fantasies. If I'm doin' things right, and believe me, I intend to, you'll be pleasured, whichever one of us is callin' the shots."

Emma believed that. Because everything about Gabe gave her pleasure.

"I want to push your limits," he said. "To show you how far you can go. How far we can go together. I may command you to do things your logical mind never thought you'd do. Things that may even frighten you. But you'll do them. Willingly. Eagerly."

"You're that sure of me?"

His lips curved in a slow, wickedly erotic smile that could have been one Lucifer had pulled out to convince all those heavenly angels to join him in hell. "I'm that sure of *us*. You'll do them because you've dreamed of them, in the darkest, most secret corners of your mind and heart. You'll do them because, deep down inside that magnificently lush body, is the soul of a sexual adventuress."

The certainty of his growled words made her wet. But the part of her who'd overcome the humiliation of being the cheated upon wife, needed to get one last thing clear before surrendering power.

"If you're looking for a submissive to play French maid to your macho, sexual dominant, you've got the wrong woman."

He laughed at that. A rich, hearty, bold rumble of sound that vibrated inside her every cell.

"Lucky for me the store was all out of French maid outfits," he said. "I want you, Emma." He skimmed his palm down the front of her top. "And, if the way your nipples harden at my touch, and watching your blood beating like a bunny in your pretty white throat are any indication, you want me, too." His words were as soft as ebony silk; his touch, as his fingers plucked at her taut nipples, stole her breath. "Would it make you feel any safer if I promised never to hurt you?"

She believed him with every fiber of her being. And that belief made her bolder than she would have ever thought possible.

She met his hot, sexy gaze with a sizzling, challenging one of her own. "What kind of pirate would that be?"

His bold, pleased grin was echoed in his eyes. "Not a very good fantasy one, that's for certain." He tangled a hand in her hair and tugged with a sensual force that sent a frisson of delicious anticipation/fear skimming down her spine. "How about I rephrase that?" The hand that was still on her breast tightened, squeezing her flesh. "I'd never intentionally harm anyone. Especially a woman. Most especially you, *mon douce ami*."

My sweet love. Endearments seemed to come trippingly off Gabe's tongue. But tonight, for this stolen time of midnight fantasies, Emma chose to believe him.

"You've got to believe that I'd rather break my own bones than cause you any injury," he continued. "And I'd never inflict any pain that you're not willing—and eager—to accept. Or that doesn't give you pleasure."

The idea of a painful pleasure was frightening. Exciting. And impossible to turn down.

Having grown up under the disapproving thumb of her mother, it had taken Emma a great deal of effort to develop the self-esteem necessary to rise from the rubble of her marriage and reinvent herself into a woman she could be proud of. If asked, she would have insisted there was no longer a submissive cell in her body.

She was discovering she'd be wrong.

Submission to Richard the dickhead would be a waste of energy.

Submission to a man strong enough to know what to do with such a valuable gift was proving thrilling.

Emma lowered her gaze to the floor. Gathered herself inward. Then, slipping more easily into character than she would have ever believed possible, she gazed demurely up at Gabe through her lashes. Her thighs were quaking; her entire body was pulsating with need with the instinctive, eons-old biological need of a sexual female for a dominant male.

"I believe you, Gabriel."

Fifteen

A blue flame rose in Gabe's eyes. Watching him carefully through her lowered lashes, she saw the flare of masculine satisfaction.

"Now, there's a good wench." She wasn't the only one who could play a role. Then again, she reminded herself, role-playing was what Gabe did for a living.

Did he play these kinds of sexual games with his other women?

Don't go there.

His gaze was that of a predator, confident of its prey. "Your fate is ultimately in your hands, Emma. Whenever I command you to do something, you'll respond, 'Yes, my lord.' However, if there's any barrier that goes against your moral code, or which you find too difficult to overcome, you'll answer, 'If it pleases you, my lord,' and I'll understand that it's something you honestly don't want to do."

"What happens if I respond in that second manner?"

"I suppose you'll learn the answer to that, if—and when—the time comes."

It was not the most reassuring of answers. But, even as pinpoints of anxiety prickled her skin, Emma's body was electrified by the possibilities.

"Yes, my lord."

"Good answer." He yanked her against him, his arousal a long, hard ridge between them, his mouth taking hers.

The savage, claiming kiss ended far too soon. Emma's head was still spinning when he released her and picked up the skirt and belt she'd dropped onto the floor.

"Take off your clothes. Then put this on."

She was uncomfortable about going topless, but since he seemed to honestly enjoy her breasts, Emma decided she could live with that. Fortunately, the skirt was full enough to cover a multitude of flaws.

"Yes, my lord." She took the skirt and headed toward the bedroom to change. She'd only gone two steps when Gabe grasped her arm and jerked her back towards him.

"Where do you think you're going?"

"To change." Even knowing this was just a game they were playing, the disapproving male energy emanating from him turned her mouth as dry as dust. "My lord," she tacked on.

His long, leather-clad legs were braced apart, his muscled arms crossed over his chest. "Did I give you permission to leave the room?"

"No, my lord, but—"

"There are no *buts* allowed, wench. Perhaps you don't understand your position." He cupped her chin in an unyielding grip and lifted her wary gaze to his implacably stony one. "You are my prisoner." If she hadn't known better, she might have thought she was standing before the actual Jean Lafitte. "You will do whatever I say." His fingers tightened on her jaw. "When I say it." His other hand grasped her breast and squeezed. Hard enough that Emma gasped.

"If I tell you to drop to your knees on the floor and take my cock between your glossy wet lips, you'll do so without hesitation. If I tell you to bend over that chair, so I can take you hard and fast from behind, you'll say, 'Yes, my lord, with pleasure and gratitude,' then bare that smooth white ass in a heartbeat." Her thighs trembled as he ran a wide palm over her ass. "Whatever I demand, you acquiesce to. Quickly. Willingly." She whimpered as he cupped her. "Is that understood?"

Emma felt the color flame in her cheeks. She was not used to being talked to so strongly by anyone. She was especially not accustomed to being treated like some nameless sex slave.

Yet, that was exactly what she'd agreed to. What she wanted.

She ducked her head. "Yes, my lord." She risked a glance up at the kitchen fixture that was a thousand times brighter than the muted, flattering candlelight in the cabin. "May your prisoner request that the light—"

"Will be left on." His rough tone was harsh. Implacable. Exactly, she realized, like his character's had been in *The Last Pirate,* when he'd told his frightened captive that she could expect no mercy from a pirate rogue. "Looking at you pleases me."

"Bu—" Remembering his warning against arguing, she tried a different tact. "Please, my lord." She placed a hand on his forearm and felt the stony muscle clench beneath her fingertips.

"Either you take those clothes off, or I'll do it for you." He trailed a fingertip down the row of pearl buttons at the front of her blouse. "And believe me, if you leave it to me, you'll never wear them again."

The buttons seemed to have shrunk since she'd gotten dressed this morning. Emma's fingers felt large and awkward as she took an unusually long time to unbutton the blouse. All too aware of his steady stare, she dropped it onto the floor, then shoved the billowy skirt down her legs.

"There." Resisting the urge to cross her arms over her breasts, she lifted her chin and glared at him, submissiveness temporarily replaced by anger darkened by embarrassment.

Was it so wrong for a woman to want to appear beautiful to the man she was about to sleep with? Surely even a size zero, with perky, bought boobs and a spa-toned butt and stomach would feel uncomfortable bathed in such bright, flaw-revealing artificial light.

"That's a good start." He nodded his approval. "The bra has to go. I liked the lacy one a helluva lot better."

A spark of irritation flared. Emma forced it back down again. "Excuse me, my lord. Since I didn't hear from you yesterday, I had no reason to expect you to make an appearance this evening."

Gabe arched a brow. "So, my *'tite chatte* has claws." He enjoyed her little flash of rebellion. He didn't want to bring his luscious little wench to her knees. All right, perhaps he did, but only to take his throbbing erection between her pretty lips.

He had no plans to force her to obey his commands, but preferred to accept her submission as a gift. The scarlet flush spreading across her chest like a fever revealed her struggle with her redhead's temper. A temper, he suspected, she wasn't even entirely aware she possessed.

If things went according to plan, Emma was about to discover a great many things about herself. Including the depths of her capacity for hot passion.

She reached behind her back, the quick, furious gesture pushing her breasts out in a provocative way that had him wanting to thrust his hard-on between those soft white globes. Emma wasn't the only one struggling with control. Gabe was definitely teetering on a razor's edge.

The way she tossed the bra aside suggested that she found it no more appealing than he did. He was going to have to take her shopping at one of those frou-frou lingerie shops in New Orleans. Gabe liked the idea of watching his voluptuous wench model skimpy bits of silk and lace for his approval. Of course, the trick would be managing not to take her in the dressing room.

Then again . . . That idea was unreasonably arousing. In fact, Gabe was finding everything about the lushly sexy Emma arousing.

"We'll burn those underpants," he said. "They look like something a nun might wear to keep impure thoughts at bay."

"If it pleases you to do so, my lord," she said between gritted teeth.

"Does my captive wench have a problem with my command?" He moved closer, causing her to gasp when he scraped his thumbnail across the rosy pink tips of her breasts.

"It does seem like a waste of money. My lord," she tacked on.

"Ah, but I'm filthy rich," he reminded her. "From all the plundering and looting we pirates do," he tacked on, struggling to stay in character when what he wanted to do was to drag her by that wild mass of unruly red curls into the bedroom, or hell, onto the floor, and bury himself deep into her moist, welcoming warmth. "You'll take them off. Now."

Her hands went to the elastic waistband. Then paused. She glanced up at the light again. "I don't suppose—"

"I want to see you," he repeated. More sternly this time. Both he and his privateer alter ego intended to make this point perfectly clear. "I enjoy your voluptuous body." He put his hand beneath a heavy breast and lifted it to his mouth, drawing forth a ragged moan from between her parted lips as he suckled deeply on the satiny flesh.

"It suggests you're a woman with other appetites." He moved to the other breast, dampening it with his tongue while his hand moved between them, over the soft swell of her stomach, downward over her mound, to the drenched crotch of the underpants he was tempted to feed to the gators. Who probably had enough sense in their reptilian brains not to want them, either. "God, you're wet."

Her hips were rotating in unconsciously erotic little circles, as she ground her pelvis against his caressing touch in a way that triggered primitive impulses. "I can't help it, my lord."

"Definitely a woman of lusty appetites." Growing impatient, he shoved the white cotton down, and cupped her. Which was all it took to make her come in a hard release, arching her back, practically collapsing against him.

"That's one," he said, vastly pleased with himself. And with his Emma. He'd never met a more responsive woman. Nor one whose lustiness equaled his own. Certainly not all the women he'd been with over the years since leaving Blue Bayou, women who were, according to some artificial, arbitrarily imposed standard of female looks, some of the most beautiful women in the world, who, if truth be known, more often than not failed to live up to their sexy billing.

It was, after all, hard for a woman to give a guy a blow job when she was so concerned about smearing her lip gloss or the number of calories in semen, that she totally forgot about the guy whose dick was in her mouth. And it was damn hard to have bend-each-other-into-pretzels monkey sex with a woman who was all the time sucking in her already concave stomach or clenching her nearly nonexistent butt in hopes it'd look smaller.

Once he was certain she could stand on her own, Gabe released her and lifted his hand to his mouth. "You taste sweeter than *ruiz au lait*, *chère*." With his eyes locked on her widened ones, he slowly licked her essence from his fingers, one at a time. "Now, let's try out those new clothes your lord and master bought you."

Although he'd wanted the damn ugly panties gone, Gabe nearly swallowed his tongue as she rid herself of the white cotton underwear with a sexy little shimmy of her hips. Then she stepped into the skirt and fastened the wide belt around her waist. The heavy material flowed over her hips in a way that would've obscured her smooth white thighs. If he'd left it the way it had originally been designed. Which he'd had no intention of doing.

"I had the shop sew on some extra fasteners." He reached behind her, gathered up a fistful of rough brown muslin, and attached it to the Velcro strip on the belt.

"Gabe!" Shocked, she looked back over her shoulder at her sweet, bared ass.

He glowered at her from beneath lowered brows. "What did you call me?"

"I'm sorry. My lord." She actually ducked in a cute little curtsey that had him thinking that one of these days they might revisit that French maid idea. "It's just that I'm so . . . bare."

"All the better for me to see you." He turned her around and smoothed his palm over the bared flesh. "Touch you." She yelped as he lightly smacked a rounded cheek with his palm. "Punish you if you dare to disobey my commands. Or perhaps"—he spanked her again, then let his fingers linger—"just because it pleases me to do so." He tilted his head, studying the faint mark. "Pink's a flattering color for you, *chère*. Reminds me of ripe strawberries on cream. I'm thinkin' I could eat you up with a spoon."

He splayed his hands on her hips in fine pirate fashion, turned her back to face him again, making the same adjustments with the front of the skirt. "It keeps you accessible to me at all times," he explained in a voice roughened with his own almost unbearable hunger. This master stuff was proving harder than he'd imagined. "And you've got such a sweet little pussy, you should show it off more often."

Color even brighter than that on her bottom rose in her face. "What an intriguing idea. And would my lord visit me in prison after I got arrested for flashing the good citizens of Blue Bayou?"

He laughed. *Dieu*, he loved her spunk! "We'd have conjugal visits every day, *ma jolie fille*." He tugged playfully at the gossamer flame fluff between her thighs. "And twice on Sunday." He bent his head.

Emma sank into the kiss he bestowed upon her. A surprisingly gentle, even tender kiss that was totally at odds with the out-of-control pounding of her heart.

"We'd best be going," he groaned against her lips. "Before I forget my resolution to make this last and take you here and now."

"Going?" The words sliced through her sensual lassitude. When he placed his hand against the small of her bare back, just above the wide leather belt, and began leading her toward the kitchen door, she dug in her heels. "Where?"

He tilted his head. Something hot and dangerous shimmered in the midnight depths of his eyes. "Dare you question your lord and master?" His tone was dark. Ominous, almost, Emma thought as apprehension battled hotly with anticipation in her loins.

Was he still acting? Or had they crossed a line she hadn't realized existed?

She drew in a breath and tried to sort through her spinning, tumultuous thoughts. It was one thing to act out her fantasy here, in the privacy of her own home. But to risk being caught in such an embarrassing, compromising situation . . . How would she ever live it down?

He stared at her intently. "It's not that difficult a question." With deliberate slowness, he curled his long dark fingers around her throat. "Either you trust me"—his thumb brushed a feathery caress at the hollow of her neck where her pulse leaped, quickened—"or you don't." He put a booted foot between her bare ones, spreading her legs farther apart, then pulling her tightly against him so she could feel the thick, cylindrical outline of his penis against her naked belly. "Which is it, Emma? *Oui?*"

When he lifted his knee against her mound, stimulating already overly sensitized tissue, she moaned.

"Or *non?*" The question—the challenge—hovered between them, as hot and dangerous as a thunderstorm rumbling on the horizon. A sizzle of electric charge arced between them, from him to her and back again. More heat burned between her legs.

But it was the use of her name, personalizing this game that could have, with some men, turned ugly, that assured Emma she had nothing to fear from this fallen angel in black leather.

She framed his tragically beautiful face between her hands. "There is nothing I will say no to." She went up on her toes to press a submissive kiss of surrender against his boldly cut lips. "My lord."

Sixteen

Sitting beside Gabe in the Callahan and Son construction truck, racing through the dark clad only in her wench skirt and belt, Emma was relieved when he'd shown her the shirt he'd tossed into the backseat of the crew cab, along with the suitcase he'd packed while waiting for her to arrive home. "For you to put on in case we get stopped for some reason," he'd said.

The night air was thick as gumbo and swirled with tension. Emma was quickly realizing that there was a vast difference between fantasy and reality. In her fantasies there weren't any edgy, "what am I supposed to do now" moments. Things just flowed together, erotically, seamlessly.

"You havin' second thoughts 'bout this?"

His voice rumbled in the dark, his accent even thicker than usual.

"Not at all," she hedged.

"Wouldn't be surprising if you were," he assured her. "One of the first things I learned when Mrs. Herlihy put me in her drama class back in high school is that playin' make-believe isn't always as easy as it looks." He reached across the stick shift, captured her hand and pressed it against his groin. "Maybe you need a little something to occupy your mind.

Keep it from fussin' about the logistics of gettin' from your house to mine."

The tensed steel beneath the black leather fly stirred in a way that sent a delicious, forbidden thrill through Emma. She squeezed the thick bulge of his erection, feeling it grow gloriously thicker. Longer.

Although she was playing the role of a submissive, sexual prisoner, Emma felt a surge of power that she could cause such a reaction. Intrigued, she stroked his groin with her palm and was thrilled by the growl that rumbled upward from his chest.

The black pants fastened with a metal snap and zipper. She tapped the snap with her fingernail. "May I have permission to touch?"

"*Mais,* yeah." He arched his hips up. The truck picked up speed when his boot hit the gas.

"Thank you, my lord." Her gratitude was far from feigned. The truth was that she was aching to rip away the barrier between her fingers and that hard male flesh.

Gabe sucked in a sharp breath as she slipped her fingertips between the trousers and his burning hot flesh, taking care of the snap with a deft twist of the wrist. He was naked beneath the glove-soft leather. Naked and, for now, at least, all hers.

"I've been dreaming of this," she murmured as she lowered the zipper.

"Don't feel like the fuckin' Lone Ranger," he groaned as she freed his penis. "I've been so hot the past two days away from you, I thought I'd explode."

"You could have taken care of it." She wrapped her fingers around the base of his straining shaft. "By solo flying."

"What fun would there be in that?" He took one hand from the wheel, covered hers, and began moving them together, in a slow, upward motion. "When I can command my little slave to get me off?"

"Your slave is honored to be allowed the privilege of getting you off, my lord."

A vein bulged blue and thick in the muted glow of the dashboard lights. Emma could feel the blood pulsing beneath her stroking touch, a powerful thrumming that echoed the pulsing in the wet, slick, *needy* place between her thighs.

Emma desperately wanted Gabe to pull over and take her then, but knew that by staying in the role, he'd insist on fucking her in his way. On his terms, in his time. Which made her want him even more.

"Harder." His fingers tightened on hers, increasing the pace. "That's the way." He returned his hand to the steering wheel, knuckles whitening from the power of his grip. He spread his thighs farther apart. "*Mon Dieu*, you've got my balls practically jammed into my tonsils."

"Oh, dear." She skimmed her palm over the knobby tip, experimented with a little twist at the top end of the long stroke and was rewarded when he expelled a sharp hiss between his teeth. "We wouldn't want them to feel ignored, they," she said on a fair imitation of his Cajun patois.

She delved a little deeper, cupping first one, then the other. When she lightly skimmed her fingertips between the scrotum dividing them, he cursed. But not, Emma thought, as she spread the moisture down his rampant penis, in a bad way. Snowy white oyster shells sprayed upward in a fantail beneath the tires as he jerked the wheel, pulling over to the side of the road, and cutting the engine.

He closed his eyes and arched his back, lifting his hips, grinding them against her stroking hand, encouraging her with an intoxicating guttural string of French dirty words.

And then he was erupting in an explosive orgasm that was the most amazing, thrilling thing she'd ever witnessed.

"Christ," Gabe gasped. Finally replete, he sagged against the back of the seat, eyes shut, chest heaving. "That was the most fucking amazing hand job anyone's ever given me."

Emma instinctively opened her mouth to deny the compliment. Then she realized that she had, after all, been the one who'd done that. She was the one who'd made him so dramatically lose control.

Feeling pretty damn spectacular, she fought the grin that was threatening to break free. "I merely aim to please, my lord."

Gabe opened one eye. "Oh, you do that, sugar. Spectacularly." He grabbed a handful of tissues from the glove box and was prepared to clean himself off when Emma plucked them from his hand.

"I believe that's my responsibility."

He slumped back. "I believe you're right." He shut his eyes again, but reached out with unerring accuracy and stroked her hair. "*Merci.*"

"It was my pleasure, my lord," Emma murmured, touching a kiss to the still semi-erect flesh. Truer words had never been spoken.

The hours passed in a sensual blur, a stolen, fantastic time apart from reality. When she'd agreed to Gabe's proposition, there'd been a secret part of Emma that had feared the reality of acting out her long-held fantasies would not live up to the erotic images in her head.

But she'd been wrong. The reality proved amazingly better.

As soon as they'd arrived at the camp, he'd tied her to the iron bed, arms above her head, legs splayed, giving his hands, his mouth, his tongue absolute access to her most private, secret places.

Except for that unforgettable graduation night with Gabe, when he'd taken her to heights she'd never imagined possible, oral sex had always made Emma nervous. Unfortunately, the more nervous she got, the more tense she became, until it became nearly impossible for her to climax.

Once, at a Christmas party at the country club, she'd overheard Richard complain to a golfing buddy that it took so long for Emma to get off, a guy was risking lockjaw trying to go down on his wife.

At the time, instead of being furious, Emma had been suffused with shame. From then on, she'd faked orgasms to get the unfulfilling act over quickly.

There was no need to fake anything with Gabe. He was the first person, other than Roxi, with whom she didn't have to pretend to be anything but what she was. Which, if she were to believe Gabe, was damn near perfect.

His absolute appreciation of her, of every inch of the body she'd spent so many years trying to cover up, soon had the last of her self-consciousness disintegrating, like morning fog beneath a hot July sun.

She enthusiastically explored her sensuality, allowing Gabe to do as he'd promised, to take her to places she'd never imagined possible. Including the wax.

"This won't hurt," he assured her as he stood over the bed, holding a burning candle in a tall, red glass container. More candles glowed around the room, their flames flickering in dancing patterns against the walls.

She was tied up again, her wrists and ankles encased in fleece-lined leather shackles that could only be opened with the key Gabe was wearing on a black cord around his neck. "Well, it might. But in a good way."

She smiled up at him, utterly confident. "I trust you. My lord." They'd already moved far beyond that initial pirate/captive fantasy, but she'd discovered she enjoyed, in certain instances, such as now, when she was lying helpless and naked, giving Gabe the words along with the power.

"You are beyond incredible." When he bent down and kissed her, a flare of heat scorched through her body. Smoke billowed in her mind. Then he straightened.

Although she did truly trust him implicitly, Emma couldn't help tensing as he lifted the candle. As he tipped the red glass.

Instinct had her crying out at the feel of the melted wax hitting her breast. Her body jerked against the restraints. An instant later, she realized she hadn't been burned. The wax felt warm on her skin. Sensual.

Time seemed to slow down to a crawl as Gabe continued to dribble the wax over her helpless, supine body. Emma never knew where, exactly, he was going to place the wax next, moving from her left breast, to her right thigh, then back up to her right nipple, the other breast, her nipples, her stomach, her thighs, even the tops of her feet and the little round bone at the inside of her ankle. That not knowing was both unnerving and exciting. He also varied the temperature—not allowing the wax to get hot enough to scorch her skin, but no two drops felt the same, which added a slightly dangerous, fantasy edge to the sex play.

Much, much later, he put the candle down atop a heavy pine dresser and stood, arms folded, studying his handiwork.

"That wax looks like sperm," he said. Humor laced his deep voice. "You look as if your luscious body is covered with my sperm, *chère*."

The idea was more than a little arousing. "I can only hope. My lord."

The laughter in his tone gleamed wickedly in his midnight eyes. "Your captor will take his wench's request under advisement. Meanwhile—"

He turned his back to retrieve something from the top drawer of the dresser. Emma drew in a sharp breath when he turned around and she viewed the knife he held in his hand. The light from the burning candles glistened threateningly on the sharpened steel.

"We'd best clean you off."

This was Gabe, Emma reminded herself as an unwilling stab of fear struck. The man she loved. The man who'd sworn never to hurt her.

"Yes, please." It was barely a whisper, but easily heard in the hush stillness of the candlelit room. Her lids drifted closed as she waited for the touch of the blade against her naked flesh.

"You'll watch me."

It was not a request. Emma opened her eyes. The primitive sight of the rampantly aroused male, the cold steel of the hunting weapon, the taboo situation he'd created for them, had her body quaking with lust.

"Yes."

He smiled. Pressed the side of the blade to her breast, which flamed beneath the darkly dangerous touch. "You'll need to hold absolutely still, *chère*," he said gently. "So I don't cut you."

"That may be," Emma admitted on a voice thickened with desire, "the hardest thing you've asked of me, yet."

His smile promised yet more wicked delights. "A woman of appetites," he murmured. "And she's all mine."

Emma had no concept of how long it took for Gabe to scrape the cool wax off her body. She did know that by the time he'd finished cleaning her, she was nearly out of her mind with lust.

"You're wet." He slipped his fingers into her. "And hot." There was a deep, sucking sound as he pulled them back out again. "Are you hungry, *ma belle*?"

"Starving," she moaned, arching against his touch, lifting her hips as high as the restraints would allow. Had it not been for the fleece linings, she could have cut her skin, she was so desperate for relief.

"A woman of strong appetites," he murmured approvingly, as he took the key from around his neck and one by one, opened the locks. He ran his hand possessively down her body, from her throat to her knees. "And you're all mine."

"Yours," Emma said on a gasp as he surged into her.

It was the last either of them would say for a very long time.

Seventeen

"Why did you leave?" she asked, over a supper of shrimp etouffee. Not only had Gabe given her more orgasms than she could count, he'd also fed her the best meals of her life.

"I figured it was the right thing to do." When the crocodile kitchen timer dinged, he crossed the room and took a pan of bread pudding from the oven. Emma couldn't decide which made her drool more—the scent of that sweet baked pudding or the sight of Gabe's firm hard butt in those jeans he'd put back on. "I didn't have any prospects. You were going off to college in the fall. No way was I going to ask you to give up your dreams to chase mine."

"You were my dream." She was no longer embarrassed to admit it.

"Could've been a dead-end one," he said. "By the time it looked like I was goin' to be working pretty regular, you'd gotten married."

Gabe remembered Nate's phone call as if it had been yesterday. He was admittedly foggy about the next few days, having spent them in a drunken pity party of self-recrimination.

"You could have written."

"Last time I checked, the mail goes both ways," he said mildly, as he poured the hot whiskey sauce over the pudding.

"You didn't exactly leave a forwarding address."

"Nate always knew where I was."

During the past few days Gabe had come to the conclusion that Nate knew a lot of things. He also suspected that if he'd checked, that so-called construction emergency that had Emma meeting him at the airport would turn out to be as bogus as Richard the dickhead's tax return.

Not that he minded. In fact, Gabe decided, as he carried the two bowls of pudding back to the bed they'd hardly left this weekend, maybe he'd buy his best friend a case of Scotch as a thank-you gift.

"Let's not rehash the past, Emma," he said, handing her one of the heavy earthenware bowls. "We'll leave yesterday behind, worry about tomorrow when it comes." He stuck a finger into his bowl, scooped out some of the brown sugar whiskey sauce and drew a ring around Emma's plump pink nipple. "Right now, I'm suddenly feelin' hungry again, me."

Eighteen

Emma was in the bathroom, getting dressed for the presentation ceremony when the phone rang.

"I think the jig's up," Nate said without preamble. "A couple reporters from the *Enquirer* just dropped by the mayor's office, asking questions about you."

"I'm surprised it took them this long," Gabe said. He'd been half expecting the hungry hoards to descend on him since he'd first arrived. He'd also decided that if any reporter tried to intrude on his and Emma's weekend, he would've dug out Nate's old twelve-gauge shotgun. "Do me a favor." He told Nate what he had in mind.

"No problem. Just make sure you send Regan and me an invite to the wedding."

"The lady hasn't said yes, yet."

"Women can be funny that way," Nate allowed. "Lord knows, my bride, she tested my resolve when it came to settling down. But I convinced her to see the light."

That was an understatement. When they and their adopted teenage son had visited him in L.A. last fall, Gabe had never seen two people more enthralled with each other's company.

It was then that he'd first started thinkin' that maybe that's what he wanted for himself. And, as always, whenever his mind went wandering down that path, it led straight to Emma Quinlan.

The entire town showed up for the ceremony. Even Emma's mother and father were there, looking tanned and fit after two weeks spent on a ship cruising the Greek Islands.

Neither looked all that pleased to see their daughter enter the high school auditorium with Blue Bayou's former bad boy.

"Broussard," her father said.

"Sir," Gabe responded. As far as he was concerned, the guy was nearly as much of a dickhead as Emma's ex, but since she'd been unfortunate enough to have him for a father, Gabe was going to pay him respect if it killed him. Only for her. There was nothing he wouldn't do for his lush, lusty wench.

"Gabriel." Angela Quinlan somehow managed to hold her surgically perfected nose in the air while looking down at him. Which should have been even more difficult since she was a good foot shorter than his six feet two. She was also so bony a stiff wind would blow her away. Which had him suddenly wishing for a hurricane. Or maybe a tornado.

"Miz Quinlan," he said politely, smiling as he imagined a house dropping out of a stormy sky onto Emma's mother.

"I was surprised you'd come back to Blue Bayou," she said. If her tone had been any icier, there'd be frost all over the green, purple, and gold crepe paper strung across the ceiling. "Now that you're so famous, or should I say infamous"—her teeth flashed like a barracuda's as she layered the acid scorn onto the word—"there's nothing here for you anymore."

"*Mais, oui*, there sure enough is," he drawled, rocking back on his heels as he gave Emma a look hot enough to melt the metal rafters. He put an openly possessive arm around a shoulder he knew was sporting a little love bite from this morning when they'd gotten a little frisky in bed with the beignets.

"Emma?" From her tone, Gabe figured that if it weren't for the Botox keeping her forehead an expressionless slate, Angela

Quinlan's brow would've climbed into her perfectly coiffed blond hair. "What is this"—she paused, as if seeking some word allowable in public—"actor talking about?"

Before Emma could respond, Nate was calling her name over the microphone, asking her to come present the elderly teacher with her award.

Obviously torn, Emma's concerned gaze moved from the stage to Gabe to her parents to Gabe again, then back toward the stage. Her green eyes reminded Gabe of the time a bird had gotten caught in the cabin, and had been frantically trying to find a way to escape.

"You'd better go do your deputy mayor thing," he said. "I'll just stay here and chat with your *maman* and dad."

"I don't know—"

He pulled her up against him for a quick, hard kiss and was pleased when, even while her mother was emanating enough frost and ice to cover Jupiter, he could still make her blood heat.

"It'll be okay," he said. He ran a hand down her hair, which she'd smoothed out before leaving for town, but was already breaking into those bright curls he loved. "I promise."

"Okay." She breathed out a sigh.

He caught her arm as she began making her way through the crowd, which had begun talking about that hot public kiss they'd just witnessed between Emma Quinlan and bad boy Gabriel Broussard. "When you get done with your speechifying, why don't you call me up to give Mrs. Herlihy that plaque."

"Are you sure?"

"Absolutely."

Her smile lit up her face. That lovely, generous face Gabe knew would still be able to make his heart turn over when he was an old man, retired from the movie business, sitting out on the *gallerie* at the camp, making love to his Emma in that wooden swing.

"There's somethin' you both should know," he said to her parents, who were still looking properly scandalized by that kiss as Emma walked to the stage. *Mon Dieu,* Gabe was enjoying pissing off these two! "I'm gonna marry Emma, me. Now, you can make things difficult, or you can go along with the program. Which I suggest you do, 'cause, if Emma agrees we'll be making ourselves a lot of babies. Now, personally, I don't give a rat's ass if you ever visit your grandchildren or not, but I've got the feeling Emma will care. So, we may as well all just pretend to get along. For her sake."

"You haven't changed, Broussard," her father said. "You're still a bastard coonass."

"Well, that may be. But at least I'm not doin' time in prison like the dickhead."

Suddenly he heard Emma calling his name. Gabe had never heard it sound sweeter than when it came from her sweet lips.

The elderly mentor blushed to the roots of her lavender hair as Gabe told the gathered crowd how every success he had in the movie business, he owed to his former teacher. Then he kissed her, a smack right on her scarlet tinted lips. The crowd cheered. Gabe didn't care. All that mattered to him was the pride in those faded blue eyes and the love in Emma's gaze as both women looked up at him.

"I've got one more announcement to make," he said. "And, lucky for us, we've got some esteemed members of the press, from the *Enquirer,* in the back of the room."

Heads spun around. The two reporters, thought Gabe, though those words were stretching what they did for a living, looked uncomfortable. And more than a little nervous. Which vastly added to his enjoyment of the situation.

"There's been talk about my getting engaged recently, and I'd like to go on record saying that some of that story's true."

There was an audible gasp.

"I'm lookin' to get myself married." He reached out and took Emma's hand, knowing that she'd truly trusted him when it didn't turn cold at the unexpected remark. "If the lady will accept me."

Her eyes filled with moisture as she flung her arms around

his neck. "It's about time you asked that question, Gabriel Broussard."

There was more cheering. As he carried his Emma past Nate, his friend looked nearly as pleased with himself as Gabe was feeling.

"What about Every Body's Beautiful?" Emma asked.

"Roxi says she'll be happy to run it while you open up a western branch. What do you say, Emma? There are a helluva lot of ladies out there who could use a place where they can feel pretty and pampered. Even if they haven't dieted themselves down to skin and bones. And believe me, their menfolk will be real happy with the idea, too."

"I love it." She snuggled into his arms as he marched past the reporters. Wanting to make sure the entire world knew that this story was true, Gabe made a point of pausing to kiss her again. Their cameras snapped. Busy kissing him back, Emma didn't seem to notice.

"There's just one thing," she said as he buckled her into the seat of the truck.

"What's that, *chère*?"

"Are you sure you can keep a woman of my vastly voluptuous hungers satisfied?"

He laughed, feeling, for the first time in his life, as if he'd come home.

"I gau-ran-tee it, *mon coeur*."

You Give Me Fever

Nancy Warren

One

"What we need is a decent skeleton in our family closet," Lucy Charles said to her mother. "It would make writing the family newsletter a lot more interesting."

"Don't go looking for trouble, sweetie. I'm sure the family likes recipes more than gossip," Patrice Charles said absently, flicking over the pages of a loose-leaf binder that was her personal cookbook.

They were in the big old kitchen of the family home in Halifax, Nova Scotia. Lucy lived in Toronto now, but home would always be here, where she could watch the sea from her bedroom window and fresh lobster was what you ate when hot dogs were too expensive.

"Okay, what have you got?"

"What about the *tortiere*? Your aunt Florence sent it from Quebec."

"I used that recipe year before last." She stretched her neck, which was sore from too many hours spent working on her laptop. "Maybe I'll pick up a good recipe for jambalaya when I'm in Louisiana."

Lucy was a history lecturer at the University of Toronto. Currently, she was researching her own family's background, which included the splitting up of her ancestors when the

French Acadians had been expelled from Canada in the mid 1700s. She'd recently discovered, through damn fine research, if she did say so herself, living relatives in Louisiana.

"I'm not sure you should go down there all alone, Lucy," her mom said for the hundredth time. "You don't even know these people. They could be a bunch of crazies living in the swamps."

Her mother didn't quite approve of Cajuns. According to Patrice, the way they dropped vowels and slurred a perfectly nice word like Acadian into Cajun—well, she suspected there'd been drinking involved. "And you, a professor."

"I'm not a prof, Mom. I'm a lecturer. Big difference." The biggest being a permanent job and tenure. "That's why I'm spending my summer break writing this book. Publish or perish. Besides, Beatrice LeBlanc, one of your long-lost cousins, sounds great on e-mail."

"Hmm. Internet friends. We all know where that can lead," her mother said darkly.

Lucy went back to the notes she was making on her laptop. "But first I need to fit in family recipes and the fascinating exploits of Roland Charles, Jr. on the high school baseball team," Lucy sighed. "Oh, well. I can write a nice article on the Louisiana branch of the family for the next issue."

"You be careful, honey. And for goodness' sake, book yourself a decent hotel. Don't be putting up with strangers in some swamp shack."

"They're family, Mom, and the address is in New Orleans. I can't turn down their hospitality, it would feel rude. Don't worry. If I don't like staying with Beatrice, I'll move to a hotel."

"A mother always worries." Patrice flipped to desserts. "My daughter in a shack."

Her mother could not have been more mistaken, Lucy thought a week later as the cab pulled up in front of a gracious old mansion in New Orleans' Garden District.

"Are you sure?" she asked the cab driver.

"This the address you gave me."

She felt disoriented, and from more than a few hours on a plane and a change from breezy Atlantic Canada to this hot, humid paradise.

"Thank you," she said at last and got out of the cab, still staring at the home of her newfound relatives.

Wrought iron, that wonderful curlicued twirling iron lace, fronted the mansion. Inside the gates was a walkway that ought to have been artistically crumbling but looked brand-new, winding through lush gardens. The house itself was the perfect combination of grand and charming, with balconies, rich cream stucco walls and the kind of verandah where you simply had to sit and sip a mint julep.

She hadn't been bothered by the thought that her hosts might live modestly, but she'd never thought for a second that she'd be vacationing at Tara. Wow.

She swung her overnighter over her shoulder and dragged her wheeled suitcase behind her so it bumped noisily over the sidewalk. The gate was open, so she walked through and bumped her way up the path.

When she was halfway to that inviting verandah, she had to stop and unbutton. The jacket she'd needed in Halifax was suffocating her suddenly. Her oatmeal linen trousers might as well have been made of asbestos and her *trés* fashionable beaded cotton top felt like a ski parka.

Once she'd stopped to slip off her jacket and lay it over her arm, she took another second to drink in the beauty around her. There was so much of it. An embarrassment of garden riches. From gardenia in full, perfumed splendor to massive magnolia trees sporting white blossoms the size of dinner plates. Walls spilling over with purple bougainvillea, green slinky vines, and palm trees. Peeking from among the greenery were tiny garden gnomes. Somewhere water played, which only made her feel hotter.

A prickle ran over her skin and she realized in that sudden jolt that she wasn't alone in the garden.

A quick, searching glance and she discovered a sweaty guy with black, shaggy hair leaning silently on a shovel, watching her. The sweaty guy was shirtless.

He stood to the side of the house, and he'd obviously stopped in the middle of digging to watch her. There was a patch of fresh black dirt around his feet but he wasn't digging now. He was staring. Hadn't offered her a hand with her luggage, either.

He continued to stare at her and the heat of the afternoon intensified. He was exactly the kind of man who appealed to the part of her she didn't want to encourage. His eyes appeared heavy-lidded and predatory, his hair so long past the cut-by date that it curled over where his collar would be—if he'd been wearing a shirt.

What he was wearing was a tan. The kind of tan a man gets by working outside a lot without his shirt on. Even as she willed her feet to move up the path and toward the house, that part of her that was yelling, *Yes, Yes, YESSS!* held her rooted to the spot.

She'd never entirely believed Lady Chatterley would go quite so goopy over a gardener until now. This gardener had the slightly scruffy look of a man who hasn't shaved in a day or two, blue-gray eyes staring at her as though it were perfectly all right to stare unabashedly at a stranger.

Naturally, he had broad shoulders and a muscular torso, with a nice amount of chest hair, now damp from exertion. As she stood there entranced, a drop of sweat rolled, as slow as syrup, over his collarbone, tracking a wet streak over his upper chest and finally disappearing into the damp hair. Her gaze continued to follow its path as though that drop of sweat had rolled unimpeded over the nicely defined pecs, dipping to the rib cage and finally hitting the smooth plane of tawny belly. His jeans were low enough that she saw the jut of his hipbones. The jeans were grubby and shapeless, but she saw that his thighs were powerfully muscled and his feet, in disreputable old sneakers, were long.

While her eyes had been drinking him in more thirstily than

anything long and cool she'd ever consume on that porch, the gardener had been doing the same to her. She felt scratchy and overdressed, and was aware of a wild longing to stand before him as he was, in a pair of low-riding jeans and bare torso—she even wanted her feet bare so she could curl her toes into the rich black earth he'd churned up.

Her common sense finally asserted itself. "Will I find Ms. LeBlanc in the house?" she asked in the tone she used at school when she felt she needed to exert her authority over students who were no more than five years younger than she.

Those blue-gray eyes considered her for another interminable moment and then he showed surprisingly white teeth in a quick grin. "I believe she is." Very attractive voice. Slow talking and deep with a slight hint of a French accent.

"Thank you." If her tone was cool, it was the only part of her that was.

She turned and made her way to the verandah. Based on the fact that she heard no sounds of digging behind her and that her spine prickled, she'd be willing to bet a month's salary that the gardener was checking out her back view.

Suitcases and all.

When she got to the verandah and started up the wide steps she heard a wolf whistle, so soft she could pretend she hadn't heard it if she chose.

She did not choose.

She turned to glare at the culprit only to find his head bent, watching the progress as his shovel plunged deep into the fertile ground. There was something aggressively sexual about the gesture, which she told herself was her own fault for studying too much literary symbolism. Suddenly the gardener lifted his head and she caught the carnal gleam in those eyes. Very deliberately, while holding her gaze with his, he raised the shovel and plunged it back into the yielding earth.

Her breath caught and a quiver of arousal struck, so strong it shocked her. Resolutely, she turned away from the sexiest man who'd ever planted a tulip bulb.

After taking a moment to compose herself, she knocked on the wide oak door. She wouldn't have been surprised to be met by liveried servants when the door opened, but in fact the older woman in a stylish blouse and peasant skirt took one look at Lucy standing there with her cases and beamed. "Why, you must be our cousin Lucy. Welcome, honey. I'm your cousin Beatrice."

Lucy held out her hand politely but the older woman laughed and pulled her into a huge hug, lightly scented with a perfume she couldn't identify but smelled like lily of the valley. "You're in the south now, honey. Everybody kisses everybody." For a split second she thought about that man in the garden and then forced him from her mind.

"Come in. It's wonderful to have family in the house. I swear this old place gets lonely when there aren't enough people to fill it."

Lucy smiled and pulled her cases into the wide foyer. "I really don't want to put you to any trouble. I'd be happy to stay at a hotel."

"We already had this argument on e-mail," Cousin Beatrice reminded her. "You're family. You stay with family."

"This is such a wonderful house," Lucy said, following her newfound cousin inside. "Has it been in the family long?"

"Not by New Orleans standards. It was built by a Yankee trader back in the late eighteen hundreds. We bought it in the sixties. Claude can tell you more. He's the one who knows about history."

"Your son, Claude?"

"Your Cousin Claude. Didn't you see him? He's out in the garden."

The half-dressed hottie was her cousin? "Yes. I did see him, but he didn't introduce himself."

"Probably didn't even notice you. He's very focused when he's busy with something."

He'd certainly been focused when he'd undressed her with his eyes, but she didn't feel like sharing that fact with the man's mother.

"You two will have a lot in common. You teach history and my son owns a couple of antique shops."

"Really?" It wasn't what she would have expected of the man outside. "I thought he was the gardener."

Beatrice chuckled. "He's that as well. He helps me keep up this place. I couldn't stay here if he didn't."

As Lucy was led through into the main living areas of the house, her surprise grew. "What beautiful things." She was no expert on furniture, but she could see the rich patina of age on some of the pieces. The Aubusson rug in the living room was almost too gorgeous to walk on. The whole house reeked of old money. Claude traced his distant relationship to her through his father, so the money must be on his mother's side.

"Are you hungry?"

"No, thank you. I had lunch on the plane."

"Some iced tea, then. I've got a fresh pitcher all ready in the refrigerator."

"That would be wonderful," Lucy said.

"Go on out to the porch and sit. Tell Claude to wash up and join us."

"All right. I'm going to change into something cooler first."

"You go right ahead."

Lucy slipped up to the room she'd been given. As pretty as anything in New Orleans, she figured. The wrought iron bed frame and the antique furniture were feminine and dainty. A dormer window with a padded window seat looked out over the back garden, which was as pretty as the front.

She washed up and brushed her teeth in the adjoining bathroom, which contained one of her favorite things in the world, a claw foot bathtub.

Just knowing that Claude was out there in the garden somewhere had her bringing a pale yellow cotton sundress into the bathroom to change. She freshened her lip gloss, ran a brush through her hair, and pushed her feet into sandals. She ran down the stairs, stopped and huffed a quick breath in and out before officially meeting Claude LeBlanc.

All right then. She'd made a small miscalculation about the identity of Sweaty but Gorgeous out front. He wasn't a totally hot gardener, but her distant cousin. Well, if she'd mistaken her man, Cousin Claude was about to find out that he had also mistaken his woman.

Two

"Excuse me, but I think we're related." The cool voice with its clipped Canadian accent hit him like so many snow pellets she'd brought with her from up north.

Claude raised his head slowly, taking the time to enjoy how good she looked from the tip of her strappy shoes to the green eyes staring at him with a challenge.

"We're not closely enough related for it to matter," he said.

"Well," she snapped, "if you're worrying about the gene pool, I'm not here with marriage in mind."

"It wasn't marriage I had in mind, either, *cousine,*" he said, giving it the full French inflection.

She didn't look flustered or embarrassed, which he'd expected. Somehow, she looked more amused. "Is there some reason you're acting this way with a total stranger?"

Yes. A couple of very good reasons. But he wasn't about to share them with his Canadian cousin. He played innocent. "What way?"

"Like you ordered me out of a catalogue and you're checking out the merchandise before buying."

He laughed. Couldn't help himself. Okay, so there was more brain inside that luscious package than he'd guessed. Unfortunate, but couldn't be helped. "I offer my apologies, *cousine*. Welcome to the Big Easy." He grimaced down at his filthy hands. "I'd welcome you properly but I'm filthy."

"You knew who I was when I walked through that gate, didn't you?"

"Yes."

"You let me think you were the hired help."

"I didn't encourage you to think anything," he corrected her.

"You were gardening. I took you for the gardener and you did nothing to change my impression. Why?" Her hair was a rich color, like rosewood, he thought, in a particularly fine piece of furniture that had been polished and cared for over hundreds of years. When she turned and the sun lit her hair, he watched colors from gold to burgundy spark. She had a redhead's fair skin and eyes the deep, mysterious green of the bayou at sunrise, with a few gold flecks in their depths to keep things interesting.

Her body was slim and wiry as though she never sat still long enough to gain an ounce. Some nice curves on her, though. Subtle but nice. He didn't want her to be pretty and he most certainly didn't want her to be intelligent or inquisitive, both of which she was shooting at him out of both barrels. What he wanted her to be was gone.

He'd had one of his few-ever arguments with his mama over having this unknown cousin to stay. His mother, when she'd made up her mind, was immovable, however, so all Claude could do was keep an eye on this suddenly discovered branch on a family tree he'd be perfectly happy to chop down.

"Well?" she insisted. "Why didn't you introduce yourself before?"

He decided to tell her, partly because he always preferred the truth and partly because the truth might make her run. He looked at her and let the silence lengthen. She could feel the animal attraction that arced between them, and he waited until the air around them was tinged with it and her eyes were clouding. "Cousin Claude would have had to act polite. I took one look at you and I didn't feel polite."

She didn't step back or even drop her gaze, so he began to feel as scorched by her proximity as from the sun beating down on them.

"I see," she said slowly, not looking ready to run, looking more like she might try him out for size. Shit. Trouble ahead. "Your mother said you should wash up and join us on the verandah for iced tea." And with that she turned and was gone, her body moving rapidly, the yellow dress floating behind her as though trying to catch up.

Oh, and wasn't she exactly the kind of distraction he didn't need?

And the kind of distraction he enjoyed most.

He entered the house from the back and washed up at the laundry sink, then pulled a clean T-shirt over his grubby jeans and called himself decent.

By the time he'd made it to the verandah, the tea party was in full swing. His mama loved company and he could hear the excitement in her voice as she talked to her shirttail relation. There was a tinkling burst of feminine laughter, and then he was around the corner of the house and able to see them. He was struck by how familiar they looked together. Two attractive women of different generations gathering over tea. He supposed women had been doing it for centuries—these two looked as though they had and not as though they'd met less than an hour ago.

Amazing.

When he climbed the steps they were talking about how much they both loved the ocean, and it sounded very much as though his mother had accepted an invitation to visit her new friend in Halifax. "Of course, I don't live there now, but my parents are still there. I think you'd like Halifax. It's right on the ocean and full of history."

"It's where our histories connect," he said, making his presence known. "Your people booted my people out of your country."

"Terrible the way families were split up," Lucy said, not bristling in defense as he'd half expected.

"Lucy's writing a book about the Acadians and the Cajuns. She wants to put some of our family stories in it."

And wasn't that just perfect? "Does she now?"

Lucy must have heard reluctance in his tone for she turned her big green eyes in his direction. "Your mother said it would be all right for me to look through your family records for my research."

They both gazed at him. What could he say? "Hey, it's fine by me. Knock yourself out."

"Lucy Charles," his mother said in her company voice, "this is my son, Claude LeBlanc," as though she knew damn well they hadn't bothered to properly introduce themselves.

"It's a pleasure to meet you, Lucy," he said, holding out a freshly washed hand for her to shake. As her fingers clasped his, he felt the jolt he'd expected and dreaded. *Merde*. His mother looked at him and he guessed she knew exactly what he was thinking. Why did he always go for the skinny ones with brains? Hundreds of easy-going, soft, round women passed through his life. They married his friends and turned into charming Southern wives and mothers. But it was this type, this energetic, driven, skinny brain box that would grab his interest every time.

She took back her hand and for the first time appeared flustered. Hadn't expected that jolt, huh?

Well, he had. The question that was puzzling him was what the hell he was going to do about it.

A smart man would do nothing.

When it came to skinny, driven brain boxes, Claude had never been a smart man.

Lucy watched as Claude accepted a glass of iced tea from his mother and settled into one of the wicker chairs. You could tell a lot about a man from the way he treated his mother, and in spite of the arrogant, sexually aggressive way he'd treated her, it was obvious he adored his mother and she adored him right back.

Interesting. Lucy sat back and listened as they discussed the stone patio he was making for Beatrice. She enjoyed the lilt of their voices and the smug knowledge that the two branches of the family might never have come together if not for her, when she was startled by Beatrice saying, "Why don't you take your cousin downtown tonight and show her around?"

He glanced at her from under his brows. "You like jazz?"

"Yes, very much. But—"

"I'll go home and clean up. I'll pick you up at eight. We'll have dinner."

She blinked. "Don't you live here?"

He looked amused, but it was his mother who answered. "He's crazy. I've got this big old place all to myself, but he—"

"I'm too old to live with my mother."

"Paah. You don't want me knowing what you get up to."

He shot a quick glance, full of devilry, at Lucy. "And there's that."

"Perhaps I should stay home tonight and spend the evening with you, Cousin Beatrice."

"Well, sure you could, sweetie," Cousin Beatrice said doubtfully. "Do you play bridge?"

The French Quarter restaurant was casual and funky, with a band playing in the center and diners getting up to dance whenever they felt like it. The food was amazing. She'd had a local fish she'd already forgotten the name of, and salad with pecans. Claude had chosen a dry French wine and had managed to shake his caveman manners of earlier, which had made her dread the evening. He was obviously making an effort to entertain her and his charm was so effortless, it had to come naturally.

Her date had transformed from the grubby but gorgeous

gardener to a sophisticated and even more attractive . . . what? He didn't look like an antiques dealer. He seemed more like a modern-day pirate. Maybe it was the white, open-necked linen shirt against the tanned skin, the longish dark hair—and she was almost certain she'd caught a glimpse of a small gold hoop in one ear.

An expensive-looking sleek gold watch glinted from his wrist. His hands were square and strong. He wore a heavy gold ring on his right hand, set with a large square emerald that looked very old. She could imagine those hands plundering treasure.

"You're smiling. What is it?" he asked.

"I was admiring your ring."

"Thank you. Usually I tell people it's a family heirloom."

"Is it?"

"No."

Why did the picture of him with iron-bound wooden boxes spilling with ill-gotten gains have to flash through her mind? He wasn't a cartoon character but a man who was distantly related to her and who, she was beginning to think, possessed an odd sense of humor.

"Are you going to tell me where you got it?"

He gazed down at the ring, letting it flash in the candlelight. "In my business I come across many beautiful things. Some I can pass up." He raised his head and suddenly gazed at her with intensity. "Some I can't."

Ring. He's talking about a ring. But she knew bloody well it wasn't an emerald under discussion making her blood start to pound. He was talking about her. His blue-gray eyes held hers and she felt the mysterious pull, unable to look away.

Well, he could sweet-talk her all he liked, but the ultimate decision would be hers. He was undeniably attractive. He also had trouble tattooed all over him.

Finally, she broke eye contact and took refuge in a sip of wine.

"Would you like to dance?"

Oh, what the hell. If he wasn't trouble, she wouldn't be as interested. "Yes."

Somehow she'd known it would be like this when they touched. His hands, discreetly and properly placed, one clasping her hand and the other resting at her waist, felt overly warm and intimate. She smelled his skin and knew he could smell hers. The beat of the music was sensual, insistent, and she found her feet moving and her blood pounding to the same rhythm. She wouldn't look into his eyes, that would be too dangerous, so she kept her gaze on the hollow of his throat below his Adam's apple, where his pulse beat to the same rhythm as hers.

Had she ever felt so hot for anyone in such a short time? No. She'd had her share of men, but her relationships tended to follow a certain predictable pattern. A few get-to-know-you dates, some kissing, and usually by then she knew if she wanted the man in her bed or not. Most of the ones who'd made it there had been good men who took the time to learn her body and who gave her pleasure. One lasted a couple of years and she knew the reason they'd ended things was because they weren't ready for marriage or right for each other long-term.

Lucy believed in dating, and she enjoyed it. Well, she'd been a student a lot longer than she'd been a teacher, and research was her strength. She always did her studying and research before finals. Why should sex be any different? A woman who took the time to thoroughly research her subject was far less likely to end up with a failure on her hands than one who blundered blindly into relationships.

Dancing with Claude, simply dancing with the man on a crowded floor, felt like throwing out all her careful methods and rushing blindly into an affair.

Because this wasn't dancing. It was foreplay. Somehow this man had jumped all her carefully built fences, blasted open all her gates, leapt all her walls. He was here. And if she didn't do something drastic, they'd be intimate before she knew him at all.

Part of it was the atmosphere of this city, she knew. The place pulsed with life and the drumbeat of sexuality. Her first day and night in New Orleans and already she loved it. Some cities were like that. They came right out and said, Hey, this is what I'm all about. New Orleans was one of those cities. A little faded, a little decadent, a bit seedy around the edges, but a sensual feast and, as far as she could tell, a twenty-four/seven celebration of life.

Claude's body pressed against hers as the floor grew more crowded and she felt the pulse beat of desire grow stronger. Their bodies brushed as they moved; she felt the heat coming off him and her skin grew as sensitive as though he were caressing her. She heard her breathing change to the lighter, quicker breaths of arousal. God, this was insane.

"Let's walk," he said suddenly, huskily, and she nodded. If "walk" was a euphemism for "Let's go outside and have crazy wild sex," she'd still have gone.

They returned to their table, where Claude threw money down, and then took her hand and led her out into the night. It wasn't a lot cooler outside than in, but the air was a little fresher, the insistent music muted, and her sanity made a brave attempt at a return.

There was a current of energy humming between their joined hands that both stimulated and unnerved her. Determined to get some idea of who he was before launching herself into his bed, she marshaled her thoughts.

She knew from his mother that he wasn't married and never had been. Beatrice had also made it clear that there hadn't been a steady woman in his life for a while, though he was too obviously sexual not to have had plenty of unsteady women. Which, come to think of it, was exactly how he made her feel. Unsteady. Thrown off her course. Out of control.

She breathed in the scents of New Orleans at night, the dust and flowers, the mélange of cooking styles, the saffron scent of Creole, the butter-garlic-wine of French, the spiced fish, and then, oddly, the smell of frying donuts. Beignets, she corrected herself mentally. Claude led her around a group of college-aged kids who'd been overdoing the go-cups.

Behind them a quartet of Japanese girls giggled and shot each other with digital cameras.

What exactly did she know about this man her body wanted to jump all over naked, she wondered as she stopped at a questioning gesture to take a group picture of the girls. Next to nothing.

Sense, Lucy, she chided herself. *Where's your sense?*

They walked a little farther and even as she tried to take in the atmosphere of this amazing city at night, even as the scents of one amazing restaurant after another teased her and the jazz ebbed and flowed as they approached one club after another, she found the man beside her clogging all her senses.

He looked, felt, smelled, and sounded delicious. She hadn't tasted him yet, but every part of her knew it wouldn't be long.

"Claude, I know so little about you," she said, deciding to come right out and ask. If she was cramming her study time with this man she had to go straight to the important facts.

He glanced down at her and his eyes glistened as they passed under one of the restored gaslights.

"I would like to change that," he said, tightening his hold on her hand ever so slightly.

Oh, come on. What was she, stupid to fall for this practiced seduction? They'd wandered onto Royal Street; she could see the sign. She turned to face him.

"I'm a researcher. A pretty good researcher. In thinking about this book, which I've done for some time you understand, I've studied all the branches of our family. That's why I was so excited when your mother invited me to come down and meet you. You see, I already know a lot about your family."

"Do you?"

"Yes. When the Acadians were expelled from Nova Scotia,

many of them fled to Louisiana where the only other French colony of any size existed in North America. Their descendents are the modern-day Cajuns."

"We learn this history in grade school, *cousine.*"

"Of course. And when families were split, as in our case, when the men and boys were shipped off first, and the women later sent for, they wrote letters to each other, some of which actually made it. I've got one or two. And one amazing diary. They're heartbreaking."

"That will be very helpful for your research," he said, running a single fingertip down the slope of her cheek. It was probably the practiced gesture of a professional flirt, but he did it so well it was almost as though he couldn't help himself. She shivered, feeling the finger trace its path like a tear.

"I've gathered quite a bit of information over the years. The point is, Claude"—she took a deep breath and blurted out what had been bothering her since the cab pulled up in front of the mansion—"if anyone in the family had amassed a fortune I'd have heard about it."

He stiffened slightly. Whatever he'd been expecting, it hadn't been that. "Have you perhaps shared these thoughts of yours with my mother?"

"No. Of course not. But she told me your father inherited from a distant uncle." She shrugged, letting him in on the fact that she knew every one of his uncles, distant uncles, cousins, and pretty much everyone else with a drop of shared family blood.

"Ah." She thought his eyes crinkled in amusement. "The uncle was a mistake."

"It was."

"But then my father did not know that you would one day enter our lives."

"No. I suppose not." What a strange conversation. And when was he going to get around to answering her question?

"You know what I've been thinking?"

"What?"

"How very well that ruby necklace would go with your hair and coloring," he said, pointing behind her.

Ruby necklace? She ought to be searching for her ruby slippers so she could click her heels and get the hell out of here.

In spite of herself, she turned and looked where Claude pointed. They were standing in front of one of the antique shops that crowded the street. The necklace he indicated was a thin gold filigree chain with a series of small rubies. The setting was clearly antique, but it was delicate and exactly the sort of thing she hung around antique store windows admiring.

"Yes," she said shortly. "It's very nice." And if he thought he was going to distract her with pretty things, he—

"Would you like to try it on?"

"What, now?" The shop was closed and the interior dark.

"Yes. I've a desire to see it on you." Once more that single finger was busy, this time trailing a curve from her left collarbone to her right, leaving a trail of shivery heat in his wake. "It would rest right here, I think."

She thought of the gorgeous emerald signet ring and the mental picture she'd had of him with his pirate's booty. She'd thought it fanciful at the time; now she wondered. "Claude, are you a thief?"

She was joking, but he seemed to take her words seriously.

"There are many kinds of thieves, *cousine,*" he said, his eyes seeming dark and mysterious in the dim light from the street.

"There is the greedy stock promoter who takes old ladies' life savings and loses the money. Is that not thievery of the most contemptible kind?"

"It may be, but it's not illegal."

"There is the thieving of certain politicians who sell promises for taxpayers' money and don't deliver."

He stepped closer and her heart jumped. "Then there is my favorite kind of theft," he said softly, moving closer still. "The stolen kiss," he said, and covered her mouth with his.

As his lips touched hers, lust slammed into her, flattening her the way Claude's body flattened hers against the closed door of the antique shop. She clutched at his shoulders, feeling at once overwhelmed and triumphant. He might be trouble, but he was going to be a fantastic lover. There was something about the two of them together that was magic. Her skin tingled as he pressed against her, her mouth opened under his, and he thrust inside with greedy haste but with finesse. Giving into the inevitable, she wound her arms around his neck and kissed him back.

This wasn't an experience she was ever going to forget, she thought dimly as he took her mouth with the kind of fierce focus she imagined he'd bring to his lovemaking.

He tasted of all the flavors of this city, she thought, of international spices and coffee with the dark rasp of chicory, of hot sauce and the coolness of mint. She was so far off her feet she thought she might never find her balance again when she found herself physically unbalanced and falling backwards.

With a startled cry, she took a step back and found herself inside the antique store in the darkness, with the musty smell of antiquity overlaid with some kind of sweet fragrance. Potpourri, she thought, dimly.

"What are you doing?" she whispered. She'd been mostly kidding about him being a thief but now she wasn't so sure. He chuckled, obviously enjoying her outrage, shutting the door behind him and leaning past her shoulder to punch numbers into an alarm system keypad.

She shook her head, trying to rattle her brains back into some semblance of order as the obvious answer to her question hit her. "You own this shop."

"I do. And two more like it."

She heard a deadbolt click into place and then he was reaching into the display case for the ruby necklace.

She glimpsed the price tag as he hooked it around her neck, standing so close she felt dizzy. "Claude, don't put it on. It's too expensive. What if I break it?"

"I'm more likely to break it. Besides, the markup's ridiculous on what I got it for." His fingers brushed her shoulders as he put the necklace around her neck. It felt cool and expensive against her skin, while his fingers felt hot and dangerous.

"What do you think?" he said, turning her to face a mirror.

"A light would help," she said, seeing the shadowy reflection of the two of them. A glint of gold and a single flash of red was all she saw of the necklace.

He shook his head; she saw the movement reflected. "We'll have drunk tourists banging on the door thinking we're open," he said. "Trust me, the necklace is stunning. Come on. Let me show you around."

"In the dark?"

"It's atmospheric. Use your imagination."

She rolled her eyes but let him lead her by the hand into what was obviously a high-end antique store. The most gorgeous treasures were crammed together and every surface seemed crowded with delights. A Louis XIV chest glowed with gilt, and atop it sat an ormolu clock with a graceful goddess spreading her gold skirts atop the clock's face. Crystal and silver glowed quietly in the dim light; she saw the dark squares and rectangles of paintings on the walls, and beneath her feet was the softness of expensive carpets.

She realized their immediate destination when he removed a white tent card that read, "Please Do Not Sit on the Furniture" from a pale velvet settee that she thought was blue. He pulled her onto the forbidden furniture and kissed her again.

He was too good, too slick, too amazingly sexy. She wanted to devour him and it was obvious he felt the same. He kissed her, using his lips and his tongue and his whole body, so she felt kissed everywhere. His hands were in her hair, on her shoulders, running down her arms, and then brushing across the tips of her breasts, almost by accident but not quite. She felt the brush, and the incredible tingle, the movement of the gold and ruby necklace stirring against her skin, then he was gone.

If he'd grabbed at her she might have found the strength to

push his hand away but as it was he teased, feather light touches that only made her want more.

She was pressed gently back onto the soft velvet and let herself fall. Oh, those practiced fingers could entice her skin the way his softly accented words seduced her mind. The kiss became a full-bodied affair, and from the impressive erection nudging her belly, she knew he was as aroused as she. Their breathing grew harsh in the sleeping store. Outside people wandered and she'd hear snatches of loud conversation, a laugh, a curse, the wail of a single saxophone struck up somewhere nearby, but in here it was private, dark, and intimate.

When his hand began to draw her skirt upward, she felt every inch of her thigh hum with pleasure.

The antique furniture beneath them squeaked and it was like a wake-up call to her sensible self.

"Wait," she said, grabbing his hand and pulling away. "What are we doing?"

"What comes naturally, *cousine,*" he said, running a hand over her seriously mussed hair. "I've got an apartment upstairs. I could give you a nightcap."

"I'll bet you could," she said, feeling a little wobbly but shaking her head all the same. Her body might pout big time at being left wanting, but her moral standards demanded that she find out a little more about the man before sleeping with him. She needed to know that he wasn't a criminal.

"I need to think about this," she said.

"Don't make the simple complicated, Lucy. This is the Big Easy."

"Yeah, but I'm not!"

He chuckled. "Isn't that an old-fashioned attitude?"

"Probably, but it works for me. I'm not a *laisser le bons temps rouler* kind of woman."

"You should try it. There's no better place on earth to let yourself indulge than in New Orleans." He touched her as though he couldn't help but touch her. "We are going to be incredible together. I know you feel it, too."

She sat up, nudging him out of her arousal zone and refusing to answer because they both knew he was right. "I should get back."

"All right." He rose, then held out a hand to help her up.

Once on her feet, she took the necklace off with her own hands. "It's beautiful," she said. "Thank you for letting me wear it."

"You're welcome. And," he said, white teeth flashing in a grin, "if you're interested, I give a very nice family discount."

Three

"Can you get me a cab?" she asked when he'd locked up and they were once again on Charles Street, which seemed busier than before. This really was a party town.

"I'll see you home."

"But you have your own place. I don't want to take you out of your way."

"My mother would kill me if I didn't escort you home."

Ah, mothers she understood. "Okay."

His car was a low, sleek BMW convertible. He left the top down and the air streaming through her hair felt good after an evening of far too much heat. They purred to a stop in front of his mother's house and he turned to her.

"Thanks for a . . ." What to say? "An interesting evening."

"I enjoyed it very much. I look forward to getting to know you better, *cousine*."

She licked her lips, a nervous gesture that annoyed her. "Good night."

She pushed her car door open before he could do anything really aggravating like kissing her again or running around and opening the car door for her. She needed some space and quiet in her room in order to think about this. Perhaps he understood, for he didn't move, merely sent her a smart salute and pulled away.

She stared after the car wondering what she was getting herself into and knowing there was no way out. The car purred smoothly forward, and as she turned to go up the path, the sound of the engine changed. Puzzled, she turned. To her amazement, the BMW slowed and made a sharp right into the driveway of the Italianate mansion next door to his mother's house.

No. It couldn't be. Sure enough, he cruised around a circular drive and stopped right in front of a double-doored entrance. He got out, put the roof up, beeped the car lock, and strolled to the front door.

She ran to the wrought iron fence between them. "Hey," she called in a sharp whisper.

He turned. Gorgeous, piratical, and mysterious. "Yes, Lucy?"

"You live next door?"

"Yes."

"I thought you lived in the French Quarter."

"No. I live here. I like to keep an eye on things for Mama."

"You're insane, you know that?" She had no idea why she should feel so irked, but somehow she felt like the victim of a practical joke. She'd been so delighted to find he wasn't living under the same roof, but now she found they were next-door neighbors.

"Good night, Lucy."

"Claude?"

"Yes?"

"Are you ever going to tell me where your family got all this money?"

She thought he glanced swiftly up to where his mother was no doubt sleeping. He put a quick finger to his lips. And nodded. Then he made a farewell gesture and disappeared into his house.

Slowly, she made her way back to the front door of Beatrice's home, thinking furiously. Since her hostess had furnished her with a key, she was able to let herself into the house and pad up to her own bedroom.

She washed up, undressed, and changed into a cotton nightgown. She got into bed, turned out the lights, and lay there, staring up at the ceiling. The bed was comfortable and she was tired from the combined stresses of traveling, meeting new relatives, and making out with her distant cousin.

She ought to have been sound asleep the instant her head hit the pillow, but she wasn't. She turned the clock around so she wouldn't keep watching the torturous parade as minutes and hours slipped away. She knew from experience that clock watching only made her occasional insomnia worse. She got up for some water. Went back to bed. And finally gave up. She knew herself well enough to know that sleep wasn't coming anytime soon.

Too much on her mind. Most of it concerning Claude. It was all too complicated to figure out tonight and she resented her many-times-removed cousin for robbing her of sleep.

She got out of bed to sit by the window. At least, if she couldn't sleep she could enjoy the mansions by moonlight. There was a banana tree, she thought, across the way, and some huge live oaks with waving curtains of green Spanish moss. The padded window seat was made for star gazing. Curling up with the quilt off her bed, she decided to count stars as though they were sheep until she grew sleepy.

What she counted was one man walking across his back garden at—she glanced at the clock on the bedside table that was now facing her—one-forty-five in the morning.

There was no question as to the identity of the man.

Even though he'd changed the white shirt for a black long-sleeved T-shirt and it was dark enough that she didn't see him clearly, her body recognized him instinctively. Already, after a day's acquaintance she recognized his walk, the way he held his shoulders, and the shape of his head. He was as familiar to her as a man she'd been intimate with for months.

He didn't walk with particular stealth, but the fact of him leaving his house by the back door at this time of night was in itself suspicious.

Instinctively, she shrank back from the window, and almost the second she did, she saw him turn as though he felt her gaze and glance up at her window. She knew he couldn't see her but she felt a shiver run down her spine anyway.

After a moment he turned around and opened an obviously well-oiled gate since it swung open soundlessly. He passed through and was soon lost to her sight. A minute later she heard a car pulling away.

Where was Claude going? And what was he doing?

As an aid to sleep, staring out her window tonight hadn't been a real winner. She counted thousands of stars, but it didn't help. She'd never been so wide awake.

A woman, probably, Lucy decided. One of those unsteady ones his mother didn't need or want to know about.

Lucy wouldn't care a bit if he hadn't been kissing her earlier in the evening. Had the secrecy been for her benefit? Maybe he thought, Hey, Lucy's not into sex tonight. No problem. I'll call a friend.

Well, he was going to find that Lucy didn't share. Not even for a holiday fling that would only last a few weeks.

She got back into bed deciding that this promising beginning with Claude was pretty much done for. Well, better she should learn the truth about him now, she thought, punching the pillow and bunching it under her head one more time. Perhaps this was a good lesson to her not to stray from her usual research-heavy getting-to-know-you period. Obviously, Cousin Claude was going to be receiving a failing grade. For all his sexiness and the undeniable wow factor when he touched her, kissing cousins was all they were ever going to be. Too bad, she thought, shifting around trying to get comfortable.

No. Not too bad.

Best to know in advance that this guy was a walking sex god and a man who didn't worry much which woman was on his arm, so long as there was one.

Okay. Fine. Not for her.

If only she could convince her overstimulated and currently undersexed body of that fact.

As the hours crept by she became more and more irritated with her next-door neighbor for robbing her of sleep. This was all his fault. And a man who robbed her of sleep for all the wrong reasons was going to be forced to pay.

At one point she heard sounds of movement coming from Beatrice's room and hoped she hadn't telegraphed her restlessness to her hostess.

Around five she heard something. She couldn't have said what, but her senses were so attuned to what was going on next door that, sure enough, when she crept to the dormer window to peer down at Claude's backyard, there he was, sneaking back in to his own house as stealthily as he'd snuck out earlier.

The tom cat was home from his alley prowling.

Meow.

Four

The banging on his front door roused Claude from a sleep as deep and sweet as it had been short. A glance at his bedside clock confirmed he'd been in bed for less than two hours.

Muttering a string of obscenities in French, because that was the language he'd first learned to swear in, he grabbed the gun from his bedside drawer and made his way to the window in his bedroom that overlooked the front door.

"*Merde.*" What was his all too appetizing *cousine* doing on his doorstep at seven in the morning?

For a brief moment he wondered whether she'd go away if he ignored her, then realized his car was still out front so she'd assume, rightly, that he was in the house. Sure enough, another banging on the door accompanied by the peal of his doorbell informed him that his visitor wasn't going away.

Stuffing himself into a pair of plaid boxers, and deciding that if she came calling at this time of the day, that's all the trouble he was going to take to protect her modesty, he shoved the gun back in the drawer and shuffled his way downstairs to the front door.

She was already knocking again when he yanked the door open, so she almost fell inside. He resisted the grin that tried to surface at her surprised expression.

"What?" he demanded.

She looked as fresh and cool as the country she hailed from in a white top that showed a hint of cleavage and blue shorts that gave him ideas about how fast he could get them off her. When he got a good look at her face he saw dark circles under her eyes. She started to speak and was interrupted by a yawn. Hmm. Maybe she hadn't had any sleep last night either. Wishing she'd taken him up on his offer?

"You want coffee?"

She blinked in surprise. "You've made coffee? I thought . . ."

"I haven't made coffee yet. I was in bed." He looked at her skinny but muscular body and thought about how it would feel wrapped around him. "I could be back there in under a minute, and you with me," he said, reaching to cup her cheek in his palm.

Even as her eyes darkened in response, she looked away from him and turned her head so his hand fell away.

What had happened to the passionate woman who'd been as into him last night as he'd been into her? Well, almost. He wouldn't have ended the night at the same point she did, but he didn't think she'd called a halt because she didn't want him.

"What?" he asked, looking, puzzled, at her averted face. "What is it?"

"Nothing. I came to tell you that your mother's got the stones for the patio. She wants to know if you can start laying them today."

"Yeah, I can come over," he said, not taking his eyes off her. "What's happened since we were steaming up each other's windows last night?"

As he watched, she ran a thumbnail over the fluted edge of the Directoire table in the hallway. He doubted she even knew she was doing it. Her face was still turned away, the skin fine-textured and creamy with a scatter of pale freckles across the bridge of her nose and upper cheeks.

"I saw you last night," she said, talking to the table.

"We saw each other. We had a date." He dropped his voice. "A date that ended too soon."

She turned to look straight at him and there was a hint of hurt swiftly hidden in the depths of her green eyes. "After that. Around two. I watched you go out the back way."

Merde. Fils de putain. Christ! He'd felt her watching him, he remembered now. He'd felt something and looked back at his mother's house to find it dark and still. He held his expression and his tone in check, saying evenly, "That's right. I went out."

Her gaze didn't waver. "Whatever your personal life is, it's none of my business." She said it with a tone of finality and an unspoken addendum: and it never will be. Then he understood what she was getting at.

"Lucy, I wasn't with another woman last night."

Her gaze searched his and a tiny crease appeared between her brows. "Then where were you at that time of night and why did you sneak out the back way?"

He opened his mouth and a dozen lies popped up. But he didn't spout any of them. Instead he took her hands and held them. "I can't tell you where I was and I'm sorry about that. But believe me, I'm not interested in any woman right now except you."

Her hands twitched in his grasp but she didn't pull away. She looked puzzled, frustrated, pissed. "I've known you less than twenty-four hours."

"What's that got to do with anything?" he said, letting his impatience show. He held her hands against his chest and heard her quick intake of breath. Her fingers clutched, then relaxed as though she'd forced them to let go. "I don't get this kind of rush every time I touch a woman. I'm guessing you don't get it with the men you've known, either." He paused long enough for her to decide to answer the implied question, which she did with a shake of her head.

"It wasn't pleasure that took me out last night, Lucy. It was business. I can't tell you any more. I'm sorry."

She gazed at him for a long moment more. "I'm only down here for three weeks. A vacation fling is a really bad idea, anyway."

"Seems like a good idea to me," he said, keeping his tone light.

She sent him a swift smile and took her hands back. "Well, I'll tell Cousin Beatrice the handyman's on his way," she said, backing out the door.

"Merde," he said, as he'd said far too many times this morning considering how early it was. He shut the door and stumbled back to the kitchen. When he opened the coffee tin he found a scattering of black at the bottom, exactly enough to tease his nostrils.

"Aw, shit." He tossed the tin in the sink where it made a nice loud clang and then decided that, based on the first half hour, his day was going to be a real sweetheart.

What if he told her? What if he came right out and told her where he'd been?

No, he decided. Too dangerous.

Lucy kept herself busy all that day. This was a working holiday, after all. She was glad she'd made her decision not to get involved with Claude. Glad he hadn't tried to argue her into his bed when he wore nothing but boxer shorts. There were too many excellent reasons why sex with Claude was a very bad idea. And only one reason why it was a good one. Because her body wanted his.

Now she had two burning questions. Where had the family money really come from?

And what possible business did an antiques dealer conduct between the hours of two and five A.M.?

She rode the St. Charles Streetcar to Tulane University campus where she was doing some local research.

Lucy loved research. Not only would she dig into the campus library and archives while she was here, but she wanted a sense of place, the atmosphere and conditions her ancestors would have faced. She wanted to feel their plight so that when she wrote about the expulsion and starting over in Louisiana, her book would be more than a series of dry facts.

Victims of the wars between France and England, the Acadians had been French settlers to Nova Scotia and New Brunswick. They'd displaced the Micmac Indians and settled the land for themselves and their families. Some of the Acadians had been there for generations when the British expelled the French settlers from the rich land. More than eight thousand of them were thrown out. They'd forced the young men and boys out first. The present and future soldiers were sent off on boats, the women and children to follow. She could never think about that part without hearing the wails and the tears, the begging that must have gone on. Longfellow's *Evangeline* always made her cry.

The men were shipped off, or escaped to hide in the bush. And later, when the women and children were shipped out, they didn't always end up in the same place as their fathers, husbands, and sons.

So many families broken apart, or finding each other but having to begin again from nothing. What must it have been like?

After a day with genealogy charts and obscure texts, sometimes in old French, Lucy was glad to leave. She made her way back home only to find Beatrice and Claude working together on the masonry.

Her girly bits got pretty excited when they spotted Claude. Could the man never be fully dressed when she saw him? He was shirtless again, looking manly and sweaty as he hefted flagstones in a pair of well-worn leather gloves. Beatrice was happily aiding him.

"Oh, honey, here you are home and I haven't even started supper. We got carried away in the garden. Give me a minute to clean up and I'll get your dinner on."

"No, really," Lucy said. "I'm not that hungry. And I've been inside all day. Why don't I change and then I can help you get the rest of those in."

So, she found herself five minutes later outside in one of her old running T-shirts and a pair of shorts.

It was good to have something manual to do after a gorgeous day spent inside a stuffy library. She liked the feel of the cool, rough flagstones and the dirt creeping under her nails, and there was something satisfyingly artistic about the emerging pattern. They left the big pieces to Claude, naturally, and if she indulged herself with the odd sideways peek at his muscular torso at work, that was her business.

"So, what's this book about exactly?" Beatrice asked her.

"I'm planning to write about the expulsion of the Acadians through the eyes of one family. Ours. We've got a great network because of the family newsletter and we try to have the odd family reunion, so lots of us are in touch. I'm trying to trace what happened to the ones who left and what happened to the ones who remained. I want to make it a sort of living history, I guess."

"So you're going right up to modern times?"

"That's the plan."

"Will I be in your book?"

"If you give me your permission, I'd love for you to be in my book."

"Well, imagine that Claude. We could be in Lucy's book."

"It's an interesting project," he said. Not sounding as excited as his mom about being in her book.

Beatrice wasn't a silent stone layer, and while they worked, she chattered about her day and the people she'd seen at the market and the women she'd had coffee with. She'd pause to fill Lucy in on who the characters were every once in a while, until Lucy was certain she'd recognize these people if she bumped into them at the market. Even the gossip was entertaining until Beatrice said, "Oh, and Claude, you must have heard about the robbery last night."

Lucy glanced up sharply to find Claude's gaze flash her way for a second before flicking away again. "Yes. I heard. Some customers talked about it in the shop."

"What robbery?" Lucy asked.

"The Guillotine diamonds. They're famous."

"The what?" She dusted off her hands and stood straight.

"Well, they're famous here. A French noblewoman who was to be guillotined during the French Revolution bartered her release and that of her children with a priceless set of family diamonds. Some greedy revolutionary took the diamonds one piece at a time, as her children were smuggled out of the country. I always thought she must have had a sense of humor, for she swapped the final piece, her tiara, for her head."

"That's quite a story."

Beatrice chuckled, like someone about to share a favorite joke. "The best part is that she bargained with the paste copies she'd had made years earlier. She rarely wore the real jewels—too frightened to lose them, I suppose. Anyway, her copies fooled the revolutionary and I'm sure she and her children enjoyed wearing them even more after they escaped to England.

"Her granddaughter came here, to Louisiana, bringing the set with her. They were only sold out of the family a couple of years ago." Beatrice shook her head. "They'd held on to those jewels through so many turbulent times, it was a tragedy. And dreadful dotcom people bought them. But they got a very good price, so the woman who had to sell them was able to keep her home, at least. Claude can tell you more. He handled the sale."

"You did?"

"Yes. *Cousine,* you are mangling that plant."

She hadn't even noticed, but sure enough, her right hand was pulling on a pretty flowering plant in the walled planter behind her. "Oh."

He was at her side, his skin gleaming with exertion, smelling like a hard-working, sexy man. Carefully he took out the plant and used his gloved hand to make a dent in the earth. Where had he been last night, she wondered, as she watched him engrossed in saving a small plant. Did his mysterious disappearance have anything to do with stolen diamonds? He was so close to her that his arm brushed hers when he turned the plant and carefully spread its roots before replanting it. "There," he said, turning and looking down at her. "Now it will grow better."

"Thank you." She watched him. "Were they very beautiful, those diamonds?"

"I've never seen so flawless a set."

"Must have been hard to let them go."

"If I kept everything for myself, *cousine,* I wouldn't have much of a business."

She smiled, as he'd meant her to, but she wondered.

There could be all kinds of things that took a man out in the middle of the night, she decided as they resumed work. The coincidental timing did not make Claude a thief.

No, she decided three days later. Her cousin Claude wasn't a thief. He was a liar.

She was jogging early to avoid the heat and to get her exercise out of the way before she went to the university for a few hours. Her days were already falling into a routine after being here less than a week. She ran early, although this morning was earlier than ever. It was five-thirty, and she would still be asleep if some bird hadn't mistaken her for its mother or love interest and trilled at her from outside her window.

Oh, well, Lucy decided, it was a gorgeous morning, the early light soft and mellow, and if she ran now she'd have time to catch up on her e-mails from home with her coffee.

Then she and Beatrice would breakfast together, and afterward she'd take off for the library and her hostess would go shopping or lunch out or go to one of her many activities with her wide circle of friends. Lucy had discovered her hostess was a respected New Orleans socialite and philanthropist, and few charitable or social committees existed in which she wasn't involved. She was also an inexhaustible source of information about New Orleans society past and present.

There were loads more distant relatives in the area and

Beatrice was busy planning a family get-together that would include lots of storytelling and reminiscences. Lucy was ready with her tape recorder and video recorder. Already, ideas for her book were flowing and her notes were often interspersed with a few paragraphs of her own text. Altogether, this was turning into a very productive work holiday, she thought as she jogged along dawn-quiet streets. The Lafayette Cemetery was on her right, free of tourists at this time of the morning, the dead, in their above-ground marble mausoleums, at rest in rare peace.

She was in a nice rhythm, her mind already planning ahead to the day's research, when she heard the rumble of a car engine coming toward her. It was more idleness than curiosity that caused her to look at the two people inside the car. The driver was an attractive woman in her early thirties, at a guess. She had café au lait colored skin and gold streaks in her long, dark hair. She was looking at her companion, and her expression was intense. Lucy glanced over and stumbled over her feet.

Claude was the passenger. Claude *"Oh, Lucy, trust me, I can't tell you where I was but I wasn't with another woman"* LeBlanc.

He was so busy talking to the woman in the car that he had no attention to spare for a lone, early jogger and in a second they'd passed her. She listened and sure enough heard the engine slow as it rounded the corner to the street behind Claude's house, and then a few seconds later came the slam of a car door. She wasn't positive it was the same car as the other night, but she felt certain it was. So, he hadn't been with a woman, huh? At least if he was off having sex, he couldn't have committed the diamond theft. Though, she realized, as she plodded along the street, sweat dampening her shirt so it stuck to her unpleasantly, that part of her would have preferred him stealing jewels to shagging another woman.

She decided to be philosophical about Claude and quietly celebrate that she hadn't done more than kiss him before she discovered what a rat he was. She was so busy being philosophical that she jogged an extra couple of miles out of her way. By the time she returned to Beatrice's house, she was overheated, sweating like a pig, and exhausted.

And in no mood to face the man sitting at the breakfast table sharing an early morning coffee with his mother. She was perfectly aware that she could win a one-woman wet T-shirt contest, she didn't need Claude's gaze licking at her like an eager tongue to remind her. And yep, her shorts were snug. Let him look. It was as close as he was going to get.

Refusing to bolt up to her room like a coward, she walked slowly to the fridge and drew out the jug of water with lemon slices Beatrice kept there. She drank down one huge glass and then poured another, sipping this one more slowly.

"Looks like you had quite the workout," Claude said.

"I could say the same to you," she muttered under her breath.

"What did you say, honey?" Beatrice asked.

"I asked Claude what brings him here so early."

"A party."

She turned. "Really? What kind of party?"

"The historical society's annual ball. I was offering myself as an escort for you and Mama."

"Oh, I wouldn't have thought that was your scene at all."

His smile glinted. "Surprise."

Claude would often come at some point in the day to work in his mother's garden. He spent a few hours every day at one of his stores, but he obviously had staff putting in the long hours. Leaving him more time for his late night rendezvous.

Beatrice and Claude seemed to enjoy the time together. It was difficult to hold onto her contempt for the man when he could be so sweet to his mom.

She tried, though.

A few nights he stayed to dinner and the three of them talked about family and shared history. She enjoyed him most then, for he wasn't trying to hit on her or seducing her with his eyes. Sometimes she'd catch his gaze on her and read the heat within, and she knew then that the blazing attraction between them wasn't imagined and, despite what she knew of him, it wasn't going away.

Five

It was a bit like dressing a panther in a tux, she thought, seeing Claude in his finery. If anything, the elegant evening dress only made him appear more predatory.

Not having brought anything appropriate with her for a society gala, she hadn't minded at all having an excuse to splurge in one of the amazing boutiques on Magazine Street. Her dress was a sea green silk chiffon number with a low-cut bodice featuring tiny crystal beads, a handkerchief hem, and a long wrap in the same breezy fabric, complete with its own scattering of bling.

Finding pretty, strappy shoes in the same color had consumed an entire afternoon, but the results, she decided, as she twisted in front of the mirror in her room, were worth it.

"I do love a party," said Beatrice, sparkling with excitement. She wore a long skirt and jacket in gold brocade and looked regal.

But it was Claude who took Lucy's breath away. The sight of him in evening dress was like seeing Clive Owen at the Oscars. The tux only emphasized the animal qualities of the man inside it. Her breathlessness at the sight of him irritated her so much she could barely manage to be civil. The fact that his eyes glowed with admiration when they rested on her only mildly relieved her annoyance.

Claude drove them in his BMW—the roof up in deference to their carefully styled hair—to an antebellum mansion outside of town. The place was gorgeous with an avenue of ancient oaks leading to the house, which sat on acres of sloping land.

They headed into the lavishly decorated ballroom and Lucy took a moment simply to enjoy the spectacle. Even though she didn't know a soul, she could have guessed what Beatrice had told her—that anyone who was anyone would be here. An air of money and entitlement about these people suggested they knew their worth and, based on some of the gems and fashions on display, they knew how to flaunt their wealth.

Beatrice pointed out a few of the people she thought Lucy might be interested in. Here was a famous writer, there a prominent historian. That woman had lost a son at Pearl Harbor. Over there was the mayor. She had a few anecdotes to share about some of the more colorful people, most of them good-natured.

"Oh, I should have known they'd be here," Beatrice said with unaccustomed animosity in her tone. She motioned to where a man in a toupee that seemed to be channeling Donald Trump stood with a woman so thin it hurt Lucy's bones to look at her. "She boasted to a friend of mine that she has to have her clothes custom made. Even a size two has to be taken in."

"Ouch." The form-fitting black sheath dress the woman wore certainly fit where it touched. She wore her blond hair up and her décolletage low so her long, Audrey Hepburn neck was the focal point of her ensemble. She wore a choker with three stings of fat pearls—the only thing fat on her body—centered by the biggest emerald Lucy had ever seen.

"Is that emerald real?" Lucy asked in a whisper.

"Oh, yes. The Grimmels. Husband's trying to develop land that he maintains is swamp and everyone knows is irreplaceable habitat for a rare species of frog. Horrible people." Beatrice was usually willing to give everyone his due, but Lucy had discovered that she despised people who took from society and gave nothing back.

Lucy might not know a soul, but it was quickly apparent that both Claude and his mother knew pretty much everyone. Beatrice was soon swept into a laughing group of men and women. One older gentlemen with silver hair and a tan who looked a bit like Cary Grant in his older days kissed her cheek and obviously wanted her all to himself. Another man, balding but with an attractive smile, went off to get Beatrice a drink.

"Will they fight a duel?" Lucy asked Claude.

"No. Mother says she'll never marry again. She likes men, though." He shrugged in a typically Gallic way. "You never know."

She watched Beatrice for a few minutes, feeling proud of this strong, independent woman. She realized with a start that she'd become as fond of Beatrice in the couple of weeks she'd been here as she would be if they'd known each other all their lives.

"I love your mom," she said to Claude.

"She's pretty crazy about you, too," he replied. "Come on, let's find a drink."

They made their way to the bar, and since there was some kind of bright pink punch that came out of a fountain, she went for that. How often did she go to the kind of parties where drinks came out of a very pretty mermaid's mouth? A Bud in a bottle she could get any day.

It was surprisingly fun having Claude as a date. He knew so many people that they were usually part of a group, and it didn't escape her notice that a lot of longing glances were sent his way by women in the room.

"Do you want to dance?" he asked after they'd been talking to a group of some of the younger people present.

She glanced at him under her lashes. "I haven't forgotten what happened last time we danced."

He grinned at her. "Me neither."

Oh, what the hell, she thought, putting her empty punch glass on a passing waiter's tray. They made their way to the crowded dance floor, and then she saw the woman who'd been driving the car that morning when she was jogging. The one he'd had the intense conversation with at five-thirty in the morning after who knew what had passed in the hours beforehand.

The woman was stunning. Even more so tonight in a pumpkin-colored evening dress. She was with a stern-looking man who kept a proprietary arm around her. To Lucy's surprise, the woman and Claude passed within touching distance of one another and neither made the slightest sign of recognition.

Somehow, seeing Claude and that woman pretend not to know each other took all the fun out of dancing with her sexy cousin. Why couldn't he have said, "Hey, Lucy, I'd like you to meet Ethel. She and I belong to a voodoo club that meets in the wee hours." Or, "Hey, Lucy, this here's my good friend Ethel. We're both amateur astronomers. Did you know that the best stargazing happens between two and four A.M.?"

Instead, he acted like he'd never seen the woman in his life.

"What's the matter?" he asked her after they'd been pressed together for a few minutes in with the mass of other dancers. The magic she'd felt the last time they'd danced was gone.

"Nothing."

"Your body doesn't lie to me, Lucy. Something's bothering you."

He wanted to know? Fine. *She* had no reason to hide things. Unlike some people. "That woman we passed on our way to the dance floor, the one in the orange dress. I saw her drive you home at five-thirty in the morning three days ago."

He bent his head to look down at her, and she was amazed

to see not embarrassment or contrition in his gaze, but a blaze of anger. "And you naturally decided I'm having an affair with her."

"Seemed like a logical conclusion. Now I've seen her with that possessive guy, I'd add adulterous to affair." She stared back defiantly. "Are you going to tell me I'm wrong?"

"I told you to trust me. I promised you I wasn't seeing another woman."

"I saw what I saw."

"Come on." He all but dragged her off the dance floor and outside to a floodlit garden with secret alcoves and stone benches. They passed the woman she'd seen in the car and he must have made some sign because the next thing she knew, the three of them were standing in a sheltered corner surrounded by the scent of night jasmine.

"This better be important," the woman snapped.

"Isabelle, this is my cousin, Lucy. Please tell her who you are and how we know each other."

Oh, this should be good. Voodoo club? Stargazing? She could hardly wait to hear what they'd come up with.

"Claude, you agreed—"

"It's important," he snapped. Lucy felt the tension in his body.

Isabelle must have sensed it, too, for she shot him an annoyed glance and Lucy one of exasperation. She lowered her voice. "Can we trust her?"

"She's Canadian."

Lucy didn't know what that had to do with anything and she didn't think Isabelle was overly impressed either, but after a quick glance all around, Isabelle said in a voice so soft Lucy could barely hear it. "Why does she have to know?"

"She thinks we're having an affair," Claude said in a clipped voice.

A trill of laughter, quickly suppressed, came from the woman. She then shot a much more human glance at Lucy. "I'm not sleeping with him. I'm a cop. Claude is helping me with a case."

"What kind of case?" Lucy asked, determined to show the pair of them that being Canadian did not equate with naïve, born yesterday, or stupid.

An irritated huff came from the supposed cop's direction. "Did you have to pick now, Claude?"

"Just answer her questions."

"Robbery. Claude has knowledge of gems and a network of contacts that I need. We meet at night so no one will suspect he's working with the cops. That's all I can tell you, and it's too much."

"I won't say a word to anyone," Lucy said. She stared at the woman, realizing, oddly enough that she believed her. Almost. "Do you have some I.D.?"

"Claude!"

"Show her your badge and be done with it."

A rustling in a small silk evening bag and Lucy was presented with a leather folder. Not that she knew a great deal about police identification, but this one looked official. Detective Isabelle DuBois, she read. NOPD. She nodded. "Thanks."

"Okay, keep your mouth shut. I gotta go."

Claude nodded and the woman melted away. Suddenly, Lucy realized she was in a sultry New Orleans garden all alone with a very attractive man she'd wronged. Well, one thing she'd learned in her life was to own up when she was wrong. "Claude," she said, taking a deep breath and turning resolutely to face him. "I'm sorry."

"It's not good enough," he said.

She blinked. "What? An honest apology's not good enough? Think about this from my point of view. I saw you with her and anybody would—"

"No. Sorry's not good enough. You have to pay a forfeit." There wasn't anger in his tone, more a kind of warm teasing that turned her body to mush and her brain to goo.

"A forfeit . . ."

"Yes. I think one perfect kiss should do it."

She narrowed her eyes. "Who judges whether the kiss is perfect or not?"

"The injured party, naturally."

He was so silly and so gorgeous and she was so happy to be wrong about Isabelle that she found herself smiling in the dark. The scent of night-blooming jasmine was joined by other scents, some she recognized, some not. A faint scent of roses, and the smell of rich, dark earth. Then there was the much more intoxicating scent of the man standing closer to her now than he had been a second ago.

"One perfect kiss," he said, and covered her mouth with his own.

If perfect was a wild coming together of mouths and tongues and bodies so fevered they grabbed and rubbed and pushed closer and closer until their clothes felt like cement walls keeping them apart, then it was perfect.

She was so hungry for him she shocked herself. His hands were on her bare back, slipping around the front to rub her breasts, in her hair, gripping her hips, while his mouth was busy at hers, so hungry, so demanding.

"Oh," she said, tilting her head back. "Oh."

His mouth was busy at her shoulders, her neck. Drowning her with needs and emotions she couldn't keep up with. A soft breeze ruffled the scented air and stroked her overwarm skin.

"I need you," he said raggedly.

"Oh, yes," she answered, knowing now that this had been inevitable. From the first moment she'd seen him sweaty and dangerous, staring at her over his shovel, she'd recognized an attraction more powerful than any she'd ever felt.

Here and now, she faced it.

"I've been going crazy wanting you," he muttered, his hands sliding into the silk bodice until he touched her breasts. They ached for him, and when he eased the fabric down so that she was naked to the moon and his gaze, she reveled in the freedom. Now he could see her, her skin so pale under the moonlight. Now he could touch the breasts that ached for him, now he could taste them. He bent his head and took one nipple into his mouth, and the sensation was so strong she felt that much more would be dangerous.

How had this happened? She never lost control like this.

It was as scary as it was exhilarating.

A burst of sound and she realized vaguely that a door had opened, letting out the sounds of the party. Voices nearby.

With a muttered curse, Claude rapidly pulled her dress back to cover her. "Let's get out of here," he said.

She nodded, knowing she couldn't have made a coherent sound if she'd tried.

Instead of taking her back through the party, he led her around the side of the house to the gravel parking area. Now that they weren't quite so physically entwined, and desire had subsided from a violent need to an insistent ache, she could think a little. She stopped dead. "Your mother."

He didn't even slow his pace. "One of her boyfriends will be only too happy to bring her home."

"Oh." She glanced up at him. "Did you plan this?"

He chuckled softly. "Lucy, I never planned anything that's happened with you. You're like a hurricane."

"Destructive and deadly?"

"Wild and life-altering."

"Oh." She kind of liked that view of herself. Not that anyone else had ever seen her in that light. But hey, a woman didn't knock a compliment like that. "So, should you tell Beatrice that you're taking me home?"

"Mom and I had a little talk earlier. I told her if you and I disappeared she should find her own way home."

"You discussed me with your mother?"

"She's got eyes, *cousine.*"

They walked a few more steps. She thought she'd been so discreet, but she'd probably been staring at Claude with her tongue hanging out every time he was around. How humiliating.

She'd thought she'd have time to cool off and make sure

she really wanted to sleep with this man while they were driving home. Hah. She should have known better.

No sooner had they cleared the parking area, where he'd waved good night to the last helpful attendant, and they'd turned onto the road home than he slipped a hand to her knee. And then higher. She huffed out a helpless sigh and let her thighs slip apart for him. He took his time, teasing his way up, higher, slipping the silk up her thighs so she felt the cool air on her skin. Her panties weren't more than a scrap of silk and lace but they felt like woolen long johns.

Claude obviously felt the same. He played his fingers over them, then said in a conversational tone as though discussing tomorrow's weather forecast, "Take them off."

A tiny, helpless moan slipped out of her mouth. The corners of his mouth kicked up, but that was the only indication that he'd heard her.

It wasn't easy with her seat belt on, and Lucy wasn't about to drive without a fastened seatbelt, not even for a minute, but with some wiggling and tugging, she managed to free her panties and slip them off. Because this was an equal opportunity seduction, she pulled the crisp white handkerchief from the breast pocket of his tux and replaced it with the white silk and lace panties.

He turned and looked at her, his eyes alive with devilry. She couldn't resist grinning back. They were going to be so good together. Sometimes you just knew.

The engine surged and she got the feeling he was in a hurry to get home. The notion made her just a little smug, and when he slipped a hand back under her skirt, she eased back in her seat and gave him all the access he could desire.

He took his time, slowly stroking his way up her inner thigh. She opened wider, throbbing with anticipation to feel his fingers play over her. She could see his hands as she'd watched them so many times, sturdy, capable hands that could dig a garden or clasp a fine string of rubies around her neck. He seemed to hover over her neediest place, and then, when she expected him to stroke her, he ran his fingers through her curls as though checking for tangles. He stroked and patted, and then when he delved deeper to where she was slick and needy, her hot button already quivering, it was a shock to find him touching her there, stroking her, stoking her.

A mile, maybe two they drove with him teasing her, bringing her closer to the brink and then backing away. When he eased a finger inside her she knew she couldn't take any more.

"How long until we get to your place?" she panted. She'd lost all track of time or even where they were.

"Ten, fifteen minutes." His voice was husky as though he'd smoked three packs of cigarettes in the last ten minutes.

"Pull over," she ordered, crossing her legs so his hand was clamped between her thighs, unable to toy with her.

He didn't say another word, simply wrenched his hand away from her body and suddenly turned down a dark side road she hadn't noticed.

The road bumped and grew rutted as though it wasn't used very often. The air grew damp and fragrant. She heard a frog trill and then silence.

Live oaks surrounded them, dripping Spanish moss. The headlights bounced off dark water. "Where are we? Is this the bayou?"

"Lake Pontchartrain. A secret spot I know."

She didn't care if it was the fifth crater of Mars so long as they stopped and she could have at him.

The car bumped to a stop and he killed the engine. They were suddenly alone in all the world, surrounded by the kind of darkness that teams with nocturnal creatures and sounds. The lap of water, a splash she tried to convince herself wasn't alligator-related, another frog, or maybe the same one, emitting a tentative croak.

The darkness intensified into physical form and then Claude was on her, kissing the breath out of her, his body hard and insistent against hers.

Desperate. Had she ever been so desperate for a man in her

life? It was as though all the days they'd spent together had been foreplay for this moment. She was so ready she thought she'd fly apart the second he touched her.

He must have felt the same, for when she reached out to touch him, he caught her wrist, muttering in French. "I'm sorry, *cousine*. Maybe later, ah?"

It didn't matter. She understood. He reached across her and the glove compartment flipped open, sending a soft beam of light onto her lap. He reached in and pulled out a condom. Trust cousin Claude, she thought, never to be denied the opportunity for sex.

Right now she really didn't care why he had them in his car, she was only glad that he did.

The glove box clicked shut again and the world was once more dark and private. A rip and a rustle and then they were kissing, more hungrily than before. His skin was warm beneath hers when she burrowed into his clothes, his heartbeat a crazy rhythm. Unable to wait another second, she climbed over and into his lap, banging into various bits of car as she did so. She straddled him, and this time when she reached for him, he let her.

He felt warm and very, very hard when she grasped him in hand. He made a tiny sound, a man at the end of his restraint, a feeling she knew well. She shuffled herself into place. It wasn't the most comfortable position, with one knee jammed against the door, the other wedged against the emergency brake, but she didn't care. Her body was stretched over him, eager and wet and so very hungry.

As she positioned him at the entrance to her body, their gazes locked. Only the faintest trace of moonlight made it to where they were parked, so she saw the glow of his eyes in a dark face. She held his gaze with her own as she lowered herself slowly onto him.

Oh. She realized it had been a while and he was a big man. The stretch was amazing. Delicious. He seemed to go on and on, filling her completely. When they were locked, hip to hip, she took a moment to savor the deep connection, kissing him as though she'd never stop, and then need took over. She moved on him, slowly at first as she accustomed herself to him, then faster as instinct and desire stronger than anything she'd ever known took over. His hands were all over her, hers grabbed at his shoulders to steady herself. Her knees scraped as she rode him in a frenzied rush. They kissed deep and hard and with little finesse. He grabbed her hips at last when the thrusting grew wild. She heard panting and knew it was hers. A liquid flow of French, some poetic, some gutteral, all heartfelt. Without thinking about it, she answered in the same language.

Then their words were lost as they kissed deep and hungrily, the leather seat thumping in an age-old rhythm, as they launched each other over the edge of the world. She felt as though she'd plunged right into that dark, rippling bayou. As though the water had closed over her head and she was in some quiet place of throbbing sensation. And then she was rising, up, up, breaking the surface, flying through space.

She felt his mouth kissing her even as he spoke to her. It didn't matter what he said, she heard him on some deeper level where skin spoke to skin, body to body. The message was given and received.

For a long time they stayed like that, bodies still connected, hearts talking to each other in Morse code while they caught their breath. Wow, she wanted to say. Just, wow.

When they'd cleaned up and put themselves pretty much back together, Claude drove them back to the road. "That was convenient," she said, "that that quiet spot was so handy."

Wry humor laced his voice as he answered. "I grew up here, Lucy. I know all the spots."

She chuckled softly. "You really are a hellion, aren't you?"

"Was, *cousine*. Was. I haven't been down that road in years."

Six

They drove back to the Garden District at a more sedate pace, but there was no question that they'd be stopping off at his place.

When they pulled into the circular drive, she took a quick look next door and was relieved to see no lights on. Clearly, his mother was still partying.

"It feels weird having sex next door to your mother," she said, climbing out of the car and being reminded by a sudden breeze up her skirt that her panties were still in Claude's pocket.

"Don't worry. She won't be home for a while. Mother has her own friends, too."

"Are you saying that she's out doing . . . what we're about to do?"

"She's fifty-six years old and single. Why shouldn't she enjoy her life?" He took her hand and walked her to his front door. "The last couple of years with my dad, they weren't easy on her. He was sick with cancer and she did all the nursing herself. They'd always done everything together." He was silent for a moment and she felt his grief. "We both still miss him, but it's good to see her getting on with her life."

She squeezed his hand. "You're a good son."

He smiled down at her. "It's hard sometimes, you know? I don't want to think of anybody but my daddy with her. But I'm trying."

When they got inside the house she felt suddenly like she'd jumped into that bayou without even checking to see what alligators lurked. In the morning she knew she was going to worry about what she was doing, but for tonight it was too late. The water felt good, far too good to climb out before she was ready.

So, when he took her face in his hands and kissed her slow and deep, she responded fully.

His tongue was warm and inviting in her mouth, bringing her simmering desire back to full boil.

He pulled back and she could see the effort it cost him. "Do you want something to drink?"

She let him see exactly what she wanted, let it all show in her eyes. "No."

"Good." He took her hand once more and led her up the stairs.

They didn't race, though they wanted to. Didn't stop to kiss because then they'd never make it to his bedroom.

She followed him, feeling her excitement build with each rising tread of the stairs. At the landing, he turned her to the right, to a room that she recognized the instant she saw it was exactly right for him. The furniture was rich early American. The bed was obviously new—since she didn't think a lot of early Americans had king-sized beds—but made to match the antiques. His bedding was maroon and navy, and a plush Turkish rug in the same colors graced the wide-planked floorboards. The atmosphere in the room was masculine but luxurious. On the walls were two paintings she recognized as Southern artists—very collectible.

"Are you always this neat or were you planning to bring me here?"

"I'm always this neat." He grinned at her. "But the towels in the bathroom and the sheets on the bed are fresh. That was in case I managed to get you up here."

"Well, if we're being honest"—she reached into his breast pocket and pulled out her silk and lace panties—"I don't pull these on unless I think somebody's going to see them." She tilted her head back, put her panties around the back of his neck, and used them like a rope to pull him down for a kiss.

"This time," he said, when they came up for air, "I want to take our time."

"Mmm."

"This time, I want to see you." As he spoke, he slipped a spaghetti strap off her shoulder, kissing the spot where it had sat.

She pulled off his jacket, tossed it to a nearby armchair in front of the fireplace. He tipped down the other strap, kissed her other shoulder.

Off came his tie. He held out his wrists so she could remove his cufflinks. Black ones, jet or onyx—more of those antiques he couldn't pass up, she imagined. Being with this man was like stepping back in time.

The shirt next. She took her time with the studs, letting herself savor each new inch of tawny flesh she uncovered. The little clicking noises as she dropped them onto a ceramic dish on his night table punctuated the sounds of their breathing.

She couldn't help recalling the first time she'd seen him shirtless and damp with exertion. She'd wanted to touch him then; on some cellular level her body had known the need for him. Now, he was finally hers.

He gave her his patience, and she knew it was a gift from the way she sensed the short leash he was keeping on himself. She realized that patience was near its end when she felt his hands at her back and then heard the slow hush of her zipper. The dress started to slide and she let it go, feeling the silk stroke her skin as it slid slowly to the floor. Claude watched it all the way. She wore no bra and her panties were long gone, so as the dress sighed its way down her body, she was completely exposed. His breath sucked in when her breasts appeared. He gave a guttural grunt of satisfaction when she was naked.

Small, Claude thought. Her breasts were small as he'd known they'd be. But they were perfect. Round as plums and tipped with up-tilted nipples. Her belly was runner-lean, the muscles striated but feminine. The dip of her waist curved to the slight roundness of her hips and then came those long, stong runner's legs.

He couldn't get his breath, or take his eyes off her.

"I'm not exactly voluptuous," she said with a shrug as he continued to stare, speechless.

He found his voice then. "You are perfect," he said, and to him she was.

He stripped the rest of his clothes off, unable to wait.

She sat on the edge of the bed, her spine supported against one of the posts, and watched.

Her hair hung in loose curls as she sat there regarding him, her cheeks pink with desire and her eyes big with interest.

He was glad she wasn't shy. He wanted to see the body he'd already been inside, watch her as he entered her and when she came. He wanted to know and see and savor everything with this woman. It was a new experience but he was getting used to it. He'd always known this would happen someday. He'd see a woman and be lost. His daddy and mama had been like that and he'd never known a happier pair. Now wasn't the time he'd have chosen—in fact he couldn't think of a worse moment to fall in love—but when fate threw a woman like Lucy in your path, you didn't say no.

He tossed the last of his clothes on top of his jacket and walked to the bed, and she watched him all the way.

"I am crazy about you," he said, lifting her and placing her on the bed he'd made up with such high hopes this morning.

When he had her laid out against the crisp linen sheets, he realized how good she looked in his bed. She had a timeless beauty and elegance—she was like the best pieces of furniture that never went out of style but were cherished generation after generation. In this room of the favorite treasures he'd come across in his career, she fit right in. She belonged.

"Is there some reason you're smirking at my naked body?" she asked, sounding a little pissed.

"Don't take this the wrong way, but I was thinking you fit in with my antiques."

She stared at him for a second and then reached behind her for a pillow and whacked him with it.

Shoving up an arm, he laughed. "It's your coloring," he said, grabbing her wrists before she could launch anything else at him. Her eyes were sparkling with warmth, but he explained anyway. "Your hair, the first time I saw it, I thought of how the richest woods glow when they've been around for a while and been taken care of." He let go of her wrists long enough to push his fingers through her hair, loosening the rich strands so they spilled around her on the pillow.

"Everything in this room is special," he said, kissing her lightly. Her eyes searched his and he knew he'd startled her, but after her suspicions about Isabelle, he wanted to reassure her. With Lucy living next door driving him mad with wanting her, how could he have gone with another woman?

Maybe he was talking too much. He'd do better to show her. He kissed her again, deeper this time, and felt her sigh as she opened her lips beneath his. Her arms wrapped around his neck and pulled him closer until his skin was touching hers, their bodies pressed together. There'd been no time before, no room to maneuver, and their desperate haste had been too greedy. Now that they'd taken the edge off, he felt better able to take his time. To see her, touch her everywhere, savor and explore her. And he intended to take his time.

Her body was glorious, her skin warm and silky, the muscles firm beneath. He kissed her breasts, trailing wet circles around her nipples and finally drawing one into his mouth. He loved the sounds she made, the sighs and whispered phrases.

French phrases. He couldn't believe it. Had he unconsciously triggered her tongue to switch or did she, like him, make love in French?

He made more discoveries. When he licked her nipples, her fingernails dug into his arm. When he trailed his lips down her belly, she giggled helplessly, so he felt the ripple of muscle under his mouth. When he parted her knees, she sighed, and when he kissed her inner thighs, her toes curled tight, like a ballerina *en pointe.* She was slick and beautiful, her curls darker down there. When he took his tonguc to her, her body arched with the supple grace of an athlete. He took his time, exploring her thoroughly, loving her with his mouth, and she relaxed into his rhythm, letting him build her up slowly until she shattered in a satisfying rush.

He kissed his way back up her body, feeling her tremble and sigh, and when he entered her she was as soft as melting butter.

"Where are you going?" Claude's voice was muffled with sleep.

"Next door."

"You're crazy."

"I don't want—well, I want to talk about this with your mother first."

He chuckled sleepily. "That conversation I would love to hear."

"You won't." She walked over to the bed and kissed him. He tasted sleepy and rumpled and warm. "See you later."

He grabbed her butt and squeezed. "Count on it."

Dawn was beginning to streak the sky as she padded next door, hoping very much no early rising neighbors were hanging out their windows drawing the obvious conclusion about her actions.

Well, that was just one more development in her trip to Louisiana that wouldn't make it into the family newsletter.

* * *

The smell of coffee and bacon had Lucy speeding down the stairs later that morning. It was eight. Late for her, but then she'd had a pretty active evening the night before.

She felt a quick qualm of nerves. She wasn't exactly sure what to say or how Beatrice was going to react. Her "good morning" sounded a tad too cheery and carefree to her own ears. Lighten up, she scolded herself.

He was a grownup. His mother knew he had sex. But maybe not always with her houseguests?

But Beatrice looked as happy to see her guest as she appeared every morning. "You slept in," she said, handing Lucy coffee.

"Yes, I—" She glanced up to find a broad grin on her hostess's face.

"God," she said, dropping her face in her hands, knowing she was blushing like a fool. "This is so awkward."

"Honey, I could see from the way you two looked at each other the first day what was in the wind."

"Well, I don't know that it's anything serious. I mean . . . um . . ."

"Oh, I know. It is what it is. You all take sex a lot more casually than we used to." She cracked eggs into a skillet and handed Lucy a plate of toast to butter. She shot Lucy a shrewd glance. "It's not so very casual with you two, though, is it?"

"I—I can't say for Claude."

"I can. Not to scare you, honey, but I've never seen him look at anybody the way he looks at you. First time I saw it? I'm big enough to admit I had a twinge of jealousy. Imagine. Thinking he could find a woman he'd love more than me."

"Oh, I'm sure it's not—"

"Maybe not. Don't get yourself worked up. I'm his mother. What do I know? I think you're feeling something, too, though."

Lucy buttered every square inch of toast. It gave her something to do. The eggs sizzled and Beatrice bustled around the kitchen. "I don't sleep with men casually, Beatrice. I gave myself all kinds of reasons why I wouldn't sleep with Claude, but"—she shrugged helplessly—"some things you can't help."

"I know, honey." Beatrice laughed softly. "Don't I know it."

"How was your evening?" Lucy asked, determined to change the subject.

"Wonderful. I had a nice chat with—I forget her exact position—some bigwig with Tulane. I told her all about you and your research and she said to tell you there's a position opening up in the history faculty that you might want to apply for."

"Really? I hadn't thought of . . . well. Maybe I will."

"It never hurts to look into every opportunity," Beatrice said cheerily.

"No," said Lucy. "You're right. It doesn't."

In truth, she'd seen the position posted at the university and she'd been toying with the idea of applying.

She was still thinking about it, but one thing she was sure of was that she couldn't make a career decision based on a man. Still, she'd be foolish to impede her own career for the same reason. So, she was thinking about it.

Since it was Saturday, she wasn't going to the university. She was sitting outside with her laptop, writing her mother an e-mail. She got as far as typing, "I think I've found the skeleton in the family closet," when the skeleton said from behind her, "So, did you tell her?"

Claude. Her heart skidded at the sound of his voice. She turned her head, glad of her sunglasses so she could stare at her new lover hungrily without him knowing.

"Beatrice? Yes, I told her."

He looked altogether too good. He was dressed in his usual business casual work gear and all she could think about was getting him naked. And soon.

"And?"

"She's okay with it."

"Well, that's good." He tweaked her ponytail. "Maybe you can stay over the whole night next time."

She tilted her head so she could look at him over the top of her glasses. "Maybe."

He leaned over and kissed her. "I'm going in to work for a few hours. I usually go Saturdays." He sent her a mock serious glance. "That's when we make a killing on the tourists."

"I bet."

"Come by the main store later and I'll give you a daylight tour, then we'll grab some dinner somewhere. After that I'm taking you to Preservation Hall for some of the greatest jazz you'll ever hear."

"Tourist stuff, huh?"

"You'll like it. Oh, and Lucy? Bring your toothbrush. You won't be making it home."

Seven

Lucy was having trouble concentrating on her research. She'd done it. She'd taken her resumé and a nice letter and she'd officially applied for the position of assistant professor, tenure track. She needed to get hold of her mother and get copies of reference letters and a few other things.

And, she admitted, she needed to let Claude know what she'd done. If he freaked out, well, that was a pretty clear indication that their romance was strictly short-term in his mind. That was fine, too. She'd decided that whatever happened with Claude, she wanted this job.

Somehow she needed to tell him, though.

She took the streetcar home and walked the couple of blocks to Beatrice's place. She let herself in with her key, noting that her hostess's car was gone. She was alone, which was fine by her. She needed to think about how she was going to tell them—him. She might not even get the job, but she already knew that Beatrice and Claude knew everybody and if word got out she'd applied, well, she wanted them to hear it from her first.

She slipped off her shoes and thought she'd run upstairs, get her calling card, and then phone her mother.

A slight noise from the living room made her stop. Beatrice

was out. Wasn't she? Unless her car was being serviced or she'd lent it to someone.

"Beatrice?" she called, walking into the room.

She stopped dead in her tracks, all the blood draining from her face so she felt like she might faint.

"Claude," she said, and the weight of disappointment was so great she could barely get the word around the lead weight clogging her throat.

"*Merde.* Lucy. I thought you were at the university."

"Obviously." She found she was shaking so she sat down.

He was crouched beside an open safe she hadn't even known about since it was inside a chest she'd assumed was pure furniture. In his hands was the three-string necklace with the giant emerald she'd seen on the thin, rich woman at the historical society party.

She didn't think she'd have felt any worse if she'd found her brand-new lover in the arms of another woman. The betrayal felt as sharp. "I asked you if you were a thief. You never answered me."

He'd half risen and spoken her name urgently. Now he settled back and stared down at the gems in his hand. "No. I never did answer you."

"At least you're not a liar."

He breathed a heavy sigh. "No. I'm not a liar."

The doorbell rang. He cursed again. "Now what?"

"I'll go and see who it is."

She walked to the front door and peeked out the peephole. Perfect, just perfect.

She opened the door to the glamorous police officer who stood there with a male detective at her side. "Hello, Lucy. Is Claude here?"

Her brain whirled. Should she deny him? Turn him in? While she stood there dithering, she felt Claude appear behind her.

"Isabelle, John. Hi."

"Sorry to bother you, but I saw your car out front of your

place and you didn't answer the door." She glanced at Lucy. "I thought you might be here."

Claude also glanced at Lucy. "This isn't a great time."

"It won't take long. We need your help."

There was a short pause then Claude said, "Come on in."

Lucy watched him lead the officers into the very room where she'd found him with the jewels. He had balls, she'd give him that. She headed up the stairs to her room when Isabelle stopped her. "We'd like to talk to you, too."

"Me?" She looked at all three of them. Then shrugged. This was a nightmare. A pure nightmare. "Okay."

When they'd all sat down and the police officers had turned down her offer of iced tea, Isabelle spoke.

"There's been another robbery, Claude."

"Really?" His voice was leaden. He must be waiting for her to speak.

"The Gimmels, Edward and Rose, were at the party Friday night. Do you remember seeing them?"

"Yes."

"What time was that?"

"I don't know. Early. Nine? Nine-thirty?"

"Lucy, did you see them? The Gimmels are a wealthy couple. She was wearing—"

"I know who they are. Beatrice pointed them out to me. She was wearing the tiniest black dress I've ever seen." She paused. "And a fabulous necklace."

"Right. So you definitely remember that necklace?"

"Oh yes. An amazing piece. I'd know it anywhere."

"Can you describe it?"

She looked at Claude as she spoke. "Three strings of fat pearls in a choker with a very large square emerald in the center. Claude would know more about sizes and so on. All I know is that it was stunning."

"Worth a fortune, too," Isabelle said. "It was stolen the night of the historical society's gala. Seems like it might be the same thief as the one who took the Guillotine diamonds. It went missing between two, when Mrs. Gimmel returned it to the safe, and four A.M., when their dog started barking and they found the safe open. Same M.O. Nothing else taken."

There was absolute silence in the room. Outside, Lucy heard a car drive by. In the house somewhere a clock chimed off the hour.

"Have you heard any rumblings, Claude?"

Another pause.

"No."

"Can you check with your network?"

He nodded.

"If you hear of anything, Claude, or if a fence gets in touch with you . . ."

"I'll call you right away."

Isabelle looked for a second as though she'd say more, then with a nod she and her partner got up and left.

Lucy heard the door shut behind them, and then Claude's soft tread returning to where she still sat stone still.

He didn't come all the way into the room but stood leaning on the doorjamb. "You didn't turn me in."

She felt his gaze on her but couldn't look at him. "No."

"Why not?"

Why not? Why hadn't she told the police that she'd seen him with a fortune in jewels in his hands not ten minutes ago and that they were stashed right here in this room?

Because in the moment she'd seen the police on the doorstep she'd known she was in love with her thieving cousin. "Because I'm an idiot," she said savagely, kicking the leg of her chair so hard she bruised her heel.

"Are you planning to tell them?"

"I haven't decid—" She blew out a breath. "No. I've never done one single dishonest thing in my life until now. Not one. I don't have an unpaid parking ticket, an overdue library fine. Nothing. And now I'm an accessory to jewel theft."

Claude came and squatted in front of her chair. The strained look was gone and she thought he looked smug. No, not smug, she realized. Happy.

What the hell did he have to be happy about?

"Lucy, I need your help."

"What you need is a good defense attorney."

"I want you to promise me you won't tell my mother about this."

"Of course I'm not going to tell your mother. But Claude, what are you planning to do with that thing?"

He gazed at her with a slight frown pulling his brows together. "Put it back."

"Oh." Well, it was something at least. Maybe he was going to try and go straight. A sudden qualm assailed her.

"Claude?"

"Mmm?" He was rubbing her thighs but almost as though he were thinking about something else, so she didn't stop him.

"Is Isabelle involved in the thefts?"

"Isabelle?" He looked at her like she was nuts. "Isabelle's a cop. She's trying to track down the missing jewels."

"Yeah? Well, cops can be on the take. I've seen *The Big Easy*."

He shook his head at her. "This one isn't. It's . . . complicated."

"Complicated? Calling this complicated is like calling Lake Pontchartrain a small puddle." Oh, she'd found her family skeleton all right. And he was going to rattle her right out of her mind.

She heard Beatrice come in the house, and knowing there was no way she could see her hostess while the son's criminal activities were so fresh in her mind, she excused herself quickly and ran upstairs to her room.

What was she going to do?

If only she hadn't slept with him. She'd told herself she wouldn't. Then she'd been swept away by totally inappropriate lust.

Oh, she was in trouble now.

She felt like slapping herself. Hard. The necklace had been stolen the night of the gala. The very night she'd first made love with Cousin Claude.

How could he have slept with her and then calmly gone off and stolen a fortune in jewels? She wondered which act had given him more pleasure.

She stared blindly out of the window at the garden he'd made for his mother. He was always encouraging Beatrice in her hobbies. She'd thought that was so sweet. And yet here he was living a double life. She imagined him sneaking out of his house right after she'd left it, racing out to go steal—Wait a minute.

Isabelle had said the robbery took place between the hours of two and four A.M. She remembered creeping home that morning serenaded by early birdsong. That had been after five. She was sure of it now, because she'd checked her clock when she got to her room. Five-twenty. Claude had been far too busy making love to her between the hours of two and four to be breaking and entering.

She sat down sharply on her bed. If Claude hadn't taken the necklace then what was it doing in his mother's house? And if he had taken it why would he have stashed it at his mom's? Something was wrong with this picture.

But, with a slight alteration, everything made sense.

Lucy made her way back downstairs, hearing the rise and fall of Beatrice and Claude's voices from the front room.

She walked in and they both stopped talking. Beatrice wiped her eyes and said, "Oh, Lucy. You startled me, honey."

"I'm sorry. It's just that there's a question I've been meaning to ask you. For my research."

Claude was gazing at her with a warning expression but she sat beside him on the couch anyway and patted his knee. She'd promised him she wouldn't tell his mother what she'd seen, and she wouldn't.

"What kind of question? Something about the genealogy? I think everything's in the family Bible I showed you."

"No. It's not genealogy. It's a little personal, but I'm curious where the family fortune came from. I understood it was inherited, but I can't seem to find anyone in the family who ever made a fortune. And believe me, I've looked."

"Lucy, you're being nosy," Claude snapped. "Stop it."

"I am being nosy," she said, keeping her gaze on Beatrice. "But I'd really like an answer. It's . . . important."

Beatrice heaved a huge sigh then turned to her son. "I think it's time we told Lucy the truth, don't you?"

"No. Keep your mouth shut, Mother."

"I think I've figured out most of it, anyway," Lucy said.

"I told you she was smart as a whip," Beatrice said to Claude, sounding proud.

"Mama, you can't—"

"Lucy's family. Besides, it's my business and I'll tell her if I want. I'm an international jewel thief, Lucy," she said with an unmistakable note of pride. "My husband, rest his soul, was the true talent, but I wasn't half bad either. We were a great team for more then twenty years. Never caught, you know. Came close a couple of times." She chuckled, the way another mother would, reminiscing over a particularly enjoyable family holiday. "Claude disappointed his father a little when he went straight, but you have to admit, he's made a fine success of his business and he learned everything about jewels and antiques from us, of course."

"That's nice," said Lucy, feeling something was required.

"It's very inconvenient that he's working with the police, though, very inconvenient." She turned to Lucy. "Of course, I mostly only dabble these days as a hobby. I don't keep the money. Not anymore. It's a kind of philanthropy."

"You need a new hobby, Mama," Claude said with a bite.

"Then why don't you hurry up and give me grandchildren?" She beamed at Lucy. "I'll be a wonderful grandmother."

"Back to the problem at hand," Lucy said with determination, not liking the way the fanatical grandmothering gleam was being directed at her. "What are we going to do with this necklace?"

"You aren't going to do anything," Claude said. "Either of you. I'm putting the necklace back."

"But the police know it's missing."

"I'll figure out something."

"How will you get into the safe?" Lucy asked.

Beatrice laughed. "Claude's inherited his father's gift. We used to put his allowance in different safes every week. He had to open the safe to get the money." She chuckled. "By the time he was in high school there wasn't a lock he couldn't pick or a safe he couldn't crack. That's why his father was a little disappointed he spurned the family business."

"Really?"

"Oh, yes. But the second generation often does, you know. Veronica Mills was telling me the other day that they can't get a single one of their four children interested in the Mills chain of hardware stores. Not one."

Lucy blinked. "How disappointing." She turned to the man next to her. "So, you're going to sneak into those people's home and put the necklace back?"

"No," Beatrice said. "You're not. I'm going to sell it and donate the proceeds to the Save the Swamp fund, as I was planning all along. You keep your nose out of my business and everything will be fine."

"Mama, times have changed. Law enforcement's more sophisticated now." He rose and went to stand in front of her. "I don't want my mama in jail."

"But—"

"And I'm not bringing the grandchildren on prison visiting day."

"Oh." She sniffed. "Oh. Well, that makes a difference."

Lucy was getting a funny feeling in her belly, part excitement and part fear, but this wasn't the moment to think about herself. Someone in her family was in trouble.

"The Guillotine Diamonds," Lucy suddenly said. "Isabelle said it was the same M.O."

Beatrice beamed with pride. "That Isabelle is another smart cookie."

"What did you do with the diamonds?" Lucy asked, half afraid to hear the answer.

"I returned them to their rightful owner, of course. It wasn't right they should leave the family. Those dotcom people didn't need or appreciate those diamonds. It was all for show. I merely rearranged ownership in a more satisfactory way."

"I don't want to know this," Claude said, sounding totally frustrated.

"At least she didn't try and sell them," Lucy reminded him. She wrinkled her brow. "I would think so long as the original family never tries to sell the diamonds again, no one would ever know."

"Let's hope so."

"I think it's more important that we figure out how to put the Gimmel necklace back," Lucy said again.

"It's nothing to do with you."

"Yes. It is."

"Well, I think I'll put supper on. I can't stand to think of those awful people killing all those frogs when I could have helped prevent it."

"She has a point," Lucy said, when she was alone with Claude.

"Don't you start."

She looked at him, feeling suddenly shy and fluttery. "You've never stolen anything, have you?"

He stared at her for a moment and then shook his head slowly. "I'm the black sheep. How did you figure it out?"

"Isabelle said the necklace was stolen between two and four and I knew you'd been . . . um . . . busy during those hours."

He grinned. "Very busy. And when can we—"

One kiss she allowed him; it seemed only fair after wrongly believing he was a jewel thief. Then she said, "It's too dangerous for you to return that necklace alone. Luckily, I have a plan."

Her expectations were not met when, instead of looking at her eagerly to hear her plan, he groaned and dropped his head in his hands.

Eight

Claude decided that the women in his life were going to be the death of him. Too bad he was so crazy about them both.

His mother, the international and supposedly retired jewel thief, had been as enamored of Lucy's plan as he'd feared.

"I hope this works," said Lucy, her voice sounding strained.

"If it doesn't, we'll all end up in jail," Claude said, wishing he'd been able to convince the two sweet but misguided women in his life to stay home. "Maybe they'll send us somewhere that has family cells."

When they'd announced they were going alone if he didn't feel like coming along . . . well, what could he do?

"We'll be brilliant." Beatrice sighed. "It's so nice to work with partners again."

"Last time, Mama. You promised."

"I know. Well, let's go out in style." She beamed at them, looking a good ten years younger with the glow of excitement mantling her cheeks. "You remember your part, Lucy."

"Yes. I keep the horrible husband occupied."

"Right. I'm going on the pretext of inviting that awful woman to join the garden committee. Everyone will think I've lost my mind when I announce I'm sponsoring her," his mother said bitterly.

"And I will need to use the washroom," Claude said, thinking as plans went it was about the lamest he'd ever heard. Not that he'd come up with anything better. The one good thing was that no one in their right mind would think he'd come to return a stolen item to the safe, so they at least had surprise on their side.

The Gimmels were predictably happy to see his mother and fawned all over her. Her reputation as a society woman made her the object of a lot of fawning from people like the Gimmels. They seemed surprised to see him and Lucy in tow, but his mother made their unexpected appearance sound like a treat.

"I brought my son Claude along, and our Canadian cousin Lucy. They drove me, you see, and after I'd finished telling them how lovely your home is, they were anxious to have a peek."

"Of course," the razor-thin woman said, showing teeth that were awfully big for how few workouts they must get. "Edward," she ordered her husband. "Fetch the drinks cart."

Oh, good. They were going to pretend they were in a Noel Coward play. Drinks cart. Shit.

Still, better a mild drawing room farce than, say, Tennessee Williams, who might have been a local, but the fate of families in his plays was a little too dismal for Claude's taste right now.

Soon they were all settled in an ostentatious living room, overstuffed with very expensive and very tasteless things. He almost wondered whether his mother was right and they should hock the jewels currently tucked in his pocket and give the proceeds to charity.

Lucy would never forgive him, though, and Lucy's opinion had become altogether too important.

So, he made small talk over a scotch, let his mother charm the pants off their hosts, and watched Lucy try and pretend she wasn't a bag of nerves.

After he felt they'd all had long enough to get comfortable, he said, "Excuse me, can I use your washroom?"

"Yes, of course," said Edward Gimmel. "Right through there."

"Thanks."

He slid through ornate double doors and headed in the direction of the washroom, then slipped upstairs, pulling cotton gloves on as he went. He figured he had at least seven or eight minutes before anyone wondered where he was. He ought to be done in four.

His mother had told him where to find the safe, so he wasted no time but headed directly for the master bedroom and an enormous walk-in closet that reeked of some cloying perfume. Did these people not have restraint in anything?

Closing the door and flicking on the pencil flashlight, he pushed aside a shoe rack and uncovered the safe.

Three minutes later, he had the safe open and was lifting some papers, ready to slide the necklace into place.

That was when he noticed the flaw in Lucy's plan.

They'd forgotten the damned dog.

Nine

Lucy was doing her best, but she knew—if she'd ever been curious—that she wasn't cut out for crime. Her armpits felt damp, her palms downright slippery, and the questions she posed to Edward Gimmel about the resort he'd invested in somewhere in the Bahamas couldn't have been more brainless.

A couple more minutes, she thought, and they'd be out of here.

Then the barking started. The kind of barking that comes from a hysterical, hyper little dog.

"Princess?" Mrs. Gimmel shrieked. "We shut her upstairs when guests are coming. She can be annoying, but she's a very good watch dog."

"Where's your son?" Mr. Gimmel asked, leaping to his feet.

"He'll be back," Beatrice said so serenely that Lucy had to give her credit. "Little dogs get excited about nothing, don't they? We used to have a cocker spaniel . . ."

Gimmel wasn't buying the diversion. With an ugly look, he jumped to his feet and ran out. He went first to the guest bathroom, but of course it was empty, then he charged for the stairs where the shrill, endless barking reminded Lucy of a car alarm that wouldn't shut off.

Lucy had no idea what she was going to do, but she followed her host with the bad toupee. He went straight for the sound of the hysterical barking, which was coming from behind a closed door that had to be the bedroom where Claude was.

Damn and damn. Bloody dog.

"Mr. Gimmel, I was so hoping you'd give me a tour of the house. This is wonderful," she said in a loud voice. If Claude could get out of the window or something, they could still salvage this. Gimmel ignored her and threw open the bedroom door. Still acting as imbecilic as she knew how—and it was amazing how much imbecility had lain dormant all this time—she pushed her way in front of him into the room. "Oh, is this your bedroom? What a lovely room. Oh, and this is your sweet dog."

An over-coiffed Pekingese, jumping up at a door that presumably led to the walk-in closet, was yapping its fool head off.

"Good dog," she said. "Quiet."

She turned to say something inane to her host and then froze. He held a blunt-nosed pistol in his hand and it was trained on the closet door.

"Come out of there," he ordered.

"Honestly." She tried to speak loudly enough to be heard inside the closet while simultaneously beating back the panic dancing in her chest. "Why are you holding a gun? It's probably a mouse or something."

"Get away from that door," Gimmel yelled. He pulled out a slim cell phone and before her horrified gaze called 911 to report a robbery in progress.

"I've called the cops," he yelled. "Come out where I can see you."

"Good," said Claude, calmly walking out of the door, holding a sheaf of papers. "I think the police would be very interested in seeing this."

"You bastard," said Gimmel.

"What is it?" Lucy asked.

"A list of bribes paid to certain officials he needs on his side to get his development rammed through in an ecologically sensitive area. I always wondered how you'd got so far."

"Too bad I shot you before the cops got here," Gimmel said, slipping off the safety.

"No, you didn't," said Beatrice from behind them. She had some kind of semi-automatic weapon in her hands.

"This was in your desk drawer," she said pleasantly. "I'm not the greatest shot, but at this range, I couldn't miss."

"Rose," she said, when Mrs. Gimmel came gasping up behind her, "I'm afraid I'm going to have to withdraw my support of your nomination to the garden committee. Thank you for a lovely evening."

"Beatrice, you were fantastic," Lucy exclaimed later, when the three of them had enjoyed a late supper with an excellent bottle of wine Beatrice had dug out from her cellar.

"Thanks, honey. You were great, too, for a novice. With a bit of practice—"

"Mama."

Lucy turned to Claude, mostly to shut him up. "Isabelle looked pretty happy when you handed her that list."

His mother's pleasure dimmed a notch. "I still can't believe you put the necklace back."

"I think we did more good for your frogs by uncovering this ring of corruption than selling that necklace would have."

Beatrice sighed. "I suppose. And it was very exciting." She raised her glass. "Here's to going out in style and the beginning of my retirement."

"May it last," said her son.

"I was mostly bored, but I think things are going to get a lot more interesting around here."

"Mama, I am now proposing to take Lucy next door to my house and I don't plan to bring her back before breakfast. Does anyone have a problem with that?"

"Not a one."

"Ah, no."

* * *

Lucy missed her plane home. It took almost no persuasion for the mother and son tag team to talk her into extending her stay. She still had two months before school started again and she'd found a lot of research opportunities she might otherwise have overlooked. She'd booked a swamp tour and been horrified to find that the alligators she'd been so scared of followed the tour boat because the driver threw marshmallows overboard. The sharp-toothed creatures acted like puppies when the kibble comes out, sliding with prehistoric stealth into the murky water, jaws snapping—for marshmallows.

She'd toured old homes, eaten in amazing restaurants, drunk coffee and eaten beignets in the Café du Monde, and she'd met and interviewed dozens of newfound relatives.

She found herself falling in love with Louisiana—and with this most interesting branch of her family.

Today she'd left the university early and headed straight for the French Quarter. When her steps led her to her favorite antique shop on Royal, she went inside.

After a friendly greeting, Lana, the sales clerk out front, waved her to the back where Claude had a small office.

She walked through the shop, past the pale blue velvet sofa where she'd been when she first thought there was something special about Claude, to the open door. There he was, dark head bent over. A jewelry box lay open on his desk and she saw that he was cleaning a ring.

Her body tingled as it always did when she saw him. She wanted a minute to watch him when he wasn't aware of her, but it was impossible. He glanced up even though she hadn't made a sound. He could feel her, she knew. She wondered if it would always be this way between them and suspected it would.

The smile that lit his eyes was as intimate as the things they'd done to each other last night. Under his knowing gaze, her bones melted to syrup.

"Come on in," he said.

"Thanks. I was in the neighborhood and thought I'd take you to lunch, but it looks like you're busy."

"Never too busy for you. You look pleased with yourself."

"I am. We're celebrating. I got the assistant professor job."

"Congratulations." He rose to kiss her, and she threw herself into his arms. After she was so well congratulated she could barely draw breath, he said, "Does this permanent teaching job mean you're giving up a life of crime?"

She shuddered. "Don't remind me. I've never been so scared in all my life as when that man pulled a gun and I knew you were in the closet."

They were still holding each other, so no one could see him when he ran his fingertip over her nipple so it perked to life. "Probably you should stick to teaching."

"I've been wanting to talk to you about that whole jewel heist thing," she said.

"Now's good for me."

She hiked a hip onto his desk and he settled back into his chair. She stroked the edge of the open jewelry box, feeling the old, frayed velvet. "When I found you with that necklace in your hand, you let me believe you were a thief. I felt so angry and betrayed."

"I know. And I couldn't tell you it was my mom who was the thief, not me."

"What if I'd turned you in to the police?" She shivered at the thought, which had been torturing her.

"You didn't."

She hated even thinking about those awful minutes. "I almost did, though. I almost told an NOPD detective that I'd seen you with the necklace. Once I'd told her that, you know I'd have shown her where the safe was."

"I'll never forget that moment, either. That's when I knew."

She narrowed her gaze. "Knew what?"

"That only one thing was stopping you. It had to be love."

"Are you saying I love you?"

"I'd rather you said it." He reached out and touched her hand. "A man likes to know his love is returned."

She gazed at him and saw his heart in his eyes. The gorgeous, sexy man who made her dizzy with love, loved her back.

"Oh, I do," she said, feeling her heart pound. "I do love you."

He dropped his head and went back to polishing the ring, but she saw the glow of happiness on his face.

"What a beautiful ring," she said, leaning closer. "How can you bear to sell something so lovely?"

"This ring's not for sale. It belonged to my great—I don't know how many times great-grandmother. I'd need a researcher like you to figure out the generations. It's the ring her husband gave her before they left France for the new world."

"Things probably didn't turn out the way they thought."

"Things in life rarely do. But they went on to have a dozen kids, most of whom lived, and, eventually, a pretty good life here in New Orleans. My grandmother left it to me when she died. She told me to save it for my wife."

He held the ring up, letting the light catch it so it glowed deep red. "I thought I'd clean it up. You never know when you're going to need a ring like this."

She smiled at him. "No. You never do."

"You like it?"

"I love it. I see it's a ruby."

"So it is." He placed the newly cleaned ring into the box and then tucked it into his pocket. He took her hand and grinned down at her. "Let's go have lunch."

IN GOOD HANDS

E.C. Sheedy

One

Dane looked at the clock on the lower right of his screen and cursed. He had five minutes to make up his mind. Either he went himself to pick up this Esme Shane person, or he sent Janzen.

He hit the enter key, transferred another hundred thousand, and rested his dark head on his high-backed leather chair. He wanted to close his eyes. Hell, he wanted to close his mind—but thoughts of his screwball sister skewed his normally sane and logical brain patterns. To clear the frustration nettling his chest, he let out a long sweep of air. How he'd let her sucker him into taking on this damned inconvenient houseguest, he couldn't figure. He picked up a pen, tapped it on his desk.

Marilee was up to something. Had some Machiavellian plot up that designer sleeve of hers. He was sure of it.

If it had *anything* to do with the "amazing, incredible, brilliant, charismatic" Leonardo St. James, the guy currently ranked number one on her man meter, he'd strangle her—or worse yet, make a serious cut in her allowance. Dane might spoil Marilee rotten, but no way did his stupidity extend to investing in schemes involving her boy toys. She denied any form of subterfuge—naturally—but wariness being a big part of his genetic makeup, and guile being a big part of hers, he intended to be on his guard.

"Damn it," he said to the bank of computer screens, double tiered in front of him.

When one of them beeped in response, he shook his head, again looked at the clock, and rubbed at the lines he felt deepening to wagon-size ruts in his forehead.

How the hell his sister Marilee always got the better of him was a mystery. One of those psycho-babblers would probably say their relationship got skewed after the death of their parents, and he'd had to take a more fatherly role in Marilee's life. Maybe so, but fatherly or not, he'd indulged her escapades once too often. And this latest Leonardo scheme? To run some kind of sex shop, featuring body and sexual awareness seminars in New Mexico?

Not going to happen.

Apparently, this Esme woman—due to arrive on his island retreat within the hour—fell into Marilee's breathless, "best-friend-ever" category, which meant she was probably as ditzy and irresponsible as his sister. Hell, it had taken him fifteen minutes to break through her singsong litany of the Shane woman's virtues. He remembered the conversation. . . .

"You'll love her, Dane, I know you will. She's led the most amazing life. And she won't get in your way. She's a mouse, a quiet little mouse. All she needs is two weeks near the Gulf Coast to finish some special project she's working on—a beach book for kids or something. And it's not as if you're short of space. You've got at least twenty-five rooms in that godforsaken place of yours"—anything more than ten miles from the center of New Orleans was "godforsaken" in Marilee's mind. "She's just this *ultra* special person . . . good, kind, supportive when I needed her. I owe her, Dane. I truly do. When I broke up with Richard"—or was it Philip? Dane frowned, couldn't remember—"I'd never have made it without her. She introduced me to Leonardo, you know."

She'd announced the last as if it were the clincher, then

gone on with the pleading, every word hushed, heartfelt, and packed with sincerity. His sister would make a hell of a trial lawyer—if she believed in work.

Dane idly scratched his neck. Chances were good Esme Shane was involved in this scheme of hers and Leonardo's and would be angling for a fat check within hours. Saying no wasn't a problem, the hassle was.

"You have mail," Six murmured. Dane had decided early on not to humanize the hardware arrayed in front of him by giving them names, but needing some way to identify each computer unit, he'd chosen numerals. One through twelve did the trick.

He looked at the old-style mailbox flashing on the screen. South Africa. Another message appeared. Some village in Alaska. Neither appeared urgent, but . . .

He decided to send Janzen. That would give him at least a couple more hours on the computer before his unwanted guest arrived and he'd have to face all that . . . mousiness.

The phone rang. He glanced at the call display, looked at the ceiling, and let out a noisy breath. He picked up.

"I knew you'd still be there," she accused. "I just knew it!"

Marilee. Damn. "I'm sending Janzen."

"Don't you dare!"

Marilee's exclamation-point inventory was, as usual, overstocked. "The airport is a half hour away," he said. "I'm sure Janzen can—"

"I told her *you'd* pick her up. She'll be nervous, flying on that glorified tin can of yours."

"It's a Cessna. And Granger is a first-class pilot. She'll be fine." His attention flicked over the message from South Africa.

"Dane, I don't ask you for much. I really don't."

Her pout seeped out of the receiver and bloomed in the room like a full-color hologram, forcing Dane to attempt a decode of Marilee's definition of "much." He came up empty. "Don't start, Marilee. And for God's sake, don't turn on the waterworks."

She sniffled. "I never cry . . . unless"—she sniffled again—"I absolutely have to."

Dane's lips twitched. *God, she was good.* "You are the biggest pain in the butt in Louisiana. You know that?"

"Of course I do." She paused, and Dane sensed her smile. "Dane . . . please. She's such a shy little creature. She'd be completely overwhelmed with the chauffeur thing."

"Janzen's not a chauffeur. He's . . . security." Among other things.

"Whatever he is, he'll scare the daylights out of her. I know he does me. All that ex-CIA stuff gives me the vapors."

"The what?"

"Forget it. Just, ple-e-ase, don't send Janzen. Go yourself. For me?"

"Like I said, you're a—"

"Pain in the butt. Fine. But does all that name-calling mean you'll go?"

Dane knew when he was beaten. He ran a hand over his too-long hair, his unshaven jaw, then he looked at his watch. "I'll go, but it won't be pretty. And if she's coming at me for money—"

"You're the prettiest man I know," she said, cutting him off with the subtle precision of a chain saw. "And you'll love Esme. Absolutely love her. You won't even know she's there. Thanks, big brother. I'll call you later."

Click.

Dane looked at the dead phone in his hand and shook his head. She hadn't denied the money thing. Damn.

Suckered again.

Six burped up another E-mail. He scanned it quickly.

Maybe not quite so suckered after all.

The flight was smooth and the view from the window pretty, but Esme's butt ached just the same. What with the bus, the airport, the fancy airplane, she'd been sitting for ten hours straight. She couldn't wait to get on the ground, breathe some fresh air, and walk the soles of her Nikes off.

Again she studied the posh cabin of the sleek jet, everything in shades of gray. Cushy leather seats, gleaming lacquered bar with its display of crystal glasses—all aglitter under the afternoon sun beaming in through the plane's windows—and deep, ultra-soft carpeting. Luxury on wings.

She shook her head. Hard to believe a man with this much money was so closefisted when it came to his younger sister, so determined not to help her and Leonardo. Still, that was his right and none of her business. She was just grateful to get this time on the Gulf. It was the last beach in the book due to the publisher within the month and perfect for her purpose. So far the illustrations had worked beautifully—or so Veronica, the book's author, had told her when they'd last spoken.

And Esme so welcomed the change in venue.

Doing the drawings for Leonardo's *Sex For The Seriously Inhibited* had been a tremendous amount of work. The move from a closed stuffy studio, where she'd spent days positioning naked, or almost naked, models into simulated sex positions, to open, breeze-swept beaches, was like a dose of mega-rich vitamins, as was the challenge of drawing for children. Besides, there was only so much *pretend* sex a woman could take.

"Ya'll buckle up back there now, ma'am." The pilot's voice, with its hint of the south, came over the intercom. "We'll be landing in a few minutes. Should be a smooth one."

Esme did as instructed and peered out the Cessna's generous window. Delacroix Island, its saltwater bays, lake, and bayou, stretched beneath her. The endless expanse of sea beyond, the swath of low grassy dunes, sun warmed and waiting, looked lush and tempting. She imagined a few stolen hours from her work, basking on a towel by the shore, taking some long overdue downtime.

Esme sighed and leaned back in the plush seat. No more naked bodies; just two weeks of bliss and beaches, thanks to

Marilee. All she had to do was drop off hers and Leonardo's business case and do a drawing of McCoy's home. A small price to pay for his hospitality. That done, she intended to work hard, and stay well out of his way. If Marilee was right, that wouldn't be a problem, because, according to her, he spent his days locked in a computer room making money.

Correction. *More* money.

Marilee said he'd made a gazillion running his company, some kind of electronics firm, then another gazillion when he suddenly sold it a couple of years ago. All he did now was stare at a computer screen and watch his fortune grow.

While Esme doubted it was that easy, Dane's preoccupation with moneymaking faintly repelled her.

Marilee described her older brother as a business shark, a fierce kill-the-competition-style workaholic, who was *totally* unstoppable when he wanted something. She'd also said he was *very* handsome in a middle-aged kind of way, but that he was always so "stressed to the max," he looked like an ogre on mean pills.

In what Esme called her past life, the one lived before she began seriously pursuing her art, she'd counseled more than her share of Dane McCoys. The money gods, she'd called them, and to a man they were ambitious, driven, stunningly egotistical—and when required—utterly charming.

She didn't miss them . . . those empty men with fat wallets, thin libidos, and joyless souls.

She especially didn't miss the one she'd married.

Esme rubbed at the tight spot above her breasts, the site left vacant by love and inhabited now by wariness, self-protectiveness, and a determination to live—and love—her way, or not at all.

Esme Shane was no mouse.

Tall, dark-haired, and athletic, she was built for sport—both indoor and out. Meeting her was like rounding a quiet corner and bumping into a parade.

Wearing tight jeans, a wildly bright silk shirt, and yellow sneakers, she hit the eye hard and fast, a surge of energy and color that made everything around her muddy and gray. When she extended her hand, and Dane enclosed it in his, every bone and muscle in it vibrated against his palm. Damn near electric.

Esme Shane was hot.

Dane suddenly wished he'd shaved, had a haircut. Both thoughts pissed him off, as did the thought that this "mouse" was going to be damned hard to ignore for two weeks—if he let her stay that long.

"Dane," she said, clasping his hand and smiling into his eyes. "Thanks for coming to meet me." She stopped, tilted her head. "You're as good-looking as your sister said you were."

"You're not," he said, then cringed, shaking his head at his own stupidity.

Her eyes widened.

"Sorry." He attempted a rally. "I didn't mean that the way it sounded. It's just that Marilee described you as more . . . conservative. And you're . . . not." She'd said nothing about sharp, sexy green eyes, and a lush mouth he had trouble taking his eyes from.

She laughed, tugged her hand from his. "Compared to your sister, Paris Hilton is conservative."

"Yeah." Her mouth—smiling—caused a tight feeling in his throat. He began thinking about how long it had been since he'd had sex. *Shit!*

Her smile grew and her eyelashes swept down. He had the sick feeling she knew exactly what he was thinking and was amused by it.

She was a witch. Marilee had sent him a witch—with an agenda.

Dane gestured toward the Porsche. "Your bags—"

"One bag, one portfolio case," she corrected. "I travel light, and I didn't want to scare you by bringing so much luggage you'd be afraid I'd outstay my welcome."

Not possible. "Not a problem," he muttered, again nodding toward the car, where Granger had stowed her gear. "The top's down. I can put it up if it bothers you." Her hair, loose to the middle of her back, was as thick and straight as a curtain. The wind would mess it up big time.

"Oh, no. The fresh air will be great."

When they were both in the car, she gave him a curious look. "I had you in mind as older."

He put the car in gear, reversed to make a turn, and slanted a gaze her way. "Marilee again. She thinks anyone over thirty was around when they built the Statue of Liberty."

"How old are you?" she asked, while making a rough braid from her long hair and securing it with a blue stretchy thing she'd dug from her tote.

"Thirty-nine." He eyed her, decided on tit-for-tat. "What about you?" Twenty-six, he guessed.

"Thirty-two. Next month." She finished her braid, rested her head back on the seat, and drew in some long deep breaths.

As heaving bosoms went, he rated hers an A-plus. Hell, they'd be A-plus whether they heaved or not.

With her eyes still closed, she asked, "Do you live far? I can't wait to get out of these clothes. Take a long—make that endless—shower."

Dane's mouth went dry, and his Neanderthal brain thickened with sexually charged images.

What was behind his zipper thickened, period.

"A half hour tops." He geared down, revved the Porsche's powerful motor, and screamed out the gate. For the first time he understood the relationship between a fast car and a man's libido.

They were at his house in twenty minutes. His best time ever.

Two seconds after she closed the door to her room and shut out the dour-faced Dane McCoy, Esme flipped open her cell phone and called Marilee, because one second after meeting her brother, she'd smelled a rat—and it wasn't him.

Marilee picked up.

"What's going on here?" Esme demanded, her heart thumping in her chest with enough force to damage her ribs. She'd spent the last half hour being cool, and she'd run out of ice. Nothing about McCoy jibed with Marilee's description, and she wanted to know why.

"I don't know what you mean."

"You told me your brother was some kind of middle-aged hermit, a super nerd—your exact words as I recall—with no time for—" She stopped.

"Sex?" Marilee finished. "And it's the truth . . . almost."

"Almost?" Loaded word, almost. So conveniently vague.

She sensed Marilee's shrug. "He sees women when it suits him, I guess. But he doesn't seem to like them much, and he doesn't put much effort into it, if you ask me. But sometimes they call or just . . . show up."

I'll bet! Esme thought, visions of his cobalt eyes slanting down at her with enough residual punch to make her swallow.

Marilee went on doggedly. "But mostly he never sees anyone, hardly ever goes out. Except for those weird trips he takes with Janzen, who's pretty high on the weirdness scale himself—to do business stuff. All he does is sit at his stupid computers and count his gold. Kind of like that Midas guy." She stopped. "I thought, if he met you—"

"You're matchmaking!" She sat solidly on the edge of the king-size bed. "How could I have been so stupid?"

"I am not doing anything of the kind." Marilee sounded incensed. "I just thought you could loosen him up, bring him out of himself . . . you being a therapist and everything."

"Ex-therapist. And I didn't come here to 'loosen up' your brother. I came to make a simple delivery, and do a house drawing in exchange for some hospitality. I have no intention of interfering in your brother's life."

"He's awfully cute, though, isn't he?"

My God, he's so far beyond cute he's in another dimension. "Cute has nothing to do with anything," she said, striving for prim, which was a major joke.

"Okay, I'll level with you. Leonardo and I really need Dane's help to open our spa. It just makes sense. You know Leonardo has the credentials—"

Esme couldn't deny that. Leonardo was a brilliant, caring and dedicated psychologist. He also had three degrees behind his name.

"—and I'm already back at esthetician college. But Dane won't even talk about what we want to do. I swear he thinks we plan to open some kind of high-class brothel or something. He's totally off the wall about it." She paused, took a breath. "What we want to create—in tandem with the usual reinvigorating spa environment—is a place where a person has the time and privacy to discuss sexual issues and deal with whatever inhibitions stop them from experiencing the joy and bonding inherent in a healthy, happy sex life, and—"

"Stop quoting Leonardo, Marilee. I know exactly what he wants to do." And she thought it was a fabulous idea. In her years as a sex therapist she'd learned one thing: there was a woeful shortage of understanding and a glut of confusion surrounding sexuality, much of it mired in guilt and secrecy. And a lot of people were unhappy and depressed because of it. *Shine a light where a light is needed,* Leonardo had said; Esme agreed completely.

"Well, I want it, too. For him and me." Marilee's tone was stubborn. "The idea is, I'll deal with the tense and tired body while he handles the uptight sexual psyche. It's perfect."

"Tell me something. Does Leonardo know you set me up as your business agent? Or to be more accurate, your Mata Hari."

More silence filtered down the line. "No."

"I didn't think so."

"When Dane said no, Leonardo said that was his right, that we'd find the money somewhere else."

"Sounds smart to me."

"But we haven't!" Marilee said, her voice growing desperate. "And we're running out of time."

"So you recruit me to seduce the money out of your brother?"

"No! Like I said, he refuses to talk to me about the spa. I thought if you could get close to him, he'd listen to you—or at least be polite. Then you could tell him all about Leonardo, how incredible he is . . ." She sighed. "I thought putting a face on things was so much better than dropping a file on his desk filled with a bunch of dry numbers and projections. That's all. Honestly."

"Did it occur to you that Dane might hate me on sight?"

She made a dismissive snort. "I know my brother. When he isn't antisocial, he goes for smart, ambitious women . . . with great legs. You rate on all counts."

Trust Marilee to have her own vision of things. "I'll give him your business case, because I said I would, and I'll talk about it—if he asks—but that's it," Esme said. "Then I do my drawings, and I'm out of here." A thought came, and she grimaced, afraid to ask the question that sprang from it. "Marilee, you told me your brother 'wanted' an artist's rendering of his house. Is that true?" The drawing was how she planned to repay his hospitality.

"Well . . . almost. I said he'd 'love' one . . . although he might not exactly know that."

"I can't believe this." With her free hand she shoved her hair roughly back.

"Esme, ple-e-ase. Just talk to him. If not for me, for Leonardo."

"Good-bye, Marilee." She clicked off, tossed the phone on the bed, and fell backward, arms above her head. "Damn!" she said to the ceiling.

I wonder where the closest motel is.

Two

Dane showed Esme to her room, went directly to the library, and poured himself a shot of single malt Scotch.

Janzen ambled in, took a seat on the arm of the sofa, and stretched his legs in front of him. "That is one spectacular female you drove in with," he said.

Dane ignored him. "Want a drink?" he asked, raising the bottle in his direction.

"Sure."

Dane poured a shot, walked over to where Janzen sat, and handed it to him. "You still have any of those shady connections of yours left over from your spy days?"

"One or two. Why?"

"I'm thinking of taking a contract out on Marilee." He downed his drink.

Janzen laughed. "You're talking about the woman I plan to marry."

"So you keep saying. Might be tough. She says you give her the vapors."

He frowned at that. "I think I'll take that as a compliment."

"You take everything as a compliment." Dane poured himself another drink and forced himself to sip it, then sprawled in the leather wingback across from Janzen.

"This conversation isn't about me—or my future bride," Janzen said. "It's about that beauty you just parked in the bedroom across the hall from yours."

"It's a nice room."

"It's a convenient room."

Damned if it wasn't. "Did you check out that South Africa deal?" Dane asked. Good a time as any to change the subject, get his mind off a leggy brunette who'd do nothing but distract it given half a chance.

"Yeah. It's clean. And a small investment considering the potential benefits. Fifty thousand should take care of it."

"Personnel?"

"In place. They'll make sure the money gets into the right hands."

"Good. I'll do the transfer later tonight."

Janzen stood, finished his drink, and lifted his eyes pointedly toward the ceiling, the second floor. "What about her?"

"What about her? She's a friend of Marilee's and she's here for money."

"You're a suspicious prick, McCoy."

"That, I am. And I can connect the dots when I have to. How about this?" Dane eyed his partner and friend. "First dot, Marilee's got herself a new boyfriend. His name's Leonardo."

That got Janzen's interest.

"Second dot, aforementioned boyfriend—and Marilee—want money to open some kind of sex shop."

That made Janzen blink.

"Third dot, Marilee arranges for major sexpot to spend two weeks with her brother. The brother who has refused repeatedly to finance her and Leonardo's . . . rub-and-tug operation."

Janzen narrowed his gaze. "Not necessarily connected."

"And the fourth dot?" He paused for effect. "The sexpot is the boyfriend's sister."

"You checked her out."

"With what I've got going on here, I check everyone out."

"Then why'd you let her come?"

It was Dane's turn to blink. Hell, a guy couldn't admit to an ex-CIA type he was putty in the hands of his little sister. "I didn't get the information on her until just before I left for the airport."

"What all did you get?"

"Not much. Full name, Esme Patience Shane. Divorced three years ago. No criminal record. She actually is an illustrator—been one for about four years. Successful by the sound of it. Before that she was some kind of therapist. She lives in San Diego. She doesn't lie about her age . . ." *She has intense, smart green eyes, a body created for a man's hands, and legs long enough to wrap—*

"That's it?" Janzen prodded, looking puzzled.

Dane snapped back to the present "And her brother's name is Leonardo Billings St. James. Other than her being a 'best friend' "—he made quote marks in the air—"of my irresponsible sister, she's an all-round staid and upstanding citizen."

Janzen made a show of shuddering, then grinned. "The worst kind." He stood, drained his glass, and set it on the edge of Dane's desk. "You want me to get rid of her?"

Dane turned the glass of amber liquid in his hand, mulled over Janzen's suggestion. Getting Esme Shane off the property—and off the island—would be the smart thing, the safe thing. Then his brain veered off, formed an image of her luscious mouth, the way her eyes met his, warm and confident. In the five years since he'd made *Forbes's* goddamn rich-list, that kind of look was rare. More likely, a person looking at him now, had eyes full of avarice and manufactured friendship—or they were so nervous they sputtered.

"No." He stood. "It'll be fun to let her pitch Marilee's deal and fail. Teach Marilee a damn lesson. But keep an eye on her while she's here, will you? I've got a lot on my plate."

"No can do." It was Janzen's turn to stand. "I'm out tonight, and I'm off to New York tomorrow, remember?"

No, he hadn't.

Janzen strode to the door, stopped. "You'll have to do your own 'eyeing.' " He grinned again. "And thinking of that babe upstairs, I can't bring myself to feel sorry for you. Have fun, McCoy." He walked out.

Dane stared after him. Damn. He'd been counting on pawning the woman off on Janzen. So . . . he should be disappointed and pissed off that his plan was scuttled. Which didn't account for the expectancy pacing in his tired brain, or the odd lightness in his chest. Janzen said to "have fun." Now there was a thought. Dane headed for the computer room. Hell, he wouldn't know "fun" if it hit him broadside.

And woman-type fun? More particularly Esme Shane–type fun? Uh-uh. That was an extreme sport he had neither the time nor the energy for.

He quickened his pace, but before he sat down at the computer console, he called the kitchen. "Peggy, Janzen won't be here for dinner, but I have a guest—"

He looked heavenward. "Yes, that's right, a 'living, breathing' guest of the female variety. Call her, will you? See if she needs anything. She's in the green room. And tell her dinner will be at six. Yes, I know that's early." He prayed for patience. "Six, Peggy. Thank you."

He hung up and looked at the time on the screen. He had two hours to work . . . two hours to wait.

Esme didn't expect formality, and she wasn't disappointed. Peggy Street, the woman who ran McCoy's house and cooked for him, had helped Esme get settled; she'd told her Dane didn't like the dining room, that he preferred to eat in the breakfast room off the kitchen.

When she looked at the slim silver watch on her wrist, she realized she was a few minutes early and decided to stroll through the rose garden she'd spotted from the kitchen window. She wasn't looking forward to dinner with a man who'd been coerced into having her here, so she'd resolved to be pleasant—if it killed her—until she could make a graceful exit to the nearest motel.

The blooms were full and alive with color, their scent heady and rich in the strong Louisiana sun. She had her nose buried in a pure white blossom when she heard footsteps behind her, scrunching on the crushed oyster shells that formed a path through the dozens of rosebushes. She turned and straightened.

"You comfortable? Your room okay?" Dane McCoy asked, the words clipped, his eyes cool and hot at the same time.

Esme's heart hurtled upward to fill her throat. Dane McCoy—wearing a navy shirt and tan dress slacks, a darker tan leather belt circling his lean waist, his skin clear and clean-shaven, his scarily intelligent eyes fixated on her, half angry, half wolf—was blindingly handsome, and the bolt of attraction that made her bones crumble caught her off-guard. She'd felt it earlier today, the second their eyes met. Then it was a gentle wash of warmth that made her tummy curl, but now it was a flash flood affecting a more sensitive part of her anatomy—and God, it felt good.

It had been so long . . .

She waited until her heart settled down to where it belonged, waited for her vision to widen enough to encompass more than Dane McCoy, and said in as measured a voice as she could muster, "Everything's fine. Thank you."

His eyes flicked to her mouth, stayed there. Too long. "Good," he said, finally lifting his gaze to hers. "Dinner's ready. I hope you like to eat, because Peggy's gone all out. It's been a while since she cooked for a woman."

Dane, only a few steps from the open kitchen door, went to stand beside it, waited for her. Esme followed, surprised and intrigued he'd been so honest about the lack of a woman in his life. She guessed none had called or "showed up" recently, which, according to Marilee, was how the mating game worked for Dane McCoy, the whole thing easy and effortless. No doubt women only rose on his priority list when absolutely necessary—when his body demanded them.

She twisted her lips to restrain a smile, thinking how irritating it must be for a power-hungry, money-obsessed male like Dane to have his work interrupted by an inconveniently demanding libido. Probably a quick and impatient lover, she thought. Not that she intended to confirm that. What she intended was to be polite and controlled until she could make her escape.

When she reached the door, he gestured her in, his hand briefly touching—warming—her bare elbow as she stepped ahead of him into the kitchen.

Peggy bustled around the table, setting down red beans and rice, lamb steaks, asparagus dripping in butter and parmesan, and long thin bread rolls to die for.

After she and Dane agreed on a red wine, Esme, who hadn't eaten since morning, started on dinner. "Oh," she breathed, after her first bite of asparagus. "This is beyond heavenly." After another couple of bites, she realized Dane wasn't eating. "What's wrong?" she asked, "Don't you like it?"

"Peggy's cooking? What's not to like?" He sat stone still in the chair across from her, twirling the stem of his wineglass on the white tablecloth, and looking at her as if she were a dissected frog from last week's biology class. No lust now—only enmity.

Quelling a prickle of unease, Esme set her fork down. "You're not eating."

"I'd rather watch you eat."

She met his gaze. "Why's that?"

"I like watching your mouth. The way your tongue comes out and sweeps your lips to pick up the last of the flavor."

"You like . . . my tongue?"

"Ever met a man who didn't like your tongue?" His chilly expression didn't so much as flicker.

"Never met one who admitted it so openly within"—she looked at her watch—"four hours of meeting me. A woman might consider a remark like that a bit suggestive at this point, even insulting." Esme wasn't sure what he'd meant by it. It certainly wasn't a come-on. And if it was intended as a put-down, he'd seriously miscalculated. Esme Shane was not *put-downable*.

He nodded his dark head once. "Some women would, but not you. You didn't blush, didn't turn away, and you didn't stand and walk out of the room."

"And that means what? I failed some kind of test?"

"It means you're not easily intimidated."

She wondered how he'd react if he knew she'd spent years talking about tongues, penises, and vaginas for a living. She decided to find out. "I'm not," she said. "At least not when it comes to sexuality, which is the category I'd put that remark of yours into." She picked up her knife and fork and started in on her steak. "I was a sex therapist for six years before I decided to follow my bliss, as they say."

"A sex therapist," he repeated and raised a brow. "Do I even want to know what that means?"

"You would if you needed help getting an erection, or couldn't satisfy either yourself or your partner." She looked at him, held back her smile, and adopted her clinical persona. "Do you? Because if so, while I'm here . . ." She cocked a brow in question. Yes, definitely the faintest of blushes warmed those remarkable cheekbones of his.

"I do fine, thanks."

"Well, if you change your mind, you know where to find me."

"Yeah . . . in the bedroom across the hall from mine."

She put her eating utensils down and smiled at him through her confusion. This conversation was twisting and turning a bit faster than she could handle. "Why are we having this . . . intimate a conversation when we hardly know each other?"

"We can talk about sex or we can talk about money. For now I figured sex was the simpler of the two."

She still didn't get it. "What are you talking about?"

He leaned forward. "I know why you're here, Esme Patience Shane." He enunciated her name clearly and, she thought, with obvious distaste.

She hid her bewilderment, or at least hoped she did, by taking some deep breaths and ignoring the ripple of alarm in her stomach. "Hardly a secret. I came here to draw Delacroix Island and this house, and—"

"—beg for money. For a sex shop."

"Beg for— Sex shop!" Esme tossed her napkin on the table and stood. "You've got an awful lot of things wrong, McCoy."

He leaned back in his chair, made no move to get up. "So, set me straight. Or are you more comfortable on the field of erectile dysfunction than in the arena of high finance?"

Esme stared at him, quelled her shock, the simmer of anger contracting her chest. It looked as though her exit would be a hell of lot less gracious than she'd planned, and she'd be looking for a motel room tonight instead of tomorrow. But she wasn't going anywhere until she straightened things out with this money-obsessed, tight-fisted, sister-controlling, arrogant son of a bitch she was currently having dinner with.

"All right, I will 'set you straight.'" She fixed her gaze on him, crossed her arms. "I came here to draw, not beg you for your precious money. And because your sister asked me to drop off a business proposal."

"So far we're on the same track, darlin'. A business proposal usually being a request for money. In this case, five million dollars for a sex shop."

"Five million"—Esme's jaw loosened, and she dropped her hands to her sides—"dollars?" she repeated, her voice uncomfortably close to a squeak.

"Last I heard, that was still the legal currency in the U.S. of A."

"I had no idea." She'd never gone into the financial end of

things with either Marilee or Leonardo—hadn't even thought about it. She knew their plans were ambitious, but she'd never dreamed they needed so much money.

"I've got to hand it to them," Dane said. "They think big. Five mil will stock a lot of dildoes and rubber Bettys."

"Dildoes and rubber—" She was mad again, and it felt good. "That is definitely *not* what they have in mind. My brother is a respected psychologist, and—" She stopped. One look told her McCoy was unmoved, and any further defense of Leonardo was wasted. She arched a brow. "But if they did want one of those things, so what? There are people who need—"

"To get laid, and are willing to pay good money for a reasonable facsimile when the real thing isn't handy." He nodded. "That, I know. I also know my sister doesn't know squat about business and that your brother, from what I've learned, is on a par with her." He took a drink of his wine, set the glass back on the table, and again twirled the stem, not for a moment taking those brilliant, fiercely speculative eyes of his from her face.

"How would you know anything about my brother? You've never even met him, and he's—" Light dawned. "You had him investigated!" More light dawned. "And probably me, too."

"I investigate everything, and that includes people, places, or things, that touch my home and family." He stood.

"There are some who'd call that paranoid." A part of her understood his caution, another part stung as if violated.

"And there are those who don't give a damn what it's called."

Especially when they're safely cocooned behind a wall of cash. Marilee might have been subverting the truth when she described her brother's physical appearance, but she'd sure pegged his character—flaws! Except she'd missed one. Chronic egotism.

Esme walked toward him, stood directly in his line of verbal fire, and said, "And then there are those who don't give a damn, *period*. My guess, McCoy, is that you're one of those. You don't want to help your sister, you've judged my brother without so much as shaking his hand, and . . . you've obviously got sexual issues." She met his eyes, coolly, unblinkingly. Two could play the big-time macho game. No penis required.

" 'Issues?' " He looked as if he might choke.

Score a hit for the female brigade.

He found his voice, and oddly, a thin smile that disappeared as quickly as a puff of smoke. "I'm not sure how my sexuality got in the mix," he said, his eyes a hot unreadable blue. "But as 'issues' go, it isn't one of them." He took a step closer to her. "Although I admit I've never tried the *therapeutic* approach to making love." He drew a line with his index finger down her cheek, his touch feather-light. "A man can always learn something to improve his technique."

Esme, who'd swim to Mobile buck-naked and without flippers, before she yielded him an inch, ignored the heat from his hand, the way it seeped under her skin to run up, then down her exposed throat. "There's more to making love than technique."

He ran his knuckles across her jaw. "Like what?" he asked, his voice lower.

"Feelings. You know . . . those things that get in the way of rational thought." *Like they were doing right now!*

"Uh," he said, his gaze slipping from hers to the strands of hair he was rolling between his thumb and forefinger. "Tell me more about these things, these feelings."

"You're not—"

His mouth cut her off, taking hers in a soft, compelling kiss. The scent of him entered her, a fragrance of evening forest and ruby wine.

Delicious, intoxicating. Paralyzing.

He slid his hand to her nape and ringed her neck with deft strong fingers, held her in place. When he ended the kiss, he brushed his mouth over hers and murmured, "I knew you'd taste good."

"I think—" Of course, she wasn't thinking at all, and when his mouth again settled over hers, only one hazy idea surfaced: if this man had sexuality issues . . . bring 'em on.

He ran his tongue along her lower lip, and she opened to it, offered her own. He pulled her to him, rougher now, more demanding, and her nipples hardened against his straining chest, the pounding of his heart.

And her nipples weren't the only thing getting hard . . .

"Jesus!" Dane jerked his head up, pulled back abruptly, but continued to hold her by the shoulders. His eyes were dark, shocked.

Esme, when she gained control over her legs, took a breath, and stepped back. "I think . . . you should let go of me."

He dropped his hands as if her skin had combusted, then stared at her as if seeing her for the first time. Then he rubbed at the lines in his forehead. "I don't know why I did that."

Esme looked at him, and her head, until now a kaleidoscope of colors and broken thoughts, cleared—somewhat. Determined to sound sane, alert, and sensible, she said, in what she hoped was a level voice, "And I don't know why I let you."

Those were the truest of all the words she could summon up. She was freaked! She'd spent less than an hour with this man; she didn't know him, didn't particularly like him, and considered his addiction to work—to making more and more money when he already had enough for a hundred lifetimes—not only less than admirable, but a serious character deficiency. He was the last man on earth who should make her heart race, her pulse jump, and her head fill with images of naked tangled limbs and mind-numbing sex.

Their gazes met, locked, and the air between them, thick and hot, vibrated with promise and peril. They stared at one another, the only sound two pairs of lungs struggling toward normalcy. When the quiet between them lengthened, heat coursed up Esme's neck; she couldn't find her voice. Neither, it seemed, could Dane. Mutely, they considered one another as if in thrall. As if words would kill the magic or whatever it was that had entered the room on that kiss.

"I apologize," Dane finally said, his tone low, his expression thoughtful. "I was out of line."

"And I'll leave tonight."

"No." He raised a hand. "That's not necessary."

"In the morning, then," she stated, then glanced away and attempted to reclaim her poise, which had drained away the second Dane's mouth had touched hers.

He looked as if he would argue but nodded instead.

Another layer of awkward silence tripped over the last, before he said, "Then I suggest we eat." He gestured toward the table. "Unless you feel obliged to run off immediately and start packing."

Run off? No way. She gave him an arch look. "The wounded virgin act would be overkill, I think. Besides, I'm as hungry as a she-wolf," she lied. "The packing can wait." She sat.

He sat.

Both picked up their forks. Both ate in silence, until Dane broke it. "Where will you go?"

"It's a pretty big island. There must be a decent motel. I'm not fussy." Esme had no idea where to go, but she didn't care. All she wanted was to be gone, out from under his laser blue gaze that made her hormones hopscotch and her skin quiver. She knew what this was, lust, pure and simple, and she'd counseled enough people to know it was uncertain territory. She also knew she was vulnerable. God, she could scarcely remember the last time she'd made love.

He appeared to consider her comments about the motel but offered no suggestions. "I've got a couple of calls to make in the morning, but if you can wait until nine, I'll drive you."

She thought of doing the don't-bother-I'll-manage routine, and tossing her hair, but decided against it. He didn't want her here, so damn it, he shouldn't have let her come, but he had, so let him be inconvenienced. Having nicely made the entire nonevent of their meeting his fault gave her strange comfort. "Nine will be perfect," she said.

Esme went back to her meal. She wanted to gobble her food, get up, and run to her room, but somewhere along the way, she'd lost her appetite, but she made a determined play of eating, until finally pushing her plate back. "The dinner was wonderful," she said. "Thank you. If I don't see Peggy before I leave, please tell her how much I enjoyed it."

He stood as well, glanced at her half-eaten meal. "She won't believe me."

"Nine. I'll be ready." She walked out of the room.

Regally, she hoped.

Three

Dane finally gave up on sleeping, make that *trying* to sleep, by rolling over every sixty seconds, counting a herd of all-black sheep, and pummeling his innocent pillow into violent submission. At six-fifteen, the sun barreled in his window and ended the whole lousy exercise, and he got up—or as they used to say in the locker room, pole-vaulted—out of bed with the mother of all morning erections.

He'd been over-the-top rude last night. Acted like a real shit.

Marilee accused him of being a "crabby, miserable hermit" with no life. She might be right, but, damn it, the kind of deals he was working on took time and were a hell of lot more complicated than he'd imagined. With so much on the line he couldn't afford to screw up.

Although . . . like Janzen said—he rubbed his hand over his beard-stubbled jaw—the opportunities to invest weren't going away any time soon. Probably never.

And there were other opportunities. Of the female kind. Of the Esme Shane kind . . .

He strode naked to his shower, told himself if there had been an opportunity, he'd blown it, which was probably just as well. Not only did he not want to get up close and personal with one of his sister's friends, the woman was too . . . smooth for his taste, anyway. Too much into control. She probably spent all her time in bed analyzing a guy's technique against some checklist, then, when the sex was over, grading it in her journal.

Dane stepped out of the shower to towel off in front of the floor-to-ceiling window in his bathroom. One-way glass, it offered him a panoramic view down to his private beach, boat dock, and the ocean beyond. This morning the Gulf waters were bright with sun-lightened ripples—and a woman was striding purposefully toward the seashore, wearing a billowy skirt, one of those funny fisherman-style hats that travelers wore, and carrying what looked to be an artist's case. Esme Shane.

The wind caught her hat and sent it flying, leaving her long raven-colored hair to blow wildly, shine darkly in the brilliant morning sun. She turned, took a step toward the hat now rolling across his lawn, then looked at her watch, hesitated, and again headed for the beach.

Every muscle, tendon, and sinew in Dane's body tightened, shot to a sexual alert he hadn't felt in too long to remember.

He draped the towel around his neck and tried to ignore the board-stiff erection between his legs. Feeling voyeuristic and painfully aroused, he watched Esme until she disappeared along the path to the beach, watched until her head bobbed up farther along the shore, watched until she spread a blanket on the sand and kicked off her shoes. When she'd done that, she raised a hand to cover her eyes, first scanning the ocean and shoreline, then swiveling to look back at the house.

He wondered what her reaction would be if she knew a buck-naked male with a massive hard-on watched her through an upstairs window.

As if in response to his thought, she raised her eyes and appeared to gaze straight at him. About the time he started to wonder about the effectiveness of one-way glass, she sat down on the blanket and took a large drawing pad from her case.

She centered it on her lap, bent her dark head, and started to draw. She didn't look back.

Dane studied her a few seconds longer and made his decision. Whether or not it was one of his sane and logical ones was yet to be determined. But Esme Shane had captured his interest, and what captured his interest, he pursued. Relentlessly.

Hell, he'd already made love to her all night in his mind; why not go for the real thing?

Plus, he could use the diversion.

Twenty minutes later he headed for the beach. The morning, all bright sun and warm gusts of wind rippling the water, seemed lost on the woman rapt in the drawing of sand and curves of seagrass the ocean had gifted the shore with during the night's high tide.

She didn't notice his arrival until his shadow flowed across the surface of her pad, which gave him ample time to study the glossy darkness of her hair, the enticing curve of her neck, and the dedication she gave to her work.

She blinked, shielded her eyes from the sun, and looked up at him. "Oh, good morning." She frowned, but didn't drop her gaze. "Did you want to leave early?"

He shook his head, lifted the thermos. "Coffee with chicory. And Peggy's handmade beignets. You in?" He waved the sack of beignets in front of her, not above using the aroma of Peggy's fresh baking to gain points.

She hesitated, looked momentarily confused, then moved her drawing to her side and patted the empty blanket beside her. "I'm in."

He sat, poured them two coffees, and handed her heaven with sugar on it. *Thank you, Peggy.*

"These are incredible," she said after her second bite of beignet.

Dane used his thumb to brush some sugar from beside her lip. When he touched her she froze in place. Then, in an unusually awkward movement—for her—she looped her hair behind her ear, and turned away from him to look at the glistening ocean. "You live in a breathtakingly beautiful place," she said.

"Yes, I do," he agreed, following her gaze. "I'm a lucky man." *And I've decided to get luckier.*

"That's nice."

"Nice?"

"Nice that you know that. Sometimes people don't, uh, appreciate the things they have." She took another bite of her beignet and brushed some crumbs off her skirt. She looked uneasy under his gaze. "Although I can't imagine not appreciating this. Have you lived here long?"

"Five years. I built it before I sold the business. I'd owned the property for years and finally decided to do something with it." *With the property and my life,* he amended silently.

"It's a big house—you must have—" She stopped, straightened, and shot him a piercing glance. "Why do you keep looking at me like that?"

"Like what?" He drank some coffee.

"Like . . ." She lifted her beignet. "Like I'm one of these and you've been on a month-long fast."

He leaned back and propped himself on an elbow. "You're much more interesting than that"—he gestured toward the pastry in her still-raised hand—"and if we make the beignet a metaphor for sex, it's been a lot longer than a month."

She settled her gaze on him with ferocious curiosity. "And you're telling me this because?"

"Could be because you're a therapist and I need help with those sexuality issues you mentioned." He smiled and arched a brow. "Or it could be a lot less complicated."

"Go on."

"That as beignets go, you're proving hard to resist."

"You want to have sex with me?" she said, not hiding her surprise. "And here I had the impression you didn't much like me—worse than that, you distrust me."

"You know that old saying, 'you never get a second chance to make a first impression' . . . ?"

She eyed him noncommittally. Waited.

"It's not true," he finished.

"And have I somehow done something to indicate I *actually* want to impress you?"

"Not yet."

"Are you usually so full of yourself, McCoy, or is it something I bring out in you?" Now she looked annoyed, seriously annoyed.

Okay, so he was a little rusty at the old mating game.

He studied her a moment, thought about what she'd said. "You. Definitely." He picked up a handful of sand from beside the blanket, let it sift through his fingers. "Truth is, I'm not too fond of women with agendas—even if they are initiated by my sister. So last night I wanted your butt out of here. This morning . . ." *Watching the sway of your hips when you walked to the beach, seeing the sun on your hair, remembering your nipples hard against me—* "I changed my mind."

Her mouth slackened. "You really are . . . stunningly arrogant."

"So I'm told." He got up, stood over her, and looked down at her. When she didn't say anything more, he offered her his hand to help her up.

When she was standing in front of him, he touched her cheek with the back of his hand. "Stay or go, Esme. Your call." He gestured at the arc of beach fronting his home. "But now that we understand each other, you might as well make use of the place, take the two weeks and finish what you started."

"Understand each other? You and me?" Looking puzzled, she added, "Maybe you should explain that."

He lifted her chin. "You understand I'm not interested in Marilee and your brother's business venture. You understand I want you." He stroked her jawline. "And I know you want me."

"You know I—" Her expression showed equal parts shock and amazement. "I don't know what to say."

He took his hand from her face. "Nothing to say. Unless, of course, you'd like to deny what came across in that kiss last night."

She opened her mouth, closed it, then turned away from him. When she turned back, she shook her head. "Now I *really* don't know what to say."

"Easy. Say yes. We'll have dinner tonight, try not to insult each other, and see where things lead."

That intensely curious look again claimed her face. "Do I need to lock my bedroom door?"

"No. What you need to do is decide when to open it . . . to me. Until you do, nothing happens."

"Nothing?"

He nodded.

"This conversation is utterly bizarre."

"This conversation is honest."

"And that's something that matters to you? Honesty."

"That and not wasting a lot of time going after what I want." He touched her hair. "Which doesn't mean I don't know how to go slow . . . when slow is needed."

"You're very sure of yourself, aren't you?"

"Of myself? Yes. But not of you." Another truth, because something told him Esme was a natural born challenge.

"Marilee says you're 'unstoppable' when you go after something you want."

Dane thought a moment. "She's right, but in this case all it will take is a two-letter word. No."

She studied him for a long time, then a strange, enticing smile played across her mouth. "This could be fun."

He bent his head to be sure their eyes met. "Seduction should be fun. Isn't that what you tell your clients?"

She gestured toward her sketch book, raised a brow. "I don't have clients. Not anymore. Remember?"

He brushed his lips across hers, once, lightly, because he couldn't stop himself. She tasted like sea salt and sun, and he had so much adrenaline pumping through him at the thought of what was to come, he could damn well swim in it. "You do now."

Dane headed toward the house, turned to say over his shoulder, "If the weather holds, we'll eat on the patio. The sunset's worth the wait."

Two days, I'll have her in two days.

Esme, her fingertips touching her lips where Dane had kissed her, stared after him in utter amazement. Amazed at him. And herself, because she was still standing there, like the village idiot after a lobotomy.

She was crazy. She should shake the sand out of her shoes and run at top speed to the nearest airport. She was insane if she stayed within a hundred miles of Dane McCoy.

Instead, she plunked herself on the blanket, hugged her knees, and stared at the Gulf, not moving a muscle. Her mind, on the other hand, boiled with confusion and the shivery possibilities that had arrived gift-wrapped in that kiss she'd shared with Dane last night.

Not possibilities, Esme. Lust.

Of course . . . what was happening here was pure textbook. Going back to when the female of the tribe instinctively sought out the strongest, most dominant male to mate with, believing him the one most likely to provide healthy children and protection in a harsh and hungry world.

Sexuality 101.

Nice intellectual try, but it didn't wash.

She didn't live in a harsh and hungry world, and she'd never lacked for male attention. She liked men, she loved sex—and didn't game-play to hide either fact—but she'd never met a male specimen quite like Dane McCoy, either. One who felt so . . . oddly unsettling.

Her breathing turned as choppy as the sun-crested waves she stared at. She wasn't sure she even liked Dane, let alone wanted him, sexually speaking. Did she?

She couldn't . . .

Damn it, she did want him.

Some of him.

For a while.

What she didn't want was the mess of a relationship. Her divorce, ugly and rancorous, still scabbed her psyche. She didn't relish the idea of living her life alone, but she liked the idea of walking over the flame pit of divorce even less.

And aren't I getting ahead of myself!

Dane didn't want a relationship; he wanted sex, neat.

He couldn't have been more clear, yet here she was divorcing him already. She laughed. At herself. At the situation. She stopped laughing abruptly when she thought of the other possibilities. The sexual ones. Dane, the heat of him, his long, lean body. What they might have . . .

Sex with no strings attached. Sex for sex's mind-numbing, universe-tilting sake. Stop-the-world-I-want-to-get-off sex.

She sighed, closed her eyes a moment.

Sex in a king-size bed on black satin sheets.

Sex with candles burning, their flames twisting in the air to cast shadows over naked straining bodies.

Sex with a man who looked like a god.

Sex with a man who turned her on by touching her cheek.

Making love with a . . . stranger.

The last made her frown, but the heat, rising now, encircling her throat, made it difficult to draw a full breath, more difficult still to smother the concern. Esme had always been careful, discerning, about her lovers—and she'd at least known them for more than twenty-four hours!

She straightened abruptly.

A week; she'd give it a week. That would give her time to decide for sure if she wanted Dane in her bed, and if she was ready for a short-term affair.

She smiled and picked up her pencil and sketch pad; she'd speak to him tonight, set some ground rules—give him time to cool his too-arrogant heels.

Yes, I'll give it seven days . . .

* * *

Esme stood in the patio doorway. It opened westward toward the Gulf, and the panoramic view of the silvered waters beyond took Esme's breath away.

Then she saw Dane.

Dressed in casual khakis and a blindingly white shirt, he eclipsed the view and weakened her knees. He was pouring wine when she arrived, stopped when he spied her standing in the open patio door. The wine bottle clasped in his hand, his glance slid over her, slowly, hot and invasive, from her head to her sparkling sandaled toes. Esme's mouth went dry, and she stepped onto the cobblestone terrace, determined to play the game as a sophisticated, poised woman. Which, considering inside she was more of a bitch in heat, would be a challenge.

"You look wonderful." He held her gaze a moment, then returned to pouring the wine. He brought her a glass and held it out to her.

His scent, a subtle musk and citrus, overpowered the mysterious aroma of the aged burgundy in her glass. She breathed deeply, took in more of him to savor, before he tipped her glass with his, and she took a sip of the smooth, expensive wine. "Hmm," she said, her tone a hard-won mild one, "You have great taste in wine."

"You're still here," he said, ignoring her comment, his expression unreadable.

Esme glanced around the patio. There were several tables, some larger than others, the smallest abutted the railing. It was set for two in multicolored earthenware; a nest of candles burned at its center, fighting a timid battle with the brightness of the setting sun. "It doesn't look as if you doubted I would be."

"The result of wishful thinking." He looked at her over the rim of his glass.

She smiled at him. "Thank you."

He arched a brow in question.

"For not being sure. A woman needs to retain some mystery."

"Every woman is a mystery. Impossible to solve. And endlessly intriguing." He took her glass, then her hand, and drew her to the terrace rail. Looking down at her, he added in a low voice, "You, most of all."

"Ah . . . the seduction begins." And not too badly either. Her knees suddenly felt as though they'd been built from matchsticks and paste.

"Seduction?" He smiled—or nearly did—and Esme couldn't take her eyes off the easy mobility of his mouth, the promise of it. "Maybe. Or just a simple truth? Because you definitely intrigue me." He touched her chin, turned her face from his to the seashore. "Look. I don't want you to miss it."

The sun, low in the sky, and now a deep shimmering orange, turned the Gulf into burning glass, set it aglow as if it were seeded with flaming coals.

Dane stood beside her, his shoulder touching hers. "Something, isn't it?"

Esme looked up at him, reached up to stroke his clean-shaven face. "So are you, McCoy. So are you." When he turned to look at her, she stood on her toes and kissed his mouth, a feather kiss, a stolen taste, because, for now, that was all she'd risk. She stepped back.

His eyes were an inky burning blue when they met hers. "You sure you want to eat . . ."

Ignoring her breathing, which came perilously close to a most unladylike pant, she forced a light laugh. "Oh, yes. I definitely want to eat . . ." Not above a little seduction of her own, she ran her tongue over her lower lip, touched his mouth with one finger. ". . . Peggy's wonderful cooking."

"Jesus!" he murmured on an extended breath. "This is going to be the longest meal of my life."

She cocked her head, looked at him from under her lashes. "Good sex is all about patience, the art of anticipation."

He rolled his eyes, gave her another brief smile. "If that's true, I probably do need therapy."

"Which I'll be happy to provide"—she tapped his chin

playfully—"after we eat." *And if I can get down enough to sustain a hummingbird, it will be a miracle.*

Maybe seven days was asking too much . . .

As if on cue, Peggy came out with a tray, laden with a large salad and an array of tantalizing finger food. Delicate scents drifted toward the sunset, fused with the aromatic spices of cajun cooking and the fiery kick of Mexico.

"I didn't know what you liked." Dane gestured toward the table. "So I asked Peggy for a selection."

"Perfect."

He pulled out her chair, filled her wineglass, and took the seat across from her, turning away from the table and stretching his long legs in front of him, apparently in no hurry to eat.

The setting sun shadowed half his face and burnished the other side to pale copper.

"I'm glad you stayed," he said, settling his unearthly blue eyes on her in a very earthy way.

"I'm not certain I can say the same. Not yet."

"Then I'll have to make you certain."

Four

An hour later a breeze blew in from the Gulf, light but laden with chill. When Dane saw Esme rub her bare shoulders to warm them, he rose. "It's turning cold," he said, stating the obvious, and looking for any opportunity to move, escape the sexual hunger twisting his gut like a badly applied tourniquet. "Let's go inside." The last interminable hour had rattled Dane, and he'd learned something. He'd forgotten how to wait, forgotten how not to have what he wanted when he wanted it, and forgotten how to make charm-talk.

And he'd underestimated Esme's effect on him. Jesus, he'd gone hard, then harder, watching her simply savor an oyster . . . or a goddamn cracker. Esme was trouble—and he couldn't wait to get into it.

Unless he missed his guess, she was playing him, and even knowing it, he enjoyed it. He might not trust her, but when his cock left him brain enough to think on it, he discovered that while he was frustrated, he was enjoying himself for the first time in what seemed forever.

"I'd rather take a walk." She stood beside him, dropped her napkin on the table.

He ran a finger along her collarbone. "Upstairs?" He felt the pulse jump in her throat. The breeze, not so cold now, blew between them.

"Not tonight," she said, her mouth warm, her gaze half-lidded. She placed a hand on his chest, rubbed lightly. The heat of her hand burned through his white cotton shirt. "Not that you're not tempting."

"I didn't know I was in for an exercise in willpower."

"You're not, but . . . look," she added, and gestured toward the sweeping seascape. "It's so beautiful."

He looked, saw a pale ribbon of moonlight crossing a wind-rustled sea to touch and brighten the sand on the beach. Beautiful. Yes. A detour from the bedroom? Definitely. Esme wasn't through torturing him yet. "I'll get you a jacket."

"No, thanks. I'm fine."

He offered her his hand and she took it. Hers felt small, cool, and strong in his, and he lifted it to his mouth, turned her palm to his lips and kissed it. "You're *very* 'fine.' And if you were a business deal, this . . . transaction would already be in the completed column. I think you know that."

She frowned, and for the briefest moment she looked uncertain. "I'm not a business deal, Dane. I'm a woman who intends to take her time. A woman who likes to be sure of what she's getting herself into." She squeezed his hand, smiled at him. "No matter how potent the temptation."

He didn't miss the determination in her gaze and revised his original estimate. *Three days.* "Let's go, then." He made an immediate decision to provide some sexual torment of his own. "I'll show you the *Too Much*."

"The *Too Much*?"

"My boat. I bought it last year."

"Interesting name." Her look was curious. "What does it mean?"

He hesitated. "Nothing."

* * *

A few minutes later Dane helped her board *Too Much*. The boat wasn't big—maybe thirty-five or forty feet—which, considering Dane's fortune, surprised Esme. It also wasn't new and appeared to be in the process of being restored . . . beautifully.

"A Chris-Craft from the sixties," he said. "She's a work in progress." He ran a hand lovingly along the polished wood railings, gave her a lingering look. "Like you."

"First I'm a business deal. Now I'm a boat?" She couldn't help her grin. "That's a move forward. I guess."

He took her hand. "Come with me."

He led her to the front of the boat, stopped at the prow, and nudged her ahead of him. "Not exactly the *Titanic,* but the view is good."

From behind, he gripped her by the waist and drew her flush to his chest. The heat of his body against her back, the gusts of his breath across her temple, his erection pressed against her buttocks, made her head swim. If she'd ever felt this powerful a sexual attraction, she couldn't remember it, or it had been exorcised by Dane McCoy's laying-on-of-hands. Hands he slid now to around her middle, splayed wide over her stomach. Her breath stalled in her throat.

"Like it?" he whispered into her hair.

In sensory overload, achingly aware of him, her mind was a fog, dense and blank. She couldn't for the life of her figure out what he was talking about. Nothing registered except his light, almost careless, touch, his hands sliding around her belly; first up to under her breasts, drifting down—but not down far enough to touch her in the place she yearned to be touched.

"The view, Esme. How do you like the view?" He pulled her hair back, kissed her nape, nestled his mouth close to her ear.

Seven days . . . definitely too long. Five at the max.

She turned in his arms, looked into his face, every angle of it silvered by moonlight. "I like this one better." Esme ran her hands across the muscles of his chest. They tightened under her palms, like strong ropes pulled taut, to be ready . . . able. She traced the muscles down to the belt, circling his lean waist, ran a finger along the leather, just inside the band. She looked up to see him briefly close his eyes, then open them, slam his gaze into hers, daring and dangerous. He clasped her hand, held it to his chest.

"Enough," he said gruffly. "Given that 'waiting' you're so intent on."

She didn't intend to study his mouth, but she did, drawn as if under a spell. She didn't intend the rush of moisture at the apex of her thighs, but it came, and she didn't intend to say, "Kiss me, Dane," but she did.

His mouth came down on hers hard and hungry. He spread his legs, tugged her into them and slipped his hands down to grasp her rear, hold her against the steel jut of his penis.

The kiss slowed, turned deep and voluptuous, and she gave herself to it, taking his tongue, probing his mouth with hers, until her lungs were as empty as her mind. His hot hands grew urgent on her body, and his fingers dug deep into the soft flesh of her buttocks, each an anchor to hold them fast.

"Jesus, your mouth is heaven." His expression hardened. "I don't want to wait."

Esme, breathing hard, her underwear dampened with need, her head as useless as a half-filled balloon, took a step back, out of Dane's arms, away from the heat of him.

The cold claimed her instantly, and she massaged her upper arms. "I do want to wait." She didn't, but she had to, because this instant lust, this sudden . . . blaze between them was bewildering. Too fast. Too primal. She'd always counseled her clients to relax about sex, worked to free them from inhibitions that kept them from enjoying their bodies and those of their lovers—as she did herself—but that hadn't meant leaving the brain out of the equation.

Dane didn't try to hide his frustration. "Why, for God's sake? I want you. You want me. And we're both over voting age. What could be simpler?"

"There is nothing simple about this." She looked up at him, squared her gaze with his. "Maybe you'll understand this. I have a rule and I've never broken it. I don't fuck on the first date."

For a second he stared at her, as if he couldn't assimilate what she'd said, then a smile, slow and easy, tilted his lips. "I haven't had to work this hard for a woman in a long time."

"Hard? You call having to wait a few days hard?"

He lifted her chin, brushed his mouth over hers—stopped when their breaths fused and need tore up the air between them. "When it comes to waiting for you? Beyond hard and into impossible." He rubbed her mouth with his thumb. "You have any idea what it's going to be like for me tonight? Knowing you're a bedroom away?"

She nodded. "Yes, I do. Because, believe it or not, I'll be sleeping on the identical bed of hot coals."

Maybe four days would be enough . . .

The next morning, Peggy knocked on her door. It was past eight. "Ms. Shane," Peggy said, rapping again. "I've brought you coffee."

Esme, sitting at the desk under the window, had been up since six, working on the book layout. And, yes, delaying seeing Dane, which wouldn't have been a problem if she hadn't spent the entire night acting opposite him in a triple-X movie that put *Sex And The City* on a par with Barney. Heat crawled up her throat, and her body thundered even now remembering it.

Afraid every scene she'd played with him would show on her face, she'd decided to wait, connect with real life and get her wits about her before going downstairs. If she didn't she'd attack him over the breakfast table. She smiled. Not really the worst idea she'd ever had. Although the man was going to have to be damn good in bed to top the movie version.

Still smiling, she headed to the door, clad in the cotton robe she'd put on after her shower. She opened the door to the aroma of fresh baked . . . something and sniffed appreciatively.

"Something smells so good it has to be sinful." She stepped aside to let in a tray-laden Peggy.

Peggy carried the tray to the table near the window seat, and set out a service for one. "Mr. McCoy said you liked my beignets so I brought a couple. And some fruit." She poured a big cup of steaming coffee.

Esme picked up a beignet and sighed. "Peggy, you should be bronzed. No, make that gilded—in pure gold. Thank you."

She smiled, walked to—and started making—Esme's bed. "When would you like your lunch?" she asked, smoothing the duvet.

"Whenever Mr. McCoy wants it is fine with me."

"Oh, he's not here. Mr. Janzen called on some business matter early this morning and he flew off. Didn't say exactly when he'd be back, said maybe a day or two."

So much for seduction . . .

Esme was ridiculously disappointed. "Then, twelve or twelve-thirty for lunch will be fine. Thanks."

When Peggy was gone, Esme went to the window and gave herself ten minutes to sort through her feelings. Dear God, she was actually hurt. How stupid was that! Dane was committed to his work—was crazed by it, if Marilee was to be believed—which made it insane for her to think he'd put his business on hold for her. When it came to a choice of money or sex, for men like McCoy, the decision was a no-brainer. His abrupt departure was a good lesson for her, though, a reminder to stay on her toes and keep her emotional distance.

Which left only one thing to do: get that *grip* everyone was always yammering about and do something.

She dressed and was on the beach in minutes. The Gulf water, glorious and bright under the morning sun, lifted her spirits somewhat and she settled in to work, Dane—and last night's movie—never far from her mind. But she refused to fret like an adolescent over a man she'd met only two days before. She absolutely would not. He had his life, she had hers.

It wasn't as if they were heading for hearts, flowers, and

minivans. More like a king-size bed, where, if she got really lucky—and Dane McCoy knew what he was doing—she'd enjoy some seriously fine sex. An activity, she reluctantly admitted, that had, somewhere along the way, grown stale and uninviting and been pushed to the bottom of her priority list. And wouldn't some of her old clients laugh at that, after all her lecturing about the necessity of a healthy sex life. Yes, sexual . . . release with Dane would be good for her. Healthy.

Which was all she wanted. *Wasn't it?*

Her hand slipped and the charcoal pencil she'd been holding scarred the drawing on her lap. *Damn it!* She erased her mess, told herself to focus, gritted her teeth, and started again.

The day was long and productive; another few like it and Esme figured she'd have most of the drawings she needed for the book—and one other—one she'd begun sketching late in the day. The drawing, started on a whim, had engrossed her so completely her entire body ached from the rigid posture imposed by the intense concentration.

Rubbing the tired muscles in her lower back, she got up and headed for the house. There was still light, but she was beat. It was Peggy who offered to bring her dinner to her room, and Esme accepted gratefully, her thoughts on a leisurely, warm bath.

Close to nine, there was a knock on her door. Peggy to pick up the tray, she assumed. She tightened the sash on her robe and opened the door.

Dane's eyes swept over her. "Can I talk you into a brandy on my deck?"

Esme was so surprised to see him, she had trouble finding her voice. "I thought you were away . . . for a couple of days."

"I came back early." He lounged in the open doorway. "Because you're here." He'd obviously just showered because his dark hair was damp and caught shine from the light in the hallway behind him. His eyes slid down, over her cotton robe to her bare feet. "You're ready for bed," he said, his voice intoning nothing, his eyebrows arched. "Which is either convenient for me—or another test of my willpower."

Feeling oddly disoriented, Esme scrunched up the front of her robe and held it tightly closed under her chin, as if she were a nun facing the devil himself. She had no idea why, because what she really wanted to do was throw herself into this particular devil's arms and let modesty—and any lingering reluctance—be damned. "I was thinking about going to bed," she said. "Until you showed up at my door."

"Now, what are you thinking about?" Not waiting for her answer, he touched the hand holding her robe closed and pried it open. He undid the sash, watched the robe fall open to reveal her gray silk night shift. Scoop necked, mid-thigh, and whisper light, it was her favorite sleep wear. "Nice," he said, his voice low. "Soft cotton on the outside, slick silk on the inside." He touched the rolled edge at the neck of the shift, studied it a moment, then pulled his hand back. His expression grew intense, locked with hers. "How about that brandy?"

"I don't often drink brandy."

"Another taboo? Like the no-fuck rule?"

She smiled. "I might get . . . careless, drop my defenses."

"I should be so lucky." He smiled back.

"Give me a second to change and I—"

"You don't need to change." He slid his eyes over her. "You're dressed perfectly for . . . a nightcap."

Esme looked up at him, saw the deep sensual light in his eyes, knew exactly what he meant by a nightcap. "We're talking about sex, aren't we?"

"I haven't thought about anything else all day. But not just sex. Sex with *you*." He ran a finger along her jaw. "I want you, under me, over me, and any other way that suits us both."

She hesitated, tried to think, while his demanding gaze, easy touch, and her own clamoring hormones made hash of her logic. Damn it! She didn't know him any better tonight than she did yesterday—except for her home movie. If she did this, went to his room now, it would be rash, crazy—the most foolish thing she'd ever done.

Dane began a new pattern with his finger, drew it down, under her ear to her throat, down again, stopping at the neckline of her silk shift.

She swallowed . . . decided every woman should be foolish—at least once in her life—especially when a man like Dane McCoy came along. She pulled in a breath, and with a short prayer to the angel up there who supervised the Sexual Affairs department, she said, "I hope it's good brandy."

He took her hand. "The best."

The inside of his room—no, Esme thought, looking around the spacious interior, the right word was suite, which was subtly decorated in chocolate and cream and with as little furniture in it as was necessary. Surprisingly ascetic, she thought. Dane closed his bedroom door, strode to the wall on the far side of the bed, and turned on the stereo. Soft piano jazz joined with the moonlight coming in through the high windows to fill the room.

He handed her a brandy. "Are you nervous?" he asked, sipping his drink and looking as if he had all the time in the world.

"No. I think I'm more surprised than anything."

"Surprised?"

"That I'm here, in your room. So soon." She paused, took a breath. "And given how impetuous this is—at least for me—I think it's important we're clear about our expectations." And, God, didn't she sound cool and composed, as if her heart weren't racing, her blood roaring at the sight of him—while he studied her, looking as casual as a customer in a fast-food line with a two-hour lunch.

She went on. "When this is over, we pretend it never happened. No strings. No telephone calls"—she gestured toward the computer in the corner of his room—"no e-mails. Nothing. We'll be having sex, pure and simple. A natural human expression in response to—" She stopped, knew she was babbling.

"Lust at first sight?" He eyed her quizzically, then his brow furrowed. "Are you always this detached about making love?"

"I don't know what you mean." She moved away from him.

"I mean, do you always over-think it, analyze the outcome ten ways to Sunday?" He sipped his brandy, kept his eyes on her, and waited for her answer—all the while looking vaguely amused.

Esme had no trouble seeing the effect his inscrutable and unblinking gaze would have on his competitors, no trouble seeing how he'd become so successful. Because she had no idea what he was seeing—or what he was thinking. "If you mean, am I cautious?" she said. "Yes. Always." *And growing increasingly uneasy with your questions.* She prided herself on her openness, her knowledge of sex, her possession of sexual skills that had more than satisfied lovers in the past—and would no doubt satisfy this one. "Does that bother you?" She lifted her chin.

He shook a slow negative. "Not unless you take that caution to bed. There's always the chance the . . . *detachment* required to do your job as a therapist has"—he took a step toward her, and moonlight pierced the amber liquid in his glass, gave it a dull glow—"has blunted your own hunger. Made having sex pure textbook."

"I don't—"

He touched her mouth and shook his head again. "Don't say anything. I'll answer my own question . . . soon enough." He finished his brandy, set his glass beside hers on the table. "But if what you want, to set your mind at rest, is a 'no-strings' addendum, you've got it." He let his eyes wander over her, his gaze explicit and half-lidded. "Because right now, I'm prepared to give you exactly what you want."

"So you can get what you want," she stated, eyeing him closely.

He gave her one of his half smiles. "Exactly."

"Then we agree; what's between us is sex. Only sex," she

repeated, a surge of something a lot like panic rushing up her throat. "We're moving far too fast for it to be anything else."

" 'Fast?'" he echoed, giving her an amazed look. "Hell, if it had been up to me, I'd have had you naked two seconds after you walked off my plane." His eyes darkened.

He didn't touch her. And, God, she wanted him to touch her.

So she touched him, his damp hair, the lean strong cords in his neck, his powerful shoulders. Leaving her hands to rest palm-flat against the wall of his chest, she said, "It's up to you now, Dane McCoy." She kissed his jaw, the side of his neck.

His intake of breath was sharp and deep. "I take it we're done talking the business end of this relationship?"

"Absolutely."

"Thank God," he murmured. He gripped her shoulders, vise-like, and pulled her hard to his body. He took her mouth hungrily, his tongue tasting all of her, hers tasting all of him, deeply, wetly. The heat was instant, trembling, and their bodies fused, one into the other.

Dane pulled back, took her face in his hands, and dipped his head. "If we don't slow this down, it's going to be no fun at all." A brief dark smile crossed his mouth. "I guess you know by now 'detachment' isn't one of my strengths." He slid his warm hands under the lapels of her robe, shoved it from her shoulders.

The next moment, he'd grasped the hem of her shift and pulled it over her head, let it fall to join her robe on the floor. The moment after that she was cradled in his arms, being carried naked to his giant bed.

He settled her in the center of it, stood back, and started to strip off his clothes—and he didn't waste any time doing it.

His shoulders were broad, his body lean and fit—his erection . . . breathtaking. He gazed down at her in time to see her look at him and blink. "Standard equipment," he said, his tone gruff.

If what Dane had was standard equipment, Esme had been

spending way too much time at the mini-market. Dane must have been the envy of every guy in the locker room.

When he was stretched out beside her, he nuzzled her ear, then raised himself over her to look down into her eyes. Esme forced her unruly heart to ease back a notch, find a steadier beat, but it resisted, pounded harder, seemed to grow under the intensity of his gaze until it felt too big for her chest. He blew some hair off her forehead, smoothed tendrils behind an ear.

She waited for the usual words a man said to a woman freshly naked and in his arms . . . *God, you're beautiful* . . . and waited, and waited.

"One of your earlobes is smaller than the other," he said, and ran a finger along the shell of her ear. "Did you know that?"

"Uh . . . no."

He kissed her ear. "This one," he murmured, and his breath, skittering along her neck, had the odd effect of making her eyes close.

"Good to kno—"

"Shush, no talking. You can make notes later."

"I don't under—"

He took her mouth again, shutting her down, making her breath rise, spin, and stall in her throat. He ran a hand down between her breasts, over to squeeze her waist, then slid it over the outside of her thigh, up the inside, briefly touching her mound. His hand was hot, the pressure of it expert and strong, and under the heat of it, she started to open for him.

"No, not yet. Keep your legs closed. No matter what I do, keep them closed."

Esme, dimly aware she was in bed with a man who made his own rules, nodded, met his gaze, tried to see him through the sensual fog that came and went across her line of vision.

He slid his hand up the front of her thigh, pressed his palm against her pubis, then gently probed the tight juncture at the apex of her thighs with one deft finger. Feeling his way to her clitoris, he stroked it slow and easy, building pressure, and breathless pleasure, with each precise rub and swirl of his finger.

Esme gasped and bucked.

In the limited space between her closed legs, everything was pressure, heavy and demanding; everything was confined, uncomfortably, frustratingly caged. She throbbed, tried to thrust herself up, open for him, but he straddled her, his strong legs on either side of hers, a vise, holding them together.

"Dane . . ." She looked up at him, knew her need was in her eyes. "Let me—"

He shook his head, brushed his mouth over hers, then took both her wrists in one hand and held them fast above her head. He didn't stop, neither the warm kisses across her throat and shoulders, nor the mind-numbing rub of his finger, dipping in and out of her tight crevice, making her ache all the while, forcing her to take it, legs closed.

His every move was smooth, expert, and in a distant part of her mind she remembered Marilee saying something about her brother not liking women. Well, if how he was pleasuring her was any indication, Dane McCoy had *liked* more than his share.

"You're wet," he said, his voice low. "All honeyed." He took his finger from her crease, slowly ringed her jutting nipple with it, then bent to her breast and suckled her, taking her deep and luxuriously.

His mouth drawing on her, she nearly came off the bed. Delirious, she fought him, desperate to spread herself, feel the warm air on her exposed vulva, feel *him* on her vulva. Still, he kept her pinned beneath him, immobile, desire whipping through her, a hot wind, swirling and fierce, unrelentingly contained.

He moved over her, rested the weight of his erection against her mound, making sensual primitive moves she knew tortured him as much as they tortured her.

He lifted his head, moistened her dry lips with his tongue and kissed her deeply, then he slid down—let his length and hardness rest in the valley created by her closed thighs—and gave his attention to her other breast, pulling the nipple deep into his mouth, lapping at it with his tongue.

Esme felt another rush between her legs, and lifted herself to him, crazed and increasingly desperate, every fiber and nerve in her body fire-driven and scorched.

"Now," Dane growled from somewhere above her.

She looked at him, so dazed she couldn't understand what he meant.

He released her wrists, shifted his lean hard body down, and planted his knee as a lever between her calves. "Open your legs, Esme. I want to look at you in the moonlight."

She did as she was told, and he immediately put his hands on her knees, spread her wide. He studied her with dark hungry eyes, and she saw his chest expand and contract as if he'd run a marathon in the desert. "You," he said, running a finger deeply through her drenched and oversensitized crease, "are cream, slick and rich." He tore his eyes from her pubis and met her own fogged gaze. "In the moonlight you shine like poured gold." He looked back down at her mound, now raised in full display, and his eyes went heavy lidded. He opened her more, spread the lips of her vulva until she felt the cool evening air against her heated center. "I could look at you forever." He lightly kissed her clitoris, pulled back, and stroked her softly, his eyes never leaving her sex.

Esme panted, forced her eyes open wide enough to see his face, and said as sternly as her dry voice allowed, "You'd better plan on doing a lot more than looking, McCoy."

Five

Dane went down on her. Holding her hips, he held her to his lips, seared her with his mouth and tongue.

"Oh, God. I can't . . ."

Like a flock of disturbed birds, all thought left her, and the only sound in her brain was the beat of her wild heart. Her body quaked and trembled, and she held his dark head as if it were heaven itself.

Which it was . . .

He licked her long and deeply, lifted his head, and replaced his fabulous mouth with two fingers, unmoving as if there to hold his place. "You're going to come now, Esme," he murmured, his voice hoarse and ragged. "Hard and fast, over and over again."

His eyes were midnight blue, and she didn't breathe, couldn't breathe. Her eyes fixed on his, saw the determination embedded there, the feral glow of male power. "I'm going to take you deeper."

He slipped his fingers into her and pressed her nub gently with his thumb. She moaned, thrust toward him . . .

"Easy, easy . . ."

She thrust again, high, demanding. Groaning, she grabbed

handfuls of his hair, curled her fingers in it, but still he held back, toyed with her, caressed her. Lower now.

Her head fell back against the pillow, every sense in thrall, expectant.

He swept her with his tongue, long and lavishly, nuzzled her . . . His groan vibrated against her, carried into her.

"You're incredible," he murmured against her burning, quivering flesh. "So open. Ready." He pulled her engorged, hardened nub into his mouth, sucked—

Esme exploded.

"Oh, God—" She hurled the words, hoarse and guttural, into the moonlit room and fell back.

Dane growled against her shivering, vulnerable flesh, burrowed into her heat, took her deeper, took her high. Again.

Unable to stop herself, she came again, thrust herself up, wave after wave of sensation pulsing through her depleted body.

Dane lifted his head, stared down at her with ink-blue eyes, and stroked the hot, delicate tip of her. "Again, Esme. One more time." He tugged her clitoris, the barest of pulls, a rasp of friction on her drenched, sensitized vulva . . .

"I can't, I can't." But even numb, spent, she felt it build, hover in the depths of her, far, far below.

"You will." He tugged again, skillfully, mercilessly . . . achingly gentle, as if the soft flesh of her sex was a silken thread.

Silk delicate enough to float in the heat and wind emanating from her burning, thrashing body.

Silk strong enough to reach her depths, find the coming, the rapture, the scream . . .

Esme swung her head from side to side, clasped the sheets with rigid fists. "No!" she cried, when he circled her, pulled her silk again. Once. In absolute perfection.

She imploded, convulsed, a third stunning climax rolling and shuddering to her core.

Barely able to breathe, she looked up from under heavy-lidded eyes into Dane's dark, tension-ravaged face as he pulled away from her and rolled on a condom.

He centered himself at her wet, still pulsing opening, and entered her in one strong, penetrating stroke. Esme's body, beyond ready for him, took him fully, and she widened her eyes, watched his face as he at once left her and joined with her, watched the taut, otherworldly expression that claimed his handsome features, the slow closing of his eyes as he thrust into her. She savored the thickness of him buried deep within her, then the strain and heave of his muscles when he emptied himself, gained his own blinding release.

For a time their bodies, slick and scorched from sex, were sealed to each other, their breathing the only sound in the large room. Then Dane cursed mildly, mumbled something about condom duty, and left her to go to the bathroom.

When he came back, he stretched out beside her, pulled her close and kissed her temple. "You, Esme Shane, are spectacular."

"What I am, is exhausted." She snaked a hand across his chest, played in the curls there.

"And satisfied."

"I hope that wasn't the lead-in to the *was-it-as-good-for-you-as-it-was-for-me* question."

"Wasn't a question." He ran his hand over her belly and squeezed her waist. "I'm neither blind nor deaf."

She smiled. "You really are arrogant, you know."

"Hmm." He nuzzled her neck.

And such an amazing lover, you could be addictive. She rubbed her eyes, sighed, and wondered if there was a rehab center for withdrawal from Dane McCoy. Fortunately, she had a few days before she had to find out. She nestled closer to him, and her gaze drifted to the window. The pale clouds that had covered the moon drifted away, and Esme, her energy spent, her senses languorous, watched the moonlight spill into the bedroom.

Her thoughts moved from satiation to curious.

"You're a wonderful lover," she said. "I've read about that techniq—"

"Don't," he said, propping himself up on one elbow and looking down at her.

"Don't what?"

"Don't start analyzing." He circled her nipple with a slow lazy finger, and her breath caught. God, she couldn't want him again this soon. And he couldn't possibly be . . . up for it if she did.

Maybe she could locate some of his old girlfriends and they could form their own self-help program. She stretched under his hands, and he bent to lightly kiss her peaking nipple.

"Let's go for a swim. Then come back here for"—he circled the nipple with his tongue—"more of the same."

"I didn't bring a suit," she said, trying to talk while he nibbled on her.

His head came up. "The beach is private, you don't need a suit." He rolled out of bed and stood over her, six-feet-one of gorgeous masculinity, panther-like, confident, and waiting for her. His sex, heavy between his legs, tempted her to initiate that "more of the same" he'd mentioned, right now. She couldn't take her eyes off him and couldn't resist reaching out to touch him, cup him. "A swim sounds wonderful," she said, lifting her eyes to his. "But when it's over, it's my turn to . . . play. Agreed?" She squeezed him gently.

He tensed and briefly closed his eyes, didn't hide his reaction to her fondling, and she saw his stomach contract. He gazed down at her, but his back was to the window, and she couldn't see his face. "If I didn't agree to a proposition like that, I'd have to turn in my man badge."

She smiled and pulled back her hand. "From what you just gave me, I'd say there's little or no chance of that."

The sandy beach was moon-silvered, the night warm—the water of the Gulf cold, once you got out a ways. Esme lasted sixty seconds and ran for the beach, toward the blanket and towels he'd brought from his bedroom.

Dane forced himself to stay in the water, get his goddamn sex-ravaged brain working again. If he planned to slow himself down, he'd need all the cold water he could get. Otherwise he'd never let Esme out of his bed, be all over her like a dick-brained teenager—which is exactly what he felt like.

He went under again, came up, shook his head, and finger-combed his hair back. His gaze shot to the beach and Esme waved at him, made a show of shuddering, and mouthed, *You're crazy!*

He was crazy, all right, but not in the way she meant it.

He watched her dry herself, her skin all shivery and pale. Her generous breasts, so recently in his hands, now plump and loose under the white beach towel she'd wrapped herself in.

God, she was gorgeous. All curves, all woman, all heat under his hands. The way she'd exploded under him, holding nothing back, giving him . . . all of her; if he'd had the stamina he'd have held her there forever.

Even the cool Gulf water couldn't stop him from getting hard.

He dove again, swam swiftly away from the beach, then turned and headed back. If he'd hoped muscle power would trump brain activity, he was wrong. He couldn't stop thinking about her.

Dane had read that a woman in climax was at her most beautiful, but he'd never believed it before tonight, until he'd watched Esme reach for it, her eyes heavy lidded, her mouth slack and moist, her nipples stone hard, like hot ice in his mouth. She'd glowed, like roiling, melting gold, her long black hair a spray of sin across his pillow.

He'd wanted to hold her in that place, that just-before-coming place, for hours.

Hell, he might yet.

If he didn't freeze his balls off first. He looked at the sky in time to see a drift of dark gray clouds cover it, then headed for the shore, and in a few easy strokes he was there.

Esme smiled at him and shivered theatrically. "You're a better man than I am, McCoy."

"It's not that cold if you hang in there." He reached for a towel.

She wore hers *sarong*-style and was covered from breasts to knees.

He should have brought smaller towels. He started to dry himself.

"Let me." She took the towel from his hand.

She dried his back first, then came around to his chest. Starting at his shoulders, she worked her way across his chest and headed down.

Looking up at him, she nodded at his more unpredictable anatomy, and said—damn near purring—"Do you mind?"

"I'd mind if you didn't," he said, which was the absolute fucking truth. He couldn't wait to feel her hands on him.

Esme wasn't shy—thank God—and she took her time. When she finished with him, it would have a taken a seven-mile swim off the coast of Antarctica to bring him down.

She dropped the towel to the sand and ran a finger lightly along his now fully-at-attention cock. "You've been . . . gifted." She took the weight of him in her hands, looked into his eyes, and squeezed him gently. Her smile altered subtly, shifted to intense. "Very gifted." Again she traced him.

His mouth turned into a desert, and every atom in his body waved a white flag. He spread his legs to hold ground, but if she expected an answer, he didn't have one. Hell, he'd had nothing to do with what nature endowed. All he did was try to make the most of it. Although at the moment, Esme was doing it for him.

She dropped to her knees in front of him, set her hands on his legs, pressed her thumbs in the crevice of his thighs.

His breath lumped in his throat like a goddamn medicine ball.

Jesus, she was going to do him! And he'd probably topple like a mile-high bald cypress. "I don't think this is a—" Her mouth found him, and his germ of an idea that this particular outdoor activity might not be workable was crushed by a tongue stroke.

He was toast.

Her hands slid around him, grasped his ass, and held him to her lips, her tongue—as if he needed holding. He spread his fingers on her head, forked them into her straight silky hair—managed not to crush her skull when she took his tip in her mouth, tasted him, took him deeper.

His head jerked back, and he sealed his eyelids to a tight close, let her take complete control over a piece of his anatomy that generally had a stubborn, one-track mind of its own. The sacrifice was worth every lick, stroke, and tug.

He heard the low murmuring in his throat, felt the build up, and hit the red zone. He had to move, or—

"Baby, you'd better . . ." He didn't have to finish.

She rolled on the condom he'd brought from the house and licked and kissed her way up his stomach to his chest. Taking a nipple in her teeth, she gave it a sharp bite, then looked up at him, her gaze sultry with challenge, and dropped her towel. "I'm ready for you," she said, and stretched out on the blanket.

Spreading her legs, she ran her finger through heaven. "Really ready," she murmured.

For Dane, "ready" didn't do his pounding erection justice, and he didn't need a second invitation. He covered her, grasped her buttocks, and centered himself, his raging, overheated body offering no time for finesse, for slow hands—or leisurely penetration. He went in wild, one powerful, mind-bending stroke, and she took him to the hilt. Her walls squeezed him, and he tore apart, came in a seething boil of a rush that blanked his brain and damn near stopped his fucking heart.

When he managed to drag some air into his lungs, it didn't bring clearheaded sanity. It brought confusion. And a problem.

He didn't want Esme Shane to leave.

She was stroking his hair, running her fingers through it in a gesture that was as sensual as it was soothing. "I'm . . . glad we did this," she whispered, her voice barely audible over his heart, which was still pumping like a bastard in search of its natural rhythm.

He moved to her side and immediately missed her warmth, the softness of her skin. He kissed her shoulder. "The swim or the sex?"

"The swim was cold, the sex was . . ."

"Not?" he finished, touching her hair. "Although the swim thing worked well enough for me." She turned to smile at him, the hazy, drugged smile of a tired, ultra-relaxed woman. Just then a breeze, cool and sharp, came off the water, and drops of rain hit his cheek and bare shoulder. Tropical rain could come suddenly in the Gulf—and heavily. "We'd better go," he said. "Or we'll get soaked."

He gathered up the blanket and towels, and they started toward the house, picking up their pace when the rain and wind paired up to create the beginning of a summer storm.

Back in his bedroom, Esme, still wrapped in her towel, picked up her silk shift and robe, frowned, and scanned the room's floor. "Have you seen my slippers?"

Dane came from behind and put his arms around her. "What are you doing?"

"Getting my things," she said, stating the obvious, and leaning back into him.

"Why?"

"Because"—she turned in his arms—"I'm going back to my room."

He hadn't expected this, didn't want it. "My bed's plenty big enough for two."

"Your bed is big enough for a small army." She touched his face, grinned. "And I appreciate the offer to share, but it's late, and I'm planning an early start tomorrow."

"If you're worried about Peggy or Janzen, don't be. They mind their own business."

That comment made her frown, then she smiled—a bit weaker, though. "And I take it you give them some 'business to mind' from time to time?"

"I'm not a priest, Esme."

She laughed then, but it was a cool laugh and didn't lighten her eyes much. "And I never took you for one, but we had sex, Dane, healthy, recreational sex. Great sex." She kissed his mouth lightly, one of those feathery relative-type kisses that old friends and family exchange. Then, spotting a pair of fuzzy mules at the foot of his bed, she picked them up.

What the hell was going on here? he wondered. "So if the sex was healthy and recreational, what the hell would sleeping together be?"

She paused. "Personal." She walked to the door, turned back. "Will I see you at breakfast?"

Smooth Esme was back, full force, every defense manned and barricaded; add to that, her change in attitude had taken him completely by surprise. He didn't know what the hell to do with her, so he was left to answer her question. "I generally grab a coffee from the kitchen and go to work."

"Work. Of course. Marilee said you work very hard." A fact that apparently didn't please her, because she frowned before adding, "Later in the day, then. We can have dinner, then maybe have sex again. Would that work for you? Some bondage maybe. I'm not fond of it myself, but—" She shrugged, raised a questioning brow.

Dane couldn't find his voice, and someone had put clamps on his damn brain. "I, uh . . . I'm not into that stuff." Jesus, he sounded like a choirboy. Obviously, as openminded as he was about sex, he was generations behind the ex-therapist. Hell, the next thing she'd be talking about would be—

"Leather, then? Spanking? A riding crop? Alligators in black lace? Something out of the ordinary?" She raised her brow even higher now, and he didn't miss the twist of her lip.

Okay, he was slow, but not that slow. "How about you

dress up as Little Bo Peep," he said, matching her brow-lift for brow-lift. "And don't forget to bring the sheep."

She laughed, lifted the latch on his door, and robe, shift, towel, and slippers clutched to her chest, she said, "Tomorrow, then?"

Smiling now, he said, "You can count on it."

He was still smiling when she closed the door, stopped smiling when he looked at his big—very empty—bed. She'd snookered him, and he'd damn well liked it.

He liked her.

Esme closed her bedroom door, leaned on it, and deflated like a punctured dirigible. Considering she was an intelligent, creative, educated, and extremely sensible woman, she'd put herself in danger of making the biggest blooper of her life—being attracted, hugely, frighteningly attracted—to Dane McCoy.

She dropped her slippers, kicked them out of the way, and plunked herself on the bed, her mind whirring, her body still humming from Dane's lovemaking.

"Get a friggin' grip!" she muttered to herself. "Like you told the man, it was sex, just sex." She squeezed her eyes shut, added, "Okay, monumental sex, triple orgasm sex, unforgettable sex." She stopped, before the urge to rush to the window and shout her satisfaction to the uncaring raindrops on the other side of her window overwhelmed her.

When she got herself settled down, had purged the last of Dane's sexy, ocean-scented body from her lungs by refilling them with fresh air, she managed a tenuous grip on reality. She'd got herself into this mess with her oh-so-cool-sex-professional routine, so she'd best get herself out of it, before her not-so-cool heart took a fatal body blow.

She stripped off the towel and dove naked under the covers. The first thing she had to do was remind herself that McCoy was a certified workaholic—and she'd already married one of those, and been one herself. Going back for more of the same, reliving that self-defeating craziness, wasn't an option. Maybe he was the world's greatest lover, maybe he did have a body—and smile—that would tempt an eighty-year-old nun, but he was *not* for her.

She was simply in the phase-one attraction stage; that dangerous time when emotions whacked away at common sense like a machete in tall grass. It would pass; not to worry, she advised herself, finally warming under her nest of covers. Until it did, there was nothing wrong with their enjoying each other, sexually speaking.

Because no way was she getting hooked on a man whose only goal was money, a man who dedicated endless hours of work—the time of his life—to making more of what he already had too much of.

Smart women did not make the same mistake twice. *No way.*

In a few days she'd finish her project and be out of here—and Dane McCoy would be nothing but a memory.

She punched her pillow, flushed. A very sexy memory.

Six

"McCoy!" Janzen rapped sharply on Dane's door at five A.M. "You up?"

With only three hours sleep, and that bit a patchwork of sex dreams and roll-overs, Dane not only wasn't up, he wasn't in the mood for his insomniac partner.

He opened the door. "Don't you ever sleep?"

Janzen gave him a cool once over and walked in. "Get some pants on and come with me."

"Are you nuts? It's barely five." He pulled on some jeans.

"You gotta see this," Janzen said. "You've got fifteen minutes max. Granger's already warming up the bird."

The bird was the Cessna, and Dane, awake at last, gave Janzen his full attention. "What's the deal?"

"Tennessee. The Fairtowne project. Fire."

"How bad?" Dane zipped his jeans, yanked a tee over his head, and grabbed a jacket. There was always a packed bag on the Cessna so it was all he needed.

"Bad. It looks like our investment was too little, too late. We've got at least fifteen, maybe twenty families burned out and on the pavement."

"Let's go."

"And there's another thing."

They were striding down the hall, past Esme's room. He tried not to think what losing these days with her might mean, what he'd be missing. "Yeah?"

"There's media all over the place. I'll do what I can to head them off, but I can't guarantee it."

For that Dane had only one answer. "Shit!"

Esme shaded her eyes against the brilliance of the setting sun, now a pulsing orange ball on the horizon. There'd be no more work tonight. She'd have to finish the drawing tomorrow.

She tucked her sketch pad under her arm, folded her lap easel, and headed up the dock toward the house, turning back only once to see a blaze of sun bounce off the water and ripple along the fresh white hull of the *Too Much*.

For three days, she'd worked her butt off, and she was almost finished, and she'd faxed preliminaries for approval to Veronica—who, thankfully, had faxed her okay back within twenty-four hours.

Glancing up at the house, she saw that Peggy had turned on some lights on the lower floor.

At first she'd been disappointed that Dane had disappeared, although not surprised. To give him credit, he had called to tell her some deal or another that he was working on was going to take some time and he didn't know when he'd be back. Esme guessed any woman who stayed in Dane's life would get a lot of those kinds of calls.

But, really—she told herself repeatedly in her best therapist voice—things had worked out for the best. If she'd had any lingering doubts about Dane's membership in the Workaholics-R-Us club, they'd been snugly laid to rest, and she'd made steady progress on her project, which meant she'd be able to leave sooner than she thought—probably make a clean getaway before Dane got back. Not have the . . . inconvenience of a good-bye. Then she'd take that holiday she'd promised herself.

Excellent.

She was as happy as the proverbial clam.

She frowned.

She never had understood how anyone truly knew the state of a clam's mood. For all she knew, clams were miserable, buried in cold wet sand, people always stepping on their airholes, digging them up—tossing them in boiling water. It was goddamn hell being a clam!

And it was hell trying *not* to think about Dane McCoy.

She scrunched her eyes, inhaled, then let the air out of her lungs in one long rush. Straightening her shoulders, she continued her march toward the house.

A warm bath, a good book, and bed . . . and chocolate, lots and lots of chocolate.

She'd be fine. *Absolutely fine.*

Dane watched Esme cross the lawn and disappear into the house. The Fairtowne deal had been a disaster, and he was exhausted, but the sight of her was an instant pick-me-up. He'd bet she hadn't eaten. And as peace offerings went, nothing beat Peggy's food. He headed for the kitchen.

Esme turned the water off, tossed in some rose-scented bath salts, and stepped into the outsize tub, sinking into the clear, satiny water on a long sigh. She put her head back, closed her eyes, and drew in a deep breath, let it go . . .

"As a welcome home this sure as hell beats a hot meal."

Esme nearly shot out of the tub. "Dane. What are you doing here?"

"I live here, remember?"

"I mean, in my bathroom." She crossed her arms, covered her breasts— God!

As if he'd never seen them before, never done wicked things with them, never had her nipples in his mouth—along with another even more intimate part of her anatomy. She dropped her arms. Way too late to be doing the chaste schoolgirl routine.

He watched her, his lips ticking up, as if trying not to smile. "You left the door open," he finally said.

"That's no reason for you to— What are you doing?" She knew exactly what he was doing.

He was taking off his clothes. Her heart thumped. She should say something, like maybe *no!*—

He undid the last button on his shirt, shrugged it off his shoulders, and started on his jeans.

ZZZip . . .

Her heart stopped. She was going to see that marvelous body again. She licked her dry lips. It looked mightily as if she wouldn't make that clean getaway after all.

Thank God.

Naked, Dane turned, and walked back into her bedroom. He came back with a bottle of wine, two crystal glasses, and a magnificent, truly eye-popping erection.

"I brought food, but one look at you and I decided it can wait," he said. "Move down."

She followed his terse instruction. "Some men might have asked," she said, barely managing to get the words out before his long legs slid in beside hers, and his chest hair brushed against her back. Any further complaints died in the rush of heat.

He moved her hair over her shoulder, kissed her nape, then wrapped his arms around her. "May I?" he asked softly, kissing her again. She knew any kind of answer was useless. Impossible, and a complete waste of valuable time.

Esme, encircled by strong male muscles, sighed long and deep. Although Dane held her loosely, he enveloped her completely, and the closeness of him, there, with her, dominated her senses, and banished what was left of rational thought to another galaxy. She didn't miss it. There were times when rational thought was highly overrated.

He felt so good, so warm . . . so hard against her.

"God, you feel good," he said, repeating her thought, his voice low. "So soft." Running his hands along her shoulders and down her arms, he trailed them with kisses, before sliding his hands around her and cupping her breasts. "Have I told you how much I like your breasts?" He placed a finger on each nipple and pressed lightly.

"No, but you've done a fine job of demonstrating it."

He chuckled against her hair.

She rested her head back against him, drew in a languorous breath as he played and teased her nipples. "You feel like hot . . . steel." She shifted back against his erection pressed against her buttocks and lower back, so he'd be certain of her reference point.

"Goddamn thing's been at attention for the last three days," he grumbled. "And it's your fault." He kissed her ear. "You're damned distracting, Esme Shane." He didn't sound displeased about it.

Not distracting enough, she thought, thinking of the last few days without him and feeling stupidly woeful. Not that she had any right to bitch about him doing his job—whatever it was. "Was your trip successful?" She stroked his thigh, then down to twirl the sparse springy hair on his legs.

"Uh-huh." His hand caressed her belly, moved down, covered her pubis and squeezed. His fingers probed.

"Hmm . . ." She rolled her head. She didn't have much room to open her legs, but she gave him what she could—and reveled in what he gave her, a racing heart and a glorious building anticipation.

"I've been thinking about this every second." He spread her, ran a finger along her crease, then dipped it into her. "God, you're like . . . nothing I've ever felt before." He rubbed his erect penis against her. "How about we get out of this tub, go somewhere I can do you justice."

"As justice goes"—she arched into his hand, her blood on fire, her words rocky and low—"I think I'm getting my share." She groaned the last words out and pushed her sex into his expert hand, breathlessly . . . deliriously, thoughtlessly, senselessly, incapable of any need other than Dane, what he could give her.

He smiled against her back, stroked her clitoris and made circles around it with his finger, until the taut tip of it stood achingly alone. "Even in the water I can feel the slickness of you. The heat." He gently rolled her nub. "Do you want me to make you come, Esme?

Her eyes shut tight against the hurricane in her lungs. She couldn't speak, so she nodded.

It was enough for Dane, and for the next few minutes, Esme was very glad he was a man who took this *particular* kind of work seriously.

So much better than chocolate . . .

A diagonal of light from the open bathroom door cut across the bed, and Esme lay sprawled across Dane's chest in her bed, thoroughly loved and thoroughly loving. Dane slept deeply, and she gave herself up to the pleasure of watching his easy breathing, the curve of his lashes shadowing his cheek. For the moment, he was hers, vulnerable and available to simply admire.

She touched the stubble on his chin, kissed it softly, and smiled. He smelled like a bouquet of roses. She wondered how he'd feel about that when he woke up.

Through the fuzziness of afterglow, she caught a glimpse of the clock. Already well past midnight.

By this time tomorrow, she'd be gone—a week earlier than her rose-scented man expected. She wondered even more what he'd think about that.

You know what he'll think, because there isn't a man alive who'll happily give up the sexual pleasure you've found in each other. Or a woman, for that matter.

She rubbed her eyes, sighed when another truth landed on her brain, loud and uninvited; one that totally unnerved the normally nerveless Esme Shane.

What was between her and Dane was more than sex. Much more. She knew it, but hoped he didn't, because this was not the time for the man to get in touch with his feelings.

She kissed his chest, breathed him in, then eased herself away from him. Slipping into her robe, she walked to the window, where she leaned her head against the cool glass and chewed the edge of a fingernail.

In the end it was all about work . . . No. Overwork. Imbalance.

Esme knew in the deepest part of her that Dane's obsession with work, with making money, was a relationship killer—and she knew the futility of trying to change someone—other than oneself. She'd tasted the loneliness of a work-driven life, had been caught up in it herself until the stress and emptiness became too much. Her husband, Drew, had always refused to slow down, been furious when she'd quit her lucrative, increasingly demanding practice to, as he put it, "mooch around with a pad and pencil" and ruin what he called their "profitable marriage." He'd used the term again in the divorce proceedings in an effort to mitigate her share of the marital assets. For Drew, money was more than a way of keeping score, it was his reason for getting up in the morning.

Esme preferred the brilliance of a sunrise, the wind playing in oak leaves, the mystery of the ocean. For years she'd played second-string to the quest for gold. Never again.

Which is why she'd best get at least as far as New Orleans as quickly as possible. She was already halfway in love with Dane McCoy. She didn't intend to go the distance. She intended on staying in control—and not getting hurt in the process.

After all, if they were smart about things, played the game like adults, they could still see each other from time to time, enjoy each other sexually. It didn't have to be some grand and dramatic good-bye with them never seeing each other again. Dane would be fine with that, she was sure of it.

That bit of logic made her feel better, and she decided to go back to bed. Dane might be sleeping the sleep of the dead, but she'd soon rectify that! She turned to see him, awake, his back propped against the padded headboard, one knee up. She sighed. Even with bed-head he took her breath away.

He was staring at her. "What are you thinking?"

"That the rain has finally stopped and tomorrow's going to be beautiful."

"Liar." He switched on the bedside lamp, went back to his casual position on her bed.

She joined him there, sitting on the edge, and propping one knee on it. "Okay. I was thinking about you . . . and me. And what's going on between us."

He didn't move a muscle, gave her his full attention.

She took a breath. *Tell him now, Esme, get it over with!* "I completed my sketches today—all except one that I'll finish in the morning, so . . . I'll be leaving tomorrow. Early evening, I think. I'll be stopping to visit Leonardo and Marilee, then flying home."

His eyebrows shot up. "I thought you'd be here two weeks."

She shrugged, determined to be casual if it killed her. "Things went better than expected."

She couldn't read his face, but his tone was low when he said, "Probably because I wasn't here to distract you—with sex."

Nodding and smiling, she agreed. "That definitely helped. Because as distractions go, you're world-class." She stopped, gathered her thoughts, felt her chest tighten. "And, Dane, I want you to know that, what we did, what we had? I loved every minute of it. You're a fabulous lover. Thank you." If that was the right note, it didn't feel like it. It felt like a gargantuan understatement, like she'd just called King Kong a monkey.

There was a moment of what she could only describe as electric silence, then Dane shook his head.

" 'Thank you,' " he repeated, spitting out her words. "Just like that. Thank you, Dane, for screwing my brains out, but I have to go now." He threw the sheet off, got up from the bed, strode to the bathroom, and retrieved his jeans. He yanked them on, walked over to where she sat glued into place on the edge of the bed, and glared down at her.

"Thank you doesn't cut it, Esme." His dark, furious face made rain clouds look like pink cotton candy.

"I don't know what you mean."

"No, you don't know." He quelled her with a look. "So, for now it's best you don't say another word. We'll talk about this in the morning."

"Talk about what?" Esme was stunned by his vehemence. She knew he'd be disappointed, but flat-out rage was more than she'd bargained for. "I'm not saying I'll never see you again, but I have to go. You knew that from the beginning."

"You don't 'have to go' anywhere. You're running." He put his shirt on, didn't bother doing up the buttons, and put his hands on his hips. "I can't let that happen."

"You can't—" She stood to face him, matched his hands on hips stance with her own. "You have nothing to say about it. Nothing at all."

"I think I do." He stared at her long and hard, a muscle ticking in his jaw. "And when I figure out exactly what it is, I'll say it. You may be the queen of cool, but me, I get hot. And when I get hot, I say things I regret. This is too important for that." He took her face in his hands, lifted it to his, and kissed her until her knees gave out. "Good night, Esme. He strode to the door, swung back. "Breakfast. Tomorrow. Eight o'clock." He walked out.

A few seconds later she heard his door close—none too lightly.

Esme plopped down on the bed, her knees trembling from his kiss, her mind a snowstorm—a complete whiteout. "Well, that went well," she muttered to herself. She put a hand on her pounding heart. The single-minded, get-whatever-he-wants Dane McCoy intended to be difficult.

The vanity in her was pleased; the hurt woman in her, determined not to repeat her mistake, was scared sapless.

There would be no sleep tonight.

* * *

Peggy brought some fresh-squeezed orange juice to their breakfast table and went back to the kitchen. Dane took the time to study his quarry.

Esme gave off so much cool, it chilled him from three feet away. He marveled again at how such a composed woman let herself go so wild in bed. It was as if she separated sex and passion from life and feeling. Like he used to. Before Esme walked into his life. Sitting across from him, she was as quiet as that mouse Marilee had originally described.

He took a drink of coffee, drew in a fortifying breath, and said, "I think we should get married."

When he spoke, she was reaching for some butter, and he noticed the hand holding the knife shook. Lifting her eyes to his, she said, "Can it wait until after breakfast?" Her hand steadied, and she went on to butter her toast as if he hadn't just said words that tilted his goddamn universe. Words he'd never uttered before.

Okay, not exactly the hearts and flowers version of a proposal, and definitely not a question requiring a straight yes or no answer, but hell, he wasn't going to give her that easy an out. If he planned on closing this deal—and he was determined he would—he figured he'd have to do two things: negotiate and not play fair. Giving Esme a chance to say no from the get-go wasn't in the cards. "It can wait for as long as you'd like it to—so long as it happens."

They were eating on the east patio and when the morning sun rose at the edge of his property, it illuminated Esme's face, fading out her expression—but her eyes were wide, and thoughtful.

She put down her toast and shook her head. "I hate to say this, because it makes me sound so . . . therapist-like, but I think you're confusing things. What's between us is basic biology. It's just—"

"Do *not* say it. That *just-sex* thing, you're so keen on. That's not what's going on between us. I've had my share of just-sex in my life—"

She raised a brow. "I'll bet."

"Enough that I know the difference." Why he wanted this maddening woman was a major mystery, but want her he did. "What I had with you—what we had together—was a hell of a lot more than sex. You know it, and I know it." He looked at her, wanted to see her eyes. "I'm in love with you, Esme."

"Oh, God!"

"And I think you love me." Arrogant, yes, but the truth as he saw it.

He was sure he heard her gasp, then she got up and walked to the patio railing. Stood there for a long time, her back to him. He left her to it.

Finally she turned to face him. "You're probably right. I do . . . have those feelings for you."

He stood, but she lifted a hand, telling him to keep his distance. Jesus, he couldn't believe the effect her words had on him. His heart damn near jumped out of his chest. He waited for her to go on.

"But in this case what I feel or don't feel doesn't matter. You and I—for the long-term—would be a disaster."

"Why, for God's sake?"

She chewed her lower lip. "First off, we barely know each other."

"We know enough."

"Given that you had me checked out before I came here, you're speaking for yourself, not me. I know nothing about you—other than you're fabulous in bed." She looked at him a long time, as if she were trying to photograph his brain, then she shook her head. "But the big thing is, you're married to your work."

He didn't know what he expected her to say, but that sure as hell wasn't it. But she was dead on. Hell, he *loved* his work, especially in the last couple of years, since he'd sold his company and gained the freedom to take more challenging, and ultimately more lucrative, investment directions. He'd never been more satisfied. Sure, it still took a lot of time, but every second he spent on it had a major payback. "You've got something against work? Seems to me you do your share of it."

She nodded. "Yes, I do, but from what I see and from what Marilee tells me, your work consumes you. She says it's why you never married. Why you never had a serious long-term relationship."

Damn Marilee and her pop psychology! "She's right—and wrong. Building my company, making it grow, took all I had. I decided I didn't have either the time or the energy for another commitment, so I avoided it." He eyed her, feeling oddly uncertain—a feeling he was unfamiliar with. "I was lucky. That decision was never tested, because I never met a woman like you."

"Dane, don't get me wrong, but you have enough money for a thousand lifetimes, yet you still spend all your time grasping for more." She lifted a hand, fluttered it. "Flying off to make the deal of the moment, secret meetings with Janzen, working until all hours in that computer room of yours, eating at your desk . . ." She drew in a breath, crossed her arms. "That's your choice as a way of life, but being married to it"—she shook her head—"will never be mine."

Dane's head started to hurt. Shit! As objections went, this was nuts—and unexpected. Mired in his promise to himself and Janzen to keep his mouth shut about what was going on, he could only stare at her. "Sometimes things aren't what they seem," he said. Lame, but all he could muster until he talked to Janzen—who wouldn't be back until tomorrow.

"How it *seems* is that you're asking me to play second fiddle to a bank of computers." She stood an arm's length away. There was a wash of tears in her eyes. "I'd love to . . . love you, Dane. God, what woman wouldn't? But you and I?" She shook her head. "It would never work." She took a step toward him, wrapped her arms around his neck, and kissed him softly.

He crushed her in his arms, deepened the kiss. Instantly hot, unreasonably pissed off, and uncharacteristically confused, the irony of his situation struck him like a low blow to the gut. He had to be the first man in America rejected because he'd made too much money—and he had nothing to say in his own defense. Hell, if he wasn't busy kissing the woman he loved to oblivion, he'd have laughed outright.

"Let's go upstairs," she whispered against his ear.

"What about that work you wanted to finish?" he murmured, his breathing heavy, blood pulsing in his groin.

Her eyes still shiny with tears, she moistened her lips, smiled at him, and ran her hand down his zipper. "The work can wait. Right now I'd much rather make love with you."

His lungs constricted, and he touched her face. He wanted more from this woman than a couple of hours in bed. He wanted a lifetime. "How the hell am I supposed to let you go?"

"Shush, now"—she touched his mouth—"just take me to bed, McCoy. Make love to me."

"I make you an offer—marriage—that you refuse, and you make me one I can't. Not exactly fair." But an excellent idea. Bed was the perfect place to convince her to stay—until Janzen got back. Either that or he'd wear himself out trying.

"I didn't intend it to be fair." She took a step back and brushed at her cheeks with the back of her hands, gave him a wobbly grin.

He took her hand, and to avoid Peggy's censure over the uneaten breakfast, led her through the French doors leading to the library. They'd almost cleared it when the phone rang. He glanced at the call display. Damn! It had to be about Fairtowne. "Esme, I have to take this," he said.

She hesitated, then said, "I'll wait in your room." She kissed him once, lightly on the mouth. "Don't be long."

The one call turned into three, and seventy-five minutes later he hung up the phone on the last one.

Seventy-six minutes later, he was reading Esme's note. Short and to the point, like the woman herself:

It's better this way, Dane. I'd hoped we could still see each other from time to time, enjoy each other, but after thinking about your proposal this morning, I think it's best we don't. Too hard . . .

You'll find Marilee and Leonardo's business proposal on your bed. Delivered as promised.

With love and endless regret, Esme.

When he was through cursing: Fairtowne, Janzen, and stubborn, unreasonable women everywhere, he did what every castoff man had done since they'd built their first mud hut beside a watering hole—he went back to work.

Seven

Two days later, Esme finally had the strength to pull the unfinished drawing of Dane's boat, *Too Much,* from its folder.

She was pretty, the *Too Much*. The most unlikely of Dane's possessions, she was the only one he'd shown a real affection for. Which was the reason Esme chose to draw her instead of the big house.

An incomplete drawing.

An incomplete love affair. How utterly perfect! She knew she could finish it by memory, but it wouldn't be the same. Besides, her tears would probably ruin the fine handmade paper. She sniffed.

After delivering the beach portfolio to Veronica, she hadn't drawn a line. God, all she'd done was sniffle and watch daytime TV. Something she swore she'd never do. It was hell being sane, sensible, and cool, when all she wanted was to be in Dane's arms.

Not that it would last.

She poured herself another cup of coffee, took a seat at her counter, and picked up the remote control for her tiny kitchen TV.

Might as well catch the noon news and get really depressed.

. . . all twenty-four low-income families left homeless by the

Fairtowne Apartments fire in Messing, Tennessee, are in new digs courtesy of—and here's the real news—Dane McCoy. Voted Louisiana's most wanted man—in the marriage market—for three years running, McCoy's been out of sight for a while, supposedly holed up with the zillions he made when he sold MacArte Electronics a couple of years ago. Now it seems, he's turned his attention to philanthropy. Details are sketchy, and the man himself refuses all interviews, but rumors are you can find McCoy bucks just about anywhere on the globe, be it Ethiopia or some of New Orlean's, neediest neighborhoods. And last weekend, according to the burned-out, and very grateful, tenants of the Fairtowne Apartments, a good share of those bucks ended up in Messing.

In other news . . .

Esme sat back in her chair, certain her jaw was about to hit her chest bone. When she gathered her wits, they spun in confusion. He should have told her.

Why in hell didn't he tell her?

Her phone rang. On reflex she picked it up and immediately wished she hadn't.

It was Marilee, and she was so excited, her voice was ten notches higher than normal. "Esme, thank you, thank you, thank you! I thank you and Leonardo thanks you."

Esme leaned forward, put her elbows on the counter, and tried to concentrate. *Why didn't he tell me . . .*

"Are you there, Esme. Did you hear me? Dane came through with the money. The spa is a go! There are conditions, of course, my brother's a maniac for detail, but he met with Leonardo and me—he liked Leonardo, I can tell—and now everything's set."

Guilt stabbed her. She'd forgotten about Marilee and Leonardo's spa idea, been far too busy being a righteous idiot and nursing a broken heart, which, as it turned out, was a self-inflicted wound. *Damn. Damn. Damn!*

"I'm glad," she said to her friend and meant it. "When did

you get the news?" She worked to keep her attention on her friend's happiness, her brother's good fortune.

"This morning. Dane literally flew in with the news and flew out. Said he was in a hurry, that he had to deliver some beignets or some dumb thing. I had no idea what he was talking about—"

Esme's doorbell rang.

"Marilee, I've got to go. I'm happy for you and Leonardo. Tell him I'll call him. Okay." She hung up, took a breath, walked to her front door, and opened it.

There he was.

Oh, thank God, there he was.

Holding out a sack of beignets.

She closed her eyes tight, cleared her fogged senses, and opened them again, wanting to be sure he was real.

"I knew you'd miss me," he said, not moving an inch, just standing there looking like heaven—except for the glint of devil in his blue eyes.

She rallied. "I missed the beignets." She wouldn't smile, she wouldn't. They still had things to settle. He should have told her . . .

He flashed a grin, then stepped inside, walked around, and looked around. "Nice," he said. "The kind of place I'd expect you to live. All color and light." He looked out the window, tilted his head to see the sliver of ocean, only visible to her on her tiptoes. "Great view." Then he turned from his inspection and set his gaze on her, seriously, intently, all trace of humor gone from his face. "But you don't belong here. You belong with me."

God, after the last few days without him, Esme couldn't agree more, but she had one more fret chewing at the back of her mind. "You were on TV. The noon news."

"Yeah, I know." He didn't look pleased about it.

"When I was accusing you of working too hard, trying to make more money—all those ridiculously pious things I said."

She stopped, because he'd stepped up to her, taken a long tendril of her hair in his fingers and was playing with it—like he'd done that first night at dinner. His knuckles brushed her collarbone. He was too close for her to think. When she stepped back, her hair slipped from his grasp. "Why didn't you tell me what you were doing?"

"I couldn't. Not until I'd talked to Janzen. We had an agreement that everything we did, we did in complete anonymity. And"—he hesitated—"I wasn't sure you wouldn't think I was crazy."

"For doing good things—like helping the people of Messing. I don't understand."

"Because Messing is a small piece of a big pie." He took in a breath. "I plan to spend the next few years of my life giving away my money."

"I don't—" She stopped, her eyes widening. "You mean *all* your money."

"Pretty much. It's not my intention to start eating cat food anytime soon, but"—he looked away for a moment, his expression close to apologetic—"when a man is given too much, and so many are given so little . . ." He met her stunned gaze. "He has an obligation."

"You weren't *given* it, Dane. You earned it. Every penny."

"Then I was given what I needed—talent, luck, whatever—to accomplish that. Same thing." He shrugged.

"You also changed your mind. You're backing the spa idea for Marilee and Leonardo."

"For the same reason." He ran a finger along her jaw, searched her face. "Everyone should have, should feel, what we have. What you've given to me. If your brother can help in that . . ." He let the sentence trail away, then frowned. "Plus, there's Marilee who, if I don't cough up the money, is liable to send me another sex therapist. And I can only handle one of those at a time."

Esme was still processing, still trying to understand the

complexity of the man she'd fallen in love with. "And that's what you do all day, you and Janzen, you give away money."

"It's not as simple as that—and it does take work, Esme. Lots of work," he said. "Early on we decided we'd vet our own causes. We didn't want a barrage of bogus solicitations, the hassle of a foundation, or the publicity that came with it. We keep it personal, do our own thing, limit the admin costs as much as possible, and get the cash to where it will do the most good in the shortest possible time. That's where the Internet comes in."

She turned from him, knowing a sheen of tears misted her eyes. It wasn't easy feeling the fool—with a full heart. He put his hands on her shoulders and rested his chin on her head. "So now that you know I'm not a salivating money-grabber—at least not anymore—will you marry me?"

She faced him, touched his cheek. "On one condition."

"Name it."

"I have a key to that computer room of yours and permission to enter and ravish you any time, day or night."

"So long as Janzen isn't around to watch. Done." He pulled her close and the scent of him, clean and woodsy, filled her. "Now let me hear it."

She smiled, tilted her head to look at him. "I love you, Dane. I think I have since the very first . . . beignet."

Sheets of lightning trembled against a vermilion sky curtained with rain.

Caitlin Cavanaugh stood at the apartment window in the French Quarter, looking down onto a writhing tangle of tropical plants. A crumbling stone statue stood in the center of the overgrown courtyard; Cait found the trio of satyrs chasing the comely nymph through the green, algae-choked water a perfect metaphor for this sin-drenched city.

"She wouldn't have committed suicide."

"You said it's been fifteen years since you've seen your sister." Nick Broussard was leaning against the door frame, hands in the front pockets of his dark suit trousers. "People change."

"Now there's a pithy observation." The smoky neon sign from the strip club next door flashed pink and green shimmers onto the rain-slick cobblestones below. Underlying the burned wax scent of votive candles in red glass, another vaguely unpleasant odor hung in air thick enough to drink. "Maybe you ought to embroider it onto a pillow."

"Dubois was sure enough right about you having a smart mouth on you, chère."

Cait hated the humor she heard in his voice. To her mind

there was nothing humorous about murder. "It goes along with my smart head," she said as thunder rumbled in from the Gulf. "Unlike detective Dubois, who undoubtedly found *his* shield in a box of Cracker Jacks. There's no way, given the condition of this room when he and his jerk-off partner arrived at the scene, any cop with half a brain could've called this a suicide."

Crime scene photos revealed Tara had stacked all the bedroom furniture against the door before jumping—or being thrown—out the window.

"She was trying to keep someone out of here."

"Wouldn't be the first working girl to suffer from drug-induced paranoia."

Cait wished she could have been surprised to learn that her twin had grown up to be a prostitute. *If only . . .*

No! She could give into the dark emotions battering her and wallow in guilt later. Right now the objective was to put her sister's killer behind bars. With or without the help of the local cops who were dragging their damn feet.

"I want her book." If she could only get her hands on Tara's client list, she could begin narrowing down the suspects.

"We're lookin' for that," he said with exaggerated patience that grated on Cait's last nerve. "But, being a murder cop yourself, chère—"

"It's detective," she corrected.

"Being a murder cop yourself, Detective chère," he said, his drawled Cajun patois as rich as whiskey drenched bread pudding, "you oughta know police investigations take time to do right."

Cait snorted. "What you mean is the cops are giving any city hotshots who may have paid my sister for sex, time to cover their collective asses."

He sighed heavily. Pushed himself away from the door frame and crossed the room to smooth his big hands over her shoulders.

"Hey, darlin'. This is New Orleans. Folks have a certain way of doing things here."

"The Big Easy."

"That's what we call it, all right," he agreed.

"The movie." She shrugged off his touch. "Dennis Quaid says it to Ellen Barkin."

He brightened at that, his smile a bold flash of white that Cait suspected had charmed more than its share of bayou belles into slipping out of their lace panties for him. "You like that movie, chère?"

" I *hate* any movie that glamorizes crooked cops."

He shook his dark head. "You're a hard woman, Detective Cavanaugh."

"I'm a murder cop." Rational. Logical. Tough-minded. Where others saw shades of gray, Cait's world consisted of black and white. Cops and killers. Good versus evil.

As a gust of wind rattled the leafy green leaves of the banana tree in the courtyard, Cait sensed a movement just beyond the lacy iron fence.

A man, clad all in black, and wearing a brimmed hat that shielded his face, was standing on the sidewalk, beneath an oak tree dripping with silvery green moss. The tree's thick, twisted roots had cracked the cobblestone sidewalk; the limbs Tara had crashed through on her fatal fall to the ground clawed at the window, leafy branches scratching against the glass.

"The landlord said other women had been killed in this building."

"That was before my time." Broussard was standing close enough behind her that she could feel the heat emanating from his body, along with musky male sweat and the tang of lemon, which would've seemed incongruous on a man who reeked of testosterone, if Cait hadn't known the cop trick of using lemon shampoo to wash the smell of death out of your hair. "The way the story goes, a young slave was found in the formal parlor, her dark throat slit from one pretty ear to the other."

His hands were on her again, long dark fingers massaging the boulder-like knots at the base of her neck. "Later the police discovered eight other bodies buried in the garden. They'd all been raped. Brutalized. All had a *gad* cut into their breasts."

He paused, waiting for her to ask.

The silence stretched between them, broken only by the sound of the wind, moaning like lost souls outside the window.

"So, what the hell is a *gad*?" she finally asked on a frustrated breath.

"It's a protective tattoo designed to protect the wearer from evil spirits. The guy who built this place was a *bokor*. A priest who specializes in the dark arts, what voodoo practitioners call the left-hand way. They're not all that common, though we've got a handful of 'em living here in the city."

"Sounds like the tattoos weren't all that much protection." Having grown up with a mother who staged fake séances, Cait didn't believe in magic, either white *or* black. Or any other woo-woo things that went bump in the night.

He shrugged. "Hard to stop a man with killin' on his mind."

She could not argue with him about that.

"Your sister had one."

"One what?" The rusty gate squeaked.

"A *gad*."

She glanced up at him. "The report didn't mention that."

"The autopsy's scheduled for tomorrow morning. It'll probably show up in the coroner's report."

"Dubois still should've put it in."

"Like you said, Dubois isn't the sharpest knife in the drawer."

The man was now in the courtyard, staring up at the window. A lightning blot forked across the sky, illuminating the malevolence in eyes which blazed like turquoise fire in a midnight dark face. Cait, who'd always prided herself on her control, tensed.

"What's wrong, chère?" Broussard's fingers tightened on her neck.

"That guy in the courtyard." White spots, like paper-winged moths, danced in front of her eyes. She blinked to clear them away. "He's—"

Gone. Cait stared down at the thorny tangle of scarlet bougainvillea and night-blooming jasmine.

He'd vanished. As quickly and silently as smoke.

Here's a scintillating look
at Susanna Carr's
LIP LOCK,
available now from Brava!

She scurried back into the closet, begging—absolutely begging—for him not to enter the closet. It was midnight, after all. On a Saturday.

But time meant nothing to Kyle.

She heard him enter the bathroom and hit the lights. Molly dove for the very back rack in the closet and squatted down.

Her heart pounded. Her tongue felt huge and she couldn't swallow. She kept her eyes glued on the door, but she didn't want to look.

This is why she could never play hide-and-seek as a kid. She couldn't handle the idea of being found. Couldn't tolerate the wait.

She knew she was going to get caught. She couldn't shake off the feeling. Or bravely meet the inevitable.

No, instead she was huddling in the corner, images of her work record flashing in her head. TERMINATED BECAUSE SHE WAS HIDING IN HER BOSS'S CLOSET.

Yeah, let's see how long it'll take her to get another job with that kind of reference.

She drew in a shaky breath, ready to have that door swing open. For Kyle to find her. The interrogation that would follow. She'd have to come up with a good reason why she was here. Something brilliant. Irrefutable. Logical.

So far, she had nothing.

And why wasn't he opening the door? She couldn't take much more of this.

Molly craned her neck and cocked her head to the side. All she heard was the shower.

The shower! Molly sat up straight as a plan began to form. The bathroom would get all hot and steamy. The glass would fog and she could sneak out. Perfect!

But that would mean getting out of her hiding place. Maybe she should wait until he left.

So that he could what? Go to his desk and spend the rest of the night working on the computer? Leaving her stuck here?

This was her only chance to escape. She needed to take advantage of it. Now.

Molly reluctantly crept to the door. She winced and cringed as she slowly opened it a crack. She was so nervous that Kyle might see the movement. Or that he would spot her. Look right at her. Eye to eye.

Instead she got an eyeful.

Kyle grabbed the collar of his white Rugby shirt and pulled it over his head. The bright lights bounced against the dips and swells of his toned arms.

Molly ignored the tingle deep in her belly as she stared. She already knew that guy was fit, but oh . . . my . . . *goodness*. . . .

Kyle's lean body rippled with strength. He was solid muscle. Defined and restrained.

She memorized everything from the whorls of dark hair dusting his tanned chest to the jutting hip bone. Her heart skittered to a stop as his hands went to the snap at his waistband.

Oh . . . The tingling grew hotter. Brighter. She shouldn't look. No. She really shouldn't. Not even a peek.

He drew the zipper down.

She should turn her head away.

Her neck muscles weren't cooperating as the zipper parted.

Okay, at least close your eyes! She forced herself to obey and her eyelids started to lower.

Until the jeans dropped to his ankles.

Molly's eyes widened. *Oh . . . wow.*

He was long, thick, and heavy. There was nothing elegant or refined about his penis. It looked rough. Wild. And this was before he was aroused?

She could imagine how it would feel to have him inside her. Before he even thrust. Molly pressed her legs together as the tingling blazed into an all-out ache.

Kyle turned around and she stared at his tight buttocks. *Oh, yeah.* She could go for one of those, too. She could imagine exactly how it would feel to hold onto him as he claimed her.

He stepped out of her field of vision. A shot of panic cleared her head. Where did he go? She caught a movement in the mirror and saw Kyle step into that sinfully decadent shower. She watched the reflection as he stepped under the water.

Great. Just what she needed. A hot, naked and *wet* Kyle Ashton.

The shower stall didn't hide a thing from her. Water pulsed against his body. It sluiced down his chest and ran down Kyle's powerful thighs. She wanted to lick every droplet from his sculpted muscles.

Molly pulled at the neck of her sweatshirt. How hot was that shower? It was getting really warm in here.

The scent of Kyle's soap invaded her senses. Sophisticated. Expensive. It usually made her knees knock on everyday occasions, but this was concentrated stuff. It knocked her off her feet.

The steam wafted from the shower stall and began to cloud the glass. Molly had to squint as the fog slowly streaked across the shower glass. She was half-tempted to wipe the condensation from her view when she remembered this was what she was waiting for.

Sure she was.

She glanced at the door. It was closed, but not all the way. That was her escape. She'd better get moving before he was finished. Molly glanced back at the mirror.

His head was tilted back and water streamed down the harsh angles of his face. She fought the fierce urge to join him and press her mouth against the strong column of his neck. Of running her hands along his body as his hands remained in his drenched hair.

That was never going to happen. She could fantasize about that later. Right now, she had to get away from Kyle.

She slowly opened the closet door, thankful it didn't creak. Hoping Kyle was like the rest of the world and closed his eyes when rinsing out the shampoo, Molly got on her hands and knees. She gathered up the last of her courage and began crawling along the bathroom floor.

Her heart was banging against her chest. Nerves bounced around inside her. She couldn't breathe. When she had to pass by the shower, she got down on her elbows and shimmied her way to the door.

Almost there . . . She wasn't going to look at Kyle, no matter how tempting. Her focus was solely on the door, and once she got it open, she was making a run for it.

Molly reached out and grabbed the edge of the door and slowly, oh-so-slowly opened it enough that she could squeeze through. She could feel the cool air wafting in from the other room.

Home free! Molly exhaled shakily.

"Hey, Molly," Kyle called out from the shower. "Could you grab me a towel while you're at it?"

And don't miss Susan Johnson's
sensationally romantic new novel,
WHEN YOU LOVE SOMEONE,
available in January 2006 from Brava.

Julius and Amanda dismounted before the house and were escorted to Lady Grafton.

As the footman opened the drawing room door and announced their names, Lady Grafton looked up from penning a letter and went pale.

Taking note of their hostess's stunned look, Amanda quickly said, "I thought I'd take the opportunity to call on you, Lady Grafton." Advancing into the drawing room with a warm smile, she added, "My family has a race box in Newmarket. I believe you know the marquis." She glanced at Julius who had followed her in. "I hope we're not intruding."

"No, that is . . . my husband is at the stables. I'll have him summoned." Elspeth turned to her maid as she rose to meet her guests, high color having replaced her pallor. "Sophie, have Lord Grafton called in."

"No need to interrupt his lordship," Amanda smoothly interposed. "We won't stay long. We were out for a ride and found ourselves near your house."

"I'm sure Lord Grafton would like to see you," Elspeth countered, signaling her maid to fetch the earl. She couldn't chance he'd find out later that she'd had guests without his permission. "Would you like tea?" It was impossible not to observe the social graces, although she found herself hoping her visitors might refuse.

"That would be lovely," Amanda replied with a smile.

"Sophie, tea as well," Elspeth ordered, trying to avoid eye contact with the marquis. She could feel her cheeks flushing with embarrassment. Or excitement. Or something else entirely.

"What a lovely view," Amanda exclaimed, walking over to the row of windows overlooking a bucolic vista of green fields and grazing horses. "Do you have a favorite mount you like to ride?"

Whether intentionally or unwittingly, Amanda's words incited an outrageously lewd image. Struggling to displace her wholly inappropriate thoughts, Elspeth found herself at a loss for words.

Aware of Lady Grafton's overlong silence, Julius smoothly interposed, "I've been trying to persuade Lady Grafton to take Skylark out for a ride."

Amanda spun around. "Skylark? You'll absolutely adore him! He's powerful and swift, yet gentle as a lamb. Tell her, Julius, how he took me over ten miles at top speed without even breathing hard."

"He has enormous staying power. It's characteristic of the Atlas Barb breed. You'd enjoy trying him out, Lady Grafton."

Elspeth tried not to misinterpret the marquis's comments. Get a grip, she told herself. Everyone was simply discussing horses and she was reacting like an agitated adolescent to the most benign remarks. "If it were possible, I'm sure I'd enjoy riding Skylark, my lord. However, we lead a quiet life since my husband's illness. But thank you for the offer. Won't you sit down?" she politely offered when she would have preferred pushing her guests out the door and avoiding any further complications. From her husband and otherwise.

"Oh, look!" Amanda exclaimed, gazing out the window. "The most precious basket of violets! I adore violets!" Contriving a moment alone for Julius, she opened the terrace door and stepped outside to inspect the willow basket on the balustrade.

"Why did you *come*?" Elspeth hissed the second Amanda closed the door behind her. "I'm sorry, how rude . . . please forgive me," she stammered, blushing furiously at her graceless behavior. "I shouldn't have said, I mean . . . I don't know what came—"

"I couldn't stay away." Uncharacteristically blunt words for the marquis who only played at love. And if Grafton wasn't about to appear at any moment, Julius would have taken her in his arms and kissed away her trepidation.

"You *shouldn't* have come. He might, that is . . . you don't understand my . . . situation." Nervously surveying the door to the hallway, Elspeth visibly trembled. "My husband"—she took a sustaining breath—"is very difficult."

"I'm sorry." She was so obviously alarmed he felt a twinge of conscience-a rarity for him. This frightened child was clearly not equipped to undertake any amorous games. He shouldn't have come. "I'll fetch Amanda and we'll be on our way," he offered, moving toward the terrace door.

"No."

It was the merest whisper. His pulse quickened despite his newfound conscience and he turned back.

"God help me for not having more restraint," she breathed, her hands clasped tightly to still their tremors. "I shouldn't be talking to you or even thinking what I'm thinking or—"

"Will your husband be here soon?"

She nodded, a jerky, skittish movement.

"We'll talk later, then," he calmly said when he wasn't feeling calm in the least. When he was contemplating taking the lovely Lady Grafton to bed and keeping her there until he'd had his fill or couldn't move or both. "Please, sit down." Offering her a chair with a wave of his hand, he swiftly walked to the windows, knocked on a pane and beckoned Amanda in. Turning back, he smiled. "Don't be nervous," he gently said. "Relax. We're just here on a friendly visit. Tell me something about your father's parish. I understand he was a vicar."

The marquis's voice was incredibly soothing, as though they were indeed friends. She felt an instant lessening of her anxiety. "I suppose you do this all the time," she murmured, taking a seat. "Rumor has it, you're—"

"I never do this," he said. In fact, the mindless craving he was experiencing was so outre, he thought he might still be feeling the after-effects of last night's drink. Taking a seat a respectable distance away, he added with almost an unbecoming brusqueness, "You affect me in a most unusual way."

Here's a look at MaryJanice Davidson's
hilarious new novella,
"Cuffs and Coffee Breaks" from
VALENTINE'S DAY IS KILLING ME,
available in January 2006 from Brava.

"Well, this is it." Julie Kay tossed her keys on the kitchen counter. "Home sweet hell."

"It's nice," he commented, glancing around the small house she rented from her brother-in-law. "I used to live in Inver, back when I was a student at the U."

"Yeah, what, six weeks ago?"

"Oh, you're hilarious."

"I hate apartments. I always feel like a bee in a hive. So when my brother-in-law moved into a bigger place, he let me rent this one. It's worked out for everyone."

"Mmm." Scott was prowling around the living room and dining area like a big brunette panther. "I have an apartment, and I know what you mean. But I'm almost never there."

"Where are you?"

"Work, usually. That's why I was really glad when you decided to go out with me. I mean, I have *no* social life."

"But you're so . . ." Gorgeous. Delicious. Fabulous. Tall. ". . . smart."

He shrugged. "I was always the tallest kid in my class, *and* the skinniest. But I was bad at sports. So who'd want to go out with a big gork like me?"

Oh, I dunno, anyone with half a brain?

"Uh, let me see if I can find something better than my old cardigan." She turned to go into her bedroom, but he came up behind her and put a hand on her shoulder, gently turning her around.

"It's fine," he said. "It's the least of my problems, believe me. What the hell am I going to do about that poor guy at the restaurant?"

"Uh . . . well, I . . . uh . . ." Blue eyes were filling her world, her universe. They were getting closer and closer. There was nothing else: no house, no living room, no cardigan, no dead guy.

She felt his lips touch hers and she put her arms around him—she could hardly reach, his shoulders were so broad. Her mouth opened beneath his and his tongue touched hers, tentatively and then with more assurance, licking her teeth and nibbling her lower lip. She pulled, and the cardigan was on the floor, and her hands were running across his fine chest, and—

(*Dead guy, dead guy!*)

She yanked herself away. "Stop that! This is totally inappropriate!"

"Hey, *you* kissed *me*."

"I did not!" Oh, wait. Maybe she did. "Well, it doesn't matter. This isn't the time or place."

"I *know*. That's why I didn't kiss you. Although, I have to say," he added cheerfully, "I've been dying to all night. But you're right, this isn't the right time. Bad sweetie."

"Oh, like you were really fighting it!"

"It seemed rude to give you the brush off," he said, sounding wounded. "You know, me being a guest in your home and all."

"Well, never mind that. Let's stay focused. Put your sweater back on."

"I didn't take it off," he grumbled, but did as she asked.

"Let's figure this out. We have to be back there in fourteen hours. So, if you didn't kill the guy—"

"Charley Ferrin."

She gasped. "You know him?"

"No, no." He held his hands up, palm out. "Calm down, don't have a coronary."

"I'll have one if I damned well please!"

"It's not like that. Detective Hobbes told me his name. I swear, I have no idea who he is. The name meant nothing to me."

"Okay, okay." She forced herself to calm down. He was right, this was no time to burst a blood vessel. "So, if you didn't do it, who did? Who had a motive and could do it quickly, and avoid the cops, and stick you with a murder charge?"

"Honey, I got nothin'. I've been trying to figure it out all night. I was minding my own business, waiting for you, and the next thing I know, I'm wearing handcuffs. And not in a good way."

She felt the blood rush to her face as she pictured him cuffed to her headboard. "All right. Did you overhear any arguments? See anybody fighting? Anything weird at all?"

"No."

"Come on. There must be something."

He shook his head. "No. And no, and no. I told the cops all this already."

"Well, now tell *me*," she snapped.

"Don't boss me!"

"I'll boss you if I like! If it wasn't for me you'd still be rotting in jail!"

"The hell. My lawyer would have vouched for me."

"Yeah, I could tell what a great job he did by the way it took him *hours* and *hours* to *not* show up."

"Listen-mmph!"

She had kissed him again. What was wrong with her?

"Not that I mind," he gasped, extricating himself from her grip, "but, again, don't you think this is a little inappropriate? Given the circumstances?"

She got up to pace. "Of course it's inappropriate, it's nine kinds of inappropriate! What the hell is wrong with me?"

He opened his mouth, but she beat him to the punch. "I'll tell you, it's this fucking holiday! It's killing me! It's making me act in ways I would never normally act! God, I hate it, I hate it, *I hate Valentine's Day!*"